the Olive Conspiracy

by Shira Glassman

The Olive Conspiracy by Shira Glassman, edited by Jaymi Lynn

When Ezra tries to blackmail Chef Yael about being trans, she throws him out of her restaurant and immediately reports him to the queen. But when police find Ezra stabbed to death, Queen Shulamit realizes he may have also tried to extort someone more dangerous than a feisty old lady.

Shulamit's royal investigation leads her to an international terrorist plot to destroy her country's economy—and worse, her first love, Crown Princess Carolina of Imbrio, may be involved. Since she's got a dragon-shifting wizard at her disposal, contacts with friendly foreign witches, and the support of her partner Aviva, Shulamit has hope. What she doesn't have is time.

A love story between wives, between queen and country, and between farmers and the crops they grow.

Tales of Perach by Shira Glassman, edited by Jaymi Lynn
"Your Name is Love"
An energetic royal guard takes her artist wife on a scavenger hunt around the city so she can stop having artist's block about the lesbian graphic novel she's supposed to make for the queen.
"No Whining"
A chef dithers over whether to switch wine sellers when hers is incompetent but the delivery girl is a trusted ally.
"Every Us"
A prince with anxiety is comforted in the arms of his partner when he wakes up from a nightmare.
"Take Time to Stop and Eat the Roses"
A trans teenager and his girlfriend go on a midnight quest for flowers for her sister's wedding.
"The Generous Princess"
A royal family with two moms and two dads puts their own special twist on celebrating Purim.

Cover art by Caroline C. and Jane Dominguez

"Dayenu" song verse from the Passover Haggadah, quoted in "Your Name is Love"
All quoted literature sourced from the public domain.

❖ ❖ ❖

If you're curious about the "biological weapons" used in this book, Google *sharpshooter insect*. They're a type of leafhopper. Be aware that some of what you read about them may spoil the ending of the story, though!

Chapter 1. In the Sukkah

Queen Shulamit's sukkah was everything you'd expect a queen's sukkah to be. The lush foliage that made up its roof represented the best the capital, Home City, had to offer. Its bamboo walls were reassuringly sturdy, while still fulfilling the prescribed rules about being obviously temporary.

Inside, the woman herself sat on a chair made of a piece of thick cloth slung between more bamboo. She'd turned it into a makeshift throne so that in her typical workaholic fashion, she could continue to receive subjects and conduct business during the holiday. She was still human enough, though, to have her feet up in front of her on a stool, and she was using a metal straw to slurp the juice from a scalped coconut.

"Now *this* is a throne." She grinned at her bodyguard.

The hulking blonde beside her stretched her muscular arms forward and then relaxed. "*Nu?* What's stopping you from holding court outside whenever you want? Aren't you queen?"

"Have to save some things for the holidays or they won't be special anymore," Shulamit pointed out. "Besides, I'd feel bad if I abandoned that priceless work of art I usually perch on." Even after having a baby her tiny body still only took up half her father's throne, but that left a conveniently clear view of the carvings of fruit, representing the country's agricultural riches, that adorned most of the giant wooden chair.

"This would probably get old anyway," Rivka admitted as she wiped sweat away beneath the cloth mask that covered the lower half of her face. "I mean, yes, we have shade, but there are still between those palm fronds bits of sunlight—"

"There are supposed to be bits of sunlight," Shulamit reminded her. "And I guess *I'm* supposed to see the next person in line. Who's there?"

Rivka stepped out into the sun momentarily and returned leading an older woman. She was tall and thin and bony with age. On the hips of her gold tunic Shulamit recognized kitchen stains, a familiar sight since Shulamit's partner was also her personal chef. "Aren't you...?"

"Yael, Majesty. I own the Frangipani Table."

"Yes, that's right." Shulamit didn't frequent her capital city's restaurants the way she did all the other local businesses, due to a bewildering series of digestive sensitivities that only her sweetheart respected enough to navigate. "Here, have a shake."

She handed over her lulav.

Yael took the bouquet of myrtle, willow, and palm from her, waved it around perfunctorily, then gave it back, her eyes darting around the sukkah, peering at its inhabitants. "Majesty, I'm sorry, I know it's the middle of Sukkot, but I couldn't wait. I'm just so angry; I had to report him right away."

"What's going on?"

"Someone tried to blackmail me this morning."

Shulamit lifted an eyebrow. "I'm sorry you had to sit through that. Who was it?"

"Some fool named Ezra. Came into my restaurant this morning and demanded I give him enough money to pay his next week's rent or else he'd cause me no amount of mischief."

2

"What, he threatened to vandalize the restaurant?"

"Well, no, not that." Yael craned her neck, peering around the outside of the sukkah, then dropped her voice. "My husband and I owned the restaurant together, but he died over the summer."

"I heard about that. I'm sorry," said Shulamit. "May his memory be blessed."

"Thank you, Majesty," said Yael. "His sisters would love to get their hands on the restaurant, the farm, and any other property we shared as a couple. Ezra threatened to go to my sisters-in-law and tell them that our marriage wasn't legal so they could swoop in and take my restaurant."

Shulamit rolled the edges of her filmy white scarf between her thumb and forefinger. "I take it he was wrong, and you did have a legal marriage, or you wouldn't be coming here telling me this."

"Better than that," said Yael, standing up a little straighter. Shulamit noticed she was almost as tall as Rivka but had been slouching all of her weight on one hip. "When he died he left a very clear will, leaving all his property to me *by name*, and not just my name now, but the boy's name they gave me when I was born. Ha! So there's nothing those two old bats can do."

Shulamit was surprised to hear the part about Yael's former name, but she hid it with practiced ease. She admired the way the woman spat out such private details so casually. "That was really clever!"

"As if we'd leave something like that up to chance." Yael let out a delicate sniff that reminded Shulamit of a sulking cat. "Who does he think we are?"

"I'm glad you came here to report this," said Shulamit, "but unless he comes back and bothers you again, it may be difficult for us to prove anything and arrest him."

"Well, he doesn't need to be running around Home City bothering people, so…" Yael was clearly trying to be as respectful as possible of her sovereign queen, but the agitated hands she held in front of her shook with repressed irritation.

Shulamit licked her lips. "How did it end with him? Did you flat-out tell him you wouldn't pay him?"

Yael considered this for a moment. "I don't think so. I think I just told him to get out of my restaurant before I decided he was on the lunch menu, and not to come back."

"Did he say anything after that?"

"Said… he said I'd come around, that 'people always do,'—" Yael huffed "—and that I knew where he lived when I was ready to send for him. Dung beetle," she added under her breath.

"So as far as he knows, you might still 'come around,'" said the queen.

"I am not—"

Shulamit held up her hand. "No, no, I know. I just have an idea. How we might be able to trap him into giving himself away in front of the authorities."

"I'm up for anything."

"Are you willing to wear a lizard?"

"What?"

There was a rustling noise from the vicinity of Rivka's shoulder, where a nondescript green lizard was crawling out from the thick, bushy golden straw of her hair. It stopped when it was sitting smack in the middle of her leather tunic.

Yael yelped loudly. "What the fuck is that? Oh, I'm sorry, Your Majesty." After jumping back, she quickly composed herself and now covered her mouth with embarrassment as she tried to recover from swearing in front of the queen.

"Sorry; they're sort of a matched set," Shulamit murmured as the lizard scampered to the ground and began to transform.

Soon, an impossibly tall, blond man with a healthy stomach to match his broad shoulders stood with them in the sukkah. "I am *deeply* sorry, Yael," he said in a rich and chocolatey voice with a heavy accent that matched Rivka's. "I never intended to startle you."

"You know Isaac, right?" Shulamit smiled, and hoped as usual that it looked more like a smile than a grimace, but knew that it probably didn't.

"I thought you were a dragon," said Yael. Her wide eyes and stiffened muscles showed that she hadn't entirely relaxed, even though her tone was more comfortable around Isaac's human form than the lizard. "What happened? Skip breakfast?"

"I have… other abilities," was Isaac's only explanation.

"I take it from your reaction that it might be a little uncomfortable for you to sneak him into your shirt, then?" Shulamit was thinking furiously, trying to come up with another idea.

5

"Nah, I'll… I'll deal." Yael didn't look thrilled, but her features were softening. "Your Majesty, I'm sorry, but I didn't know he was there when I told you all of that. It's all *very* personal, as you can imagine. Is anyone else hiding in here, if a commoner has a right to ask?"

Shulamit shook her head. "Not unless Captain Riv's hair counts as a whole second guard."

"I should braid it like yours for a day, see if your subjects can tell us apart," quipped the captain, who was several shades lighter and nine inches taller.

Shulamit was pleased to see that Rivka's quip loosened Yael's tense shoulders and made her smirk. "But, really," she continued, "I'm sorry about the breach of privacy. Isaac's the only one of him around here, we swear, and we also swear that you can trust him. I trust him with my life, in fact. And I'm flattered and gratified that you trust *me*. What made you trust me with something like that, by the way?"

Yael looked her over with large, frank brown eyes. "*Riv* trusts you. And I guess with someone like you trusting Isaac, he must be the real deal." This last sentence was directed at Rivka, a woman who was content to let most of the kingdom mistake her for male to avoid prejudice against women soldiers. Yael turned her attention back toward the queen. "And of course, if it's okay for me to mention, you're a little unconventional yourself, right? I mean, you and the cook—"

"I wish *more* people would mention it," Shulamit groused. "We should be recognized like any other family, without me having to make some kind of big announcement in my Rosh Hashanah speech or something."

"Oh, well, that's good, then!" Yael put her hands on her hips. "But, honestly, most of it? Most of it is just that I'm too pissed off and insulted to give a rat's ass. I'm too old, and I've worked too hard to be talked to that way. He needs to learn a lesson, and I almost taught it to him with one of my wooden spoons!"

"I'd have liked to see that," rumbled Isaac.

"Here's the plan," explained the queen. "You'll send for Ezra, and make him think you're ready to play his game. When he comes to see you, Isaac will be hiding somewhere in your clothes. That way, a representative of the Royal Guard will be witness to his crimes." Isaac wasn't technically a member of the Guard himself, but as its captain's husband, and the orphaned queen's surrogate father, he was definitely attached to it somehow even if nobody was sure what his rank really was.

"He has to be in my shirt?"

"Your hair isn't big and wild like Captain Riv's, soooo…"

Rivka tossed her head, sending the thick, golden mess everywhere.

"I understand your discomfort, but I promise he's a gentleman," Shulamit added.

Yael smirked a little. "It's not that. I've got forty years of practice with men in my shirt. I'm just not wild about lizards."

Shulamit's eyes flashed over to Isaac, but he was smirking. She reached into a small silk purse that rested beside her in the seat. It matched her violet clothes. "Here, take this," she said, placing a single coin into Yael's hand. "Send a messenger to his house and tell him to come and see you tomorrow morning before the restaurant opens."

Yael nodded. "Yes, Majesty."

"Isaac will be there at sunrise."

"If he shows up too early, I might put him to work shelling nuts," Yael quipped. "I mean, he does magic, right?"

"You can pay me in rugelach," Isaac murmured.

"Thank you for this, Majesty," said Yael, serious again. She took Shulamit's hand in both of hers and venerated it a little. "He can't do much to me, but that's only because we already thought of this." She shook her head. "Someone else in my position—some other woman might have secrets... beast. He's a beast."

"It's the only way I know how to rule," Shulamit replied. "Do my best to take care of everybody. Otherwise, why would I deserve this pretty new dress?"

"Oh, is it new? I love it," said Yael. "Love the lilac." Half of Shulamit's wardrobe was either pink or lilac, but this outfit was new off Aviva's father's sewing bench, and particularly beautiful. "Will Isaac turn human again and arrest him once he has the proof you're looking for?"

Shulamit nodded. "That's the idea. Thank you for bringing this to the crown's attention, Yael! We're lucky you're in a position to help us stop him."

Yael smiled and bowed slightly. On her way out of the sukkah, she nearly collided with Rivka's mother Mitzi, whose arms were full of the infant princess.

"Baby!" Shulamit lifted both arms and accepted her little girl into her lap. She bounced her up and down, then moved the lulav into one of her tiny hands. "Can you shake it? Shake shake?" She left the etrog in her lap so things wouldn't get too fiddly.

"Was that a man?" Mitzi asked her daughter in a stage whisper, peering outside the sukkah.

"No," said Rivka in passionless deadpan.

Heat sprang into Shulamit's cheeks, but one couldn't really expect anything different from Mitzi. She forgot her embarrassment as she pressed her lips to the side of her daughter's forehead. "Om nom nom," she mumbled. "Baby for dessert."

"I think I'll go to the market and look at fans," said Mitzi idly. "The new year's designs should be in by now."

"Could you please stop by Aviva's kitchen on the way out and ask her to bring me a snack?" Shulamit fiddled with her clothing to give Princess Naomi access to her breast.

"What do you want?" Mitzi asked.

"Oh, she'll surprise me with something good." Shulamit smiled. "She's in charge of the royal stomach for a reason." Aviva was in charge of the royal heart too, for a better reason.

"See everybody later!" Mitzi was gone, in a whirl of extremely fashionable clothing.

"I think you care about snacks just as much as I care about buying myself a ball gown," quipped Rivka. "You just want to see Aviva."

"It's not like you're wrong, but that's funny coming from the person whose husband literally rides around on her shoulder all day," Shulamit retorted, a sassy gleam in her eyes.

Isaac lifted an eyebrow. "It's only fair, considering how often it's the other way around when I'm a dragon."

"She's latched," Shulamit announced, looking up from her daughter. "Who's next out there?"

Rivka left the sukkah to go check, and Isaac resumed his lizard form. He was sitting on top of the queen's head doing a very bad impression of a fascinator when the captain returned, leading two men.

"Season's greetings, Majesty," said one of the men. The other one simply bowed.

Shulamit's arms were around the baby, so she couldn't offer the lulav. But she nodded back at them in response and gave them a serene half smile. "How did the trials work out? Was the new variety of melon resistant to the blight?"

"Moderate success, Majesty," said the one who had already spoken. "The fruit are smaller, and the yield isn't quite where we want it. But the blight only sort of... annoys it, rather than choking it off."

Shulamit nodded slowly. "That's good. That's very good."

"We have already begun to cross them, hoping to obtain a variety with both traits," said the visitor.

"I appreciate the update. I'm so grateful for all of you. Perach is grateful," she corrected herself. "Perach's wealth is in its farms, so you're almost like my soldiers out there, protecting them."

"We try our best, Majesty," said the man, "but there is always one more blight. We saw a new worm on the litchis recently, and something new is attacking the olive trees up north and down along the river."

"I trust you," said Shulamit solemnly. "I trust all of you." And alongside the babe suckling at her breast, she felt the presence of the country to which she was also a symbolic mother.

But she didn't have to mother alone, either the princess or the nation. Soon, a beautiful bosomy vision appeared in the doorway of the sukkah carrying a plate of fruit dusted with salt, sugar, and cayenne, and Shulamit's heart leapt up just as it always did.

"I like your hat," said Aviva with a giggle as she bent down to plant a sweet kiss on her queen's mouth.

"All the fashionable queens are wearing lizards instead of crowns nowadays," Shulamit shot back.

"Nobody would mistake you for anything but fashionable in that new plumage," Aviva remarked, smiling as she looked over the purple dress with its diaphanous, lilac sleeves. "Here. Fashionable queens need mangoes."

Chapter 2. The Little Green Spy

Under the veil of an aging night, Isaac left the palace walls and walked to the Frangipani Table in human form. It wasn't ideal, because if anyone saw him, his size gave him away even though he'd tossed a black, hooded cloak over his head. Most of the natives of Perach were shorter than six feet, and he stood inches above. After a few moments of feeling exposed, even though he saw no other people, he used magic to draw any nearby humidity in the air closer to him so that his path would remain slightly foggy.

He could have just walked the whole way as a lizard and remained totally unseen, but this seemed easier. What was the point of magic if you had to walk for hours to get somewhere that was really only fifteen or twenty minutes' walk in human steps?

When Isaac got to the restaurant it was still too early for Yael to be there. He shrank down into his lizard form and crawled up the wall in front of the door to rest on the mezuzah. It turned out to be made of marble, and the cool smoothness felt good against his little lizard stomach after the overdressed, humid walk.

Yael arrived as the sky edged toward silver. While she fussed with a big metal keyring attached to her belt, looking for the right key in the dark, she kissed the fingertips of her other hand and reached out toward the mezuzah.

Isaac wasn't a *total* jerk though. "Good morning," he said in a jaunty but half-volume voice.

Yael, startled, dropped her keys and spun around, tense and angular. "Who's there?"

"It's me. I'm on the mezuzah."

Yael picked up her keys and leaned in closer, squinting. When saw him, she cried out in disgust. "I almost touched you!"

"That's why I warned you, didn't I?" The lizard was smirking mischievously.

"Ugh," she said again, shaking her head, but he could see a smile forming across her face.

"What, I should wait here for my secret mission as the tallest and whitest man in the city? Some secret."

Yael finally got the door open. "Let's go inside."

Since there was plenty of time before they could reasonably expect their prey, Isaac resumed his human form once the door was safely shut. Yael began her prep work for the day's service, and just as she'd promised, she wasn't shy about sharing it with him. "Here. You have any magic that can get these shells off?"

"I'd better—it's just about the only way I can shell nuts!" He showed her the palm of his right hand. Her eyes bulged when she saw the huge ugly, raised scar that snaked from his hand down half the length of his forearm. "These fingers don't close." He demonstrated by tensing his fingers and thumb as if to try.

"That's some scar!" Yael nodded, clearly impressed. "I got this from hot oil, and this one from a knife that slipped." She was pointing to various bits of bare skin that had indeed seen action, if of a very different type than Isaac's.

As she bustled around the kitchen getting things set up to prep, Isaac could see the tension in her limbs. Her grip left dents in the sack of flour, and sometimes she walked back and forth from the dry goods storage area to the prep table without whatever she'd gone there to fetch. When he had to use magic to stop a clay bowl from shattering after she knocked it off the table, he decided he needed to distract her before her agitation set the building on fire.

"I got that scar over twenty years ago." He picked up nuts in his left hand and aimed the fingertips of his right hand at them, popping the shells open one by one with wizardry. "Far away from here, across the sea in the north lands. A young prince was taken, and in his absence, a pretender claimed his name and his throne. My wizarding order got involved, and…"

He'd been telling the story for so long that it was easy to drone on automatically while still keeping one ear open for noises outside the restaurant.

After some time, there was a sound and a knock, and Yael froze. Isaac transformed, scattering nut shells, and crawled across the table toward her.

She eyed him warily.

He frilled the red dewlap on his throat flirtatiously. "I'm not even a real lizard. Come on."

"It's not like I can control it!" She sighed in exasperation. "Don't get me wrong. I'm grateful for this. One minute!" she called out to the locked door.

Yael's hand was open and waiting for him, even if her face said otherwise.

Isaac could feel her goose bumps as he crawled up her arm. She shivered involuntarily. "I wore this specific tunic so there would be plenty of places for you to hide in the folds." It had a lot more decoration than he was used to seeing on a cook. "And, obviously, it's green too."

"That was smart." He curled up inside one of the folds, safely out of view.

Yael took a deep breath. Then she went to the door and opened it.

"Morning, madam!"

It was the dairy maid. "Oh, morning." From his unusual perch, Isaac felt Yael's chest deflate and relax.

Yael helped the dairy maid bring that day's supply of milk and cheese into the restaurant. "Macadamias today, madam?" asked the girl.

"Sour orange and macadamia roglit with every meal," said Yael, and Isaac grinned. Roglit was the same thing as rugelach, and he was excited at the prospect. "Or guava and cheese, now that you've brought the cheese."

"You don't have any ready yet, do you?" The dairy girl blinked and smiled hopefully.

"I don't even have dough rolled out yet, child!"

When the girl left, Isaac stayed in her clothing while Yael worked. He could easily monitor her mental state from being so close to her beating heart, and once he finished the story of his scar he thought of other topics to keep her mind off their mission. "I'm interested to know how you met your husband."

"Oh!" she exclaimed in happy surprise. "Well, years and years ago, down south in the Sugar Coast. There was a big cooking contest, with chefs from all over the Coast and other countries. I'd say about half the chefs were local and half from, you know, Perach, Imbrio, City of Red Clay, City of Lakes, wherever."

15

"All the way from Imbrio down there," mused Isaac. "But maybe they were already living there for other reasons." He was mostly just filling time, still distracting her.

"Yes, there're some people who go down to the Sugar Coast and stay there… people who came looking for the beach lifestyle." Yael was moving swiftly in many directions at once, and Isaac snuggled farther into the folds of her tunic. "My husband and I had never met before when we entered the contest, but we noticed each other as one of the other Perachis. Then, just after one of the first events, a couple of local guys went through some of the foreign booths and wrecked or stole half the ingredients."

"Oh no!" Isaac was used to his human conversational partners needing audible reassurances that he was still there or still listening when they spoke to him in his lizard form.

"I know. They didn't like how well some of us did in the first round and wanted only Sugar Coast competitors," said Yael. "It could have meant the end of the contest for both of us, but instead of competing we decided to combine our resources. By chance, between ourselves, everything we still had left intact was nearly a perfect pantry."

"That was very lucky!"

"I suppose it shows that the nationalistic jerks went into it without a plan," said Yael, "or they'd have all destroyed the same things. There was a catch, though."

"Oh?"

"In order to stay in the contest and not break the rules, we had to pretend to be a couple already. Group entry was only open to families."

Isaac chuckled. This was exactly his favorite kind of story. He also wondered if Yael had already been presenting as female at that point, but as someone who guarded his own personal information as if his life depended on it, he would never have actually asked.

"So we pretended," Yael concluded, "and I guess we forgot to stop pretending. It was… it was magical. It was God. God's gifts are great." Isaac felt a change in her physiology and would have bet his promised rugelach that tears had started to form in her eyes. A heavy exhalation reinforced this impression.

"May his memory—"

"Thanks," she interrupted him in a flat voice. "Sorry."

"You don't have to apologize for your feelings."

"I don't want to be like this when Ezra shows up."

"Even if you were, I'm sure he'd think it was just in reaction to him."

"Bloodsucking little gnat."

"Too bad he's not," said Isaac. "If he were a gnat, I could eat him!"

There was another knock at the door, and Yael's breathing became a loud little wind. "I can do this."

"Yes, of course you can."

He could hear her fingers fumbling on the door instead of opening it efficiently.

"Oh, good morning."

It was a man with a basket of eggs. "You don't look happy to see me! I promise they're today's."

"I'm in mourning, remember?" Yael said gently.

"I am so thoughtless. Here. Take an extra egg this morning, no charge."

"Thank you, dear."

"He was a good man. Always a good customer."

When Yael and Isaac were alone again, she started rolling out dough that she'd prepared the day before. "It's pretty busy around here!" he commented.

"Yes… and it's only going to get busier. My help will be here soon, with vegetables and chickens from the market. I expected Ezra a lot earlier."

"Did he respond to your message?"

"Yes, last night," said Yael. "He said he'd be here just after sunup, and that I didn't have to have the money with me today—today was just to talk. He said, 'I'm a reasonable man.'" There was acid in her voice.

"It's far beyond sunup."

"I know."

Once Yael's two assistants arrived, their arms full of baskets of raw ingredients, the jig was up. She'd already told him she didn't want them involved in something so personal and awkward, and if Ezra showed up at this point, she wouldn't have spoken with him with them around.

"I'll be right back," she said to the staff and slipped into the sunlight.

Isaac hopped off her fingertip and onto the outside of the building so that he could crawl down the wall instead of down her body. He transformed and stretched his arms, his human arms.

"Thank you anyway," said Yael, her face puzzled. "I don't know what happened. He seemed so... organized."

"We'll be in touch. Please let us know if you hear from him again."

"Thank you." She handed him something. "Here."

Isaac grinned when he realized the pouch contained his favorite pastry, fresh from her morning's work. "I'm looking forward to this!"

He walked back to the palace, the cloak folded over his arm now that the sun was bright and burning.

Isaac did not expect the flurry of activity he faced when he returned home. Horses and carriages were lined up in the front courtyard, just within the walls, and there were servants running around in all directions with three times as much urgency as usual. He furrowed his brow and frowned, considering which was the likeliest place to find Rivka or Shulamit in case of emergency.

A servant noticed him and called out to her coworker before addressing him directly. "Isaac is back. The queen is in her chambers—she'll be glad to see you. There isn't much time."

Isaac did *not* like the sound of that. But the carriages reassured him that nobody was dying.

Growling because he didn't like feeling left out of knowledge, he hustled toward Shulamit's private room.

19

A servant nearly smashed right into him as she hurried out of the queen's room at top speed. Isaac peered through the open door she'd left behind.

"This one and that one, and the jewelry that matches, but not the bracelet. It hurts my arm," Shulamit was rummaging through her wardrobe. Aviva hovered nearby, holding the baby and watching over Shulamit with a concerned expression.

"That bracelet was adjusted, Majesty," said the servant.

"Was it? Never mind, I can't think about this now." Then she noticed Isaac through the open door. "Oh good, you're here." She was breathless and a little frantic, and continued rummaging through her wardrobe as she spoke to him. "I was almost going to go send someone for you."

"What's going on, little one?"

"The King of Imbrio is dead. He died three days ago." Shulamit exhaled deeply and bit her lower lip. "We're all going up to Imbrio for the state funeral."

Chapter 3. Imbrio in Mourning

The people of Imbrio gathered in the streets of their capital city, feeling the teeth of an autumn chill biting at their arms even through the sleeves of their mourning clothes. It seemed appropriate that the season had turned so suddenly this year, coinciding with the loss of their king. Children huddled into their parents' arms, watching the streets for the first signs of the procession.

King Fernando's spirit had gone on to live with the Gods, but what was left of his body had been purified in fire and would be taken through the city to the great temple that housed his forebears. Sad, chilled, but a little excited by the spectacle, the Imbrians waited on both sides of the city streets, peering toward the palace for the black horses.

"There they are!"

"Praise the king!"

"All praises to King Fernando."

They couldn't see inside the black carriages, led by jet-black horses that frightened some of the children, but they knew King Fernando's ashes were inside, and they followed them anyway.

The people flowed down the street in rivers of dark fabric. A cold wind pushed them forward and swirled dead leaves over their heads as they walked.

The Temple of Dead Rulers rose over the streets in stark marble lines, a king itself among buildings. People crowded around its steps on all sides, spilling out into the street as far as the eye could see in every direction.

Their speech dwindled to silence as the carriages began to open.

First, there was the Prince-Consort, husband to their Crown Princess. It gave a sobering reminder of the nation's tragedy to see his usually jolly face without its smile. He stepped into the street, waved at the crowd, and then bent back into the carriage to fetch the little princess who was his daughter. His son, next in line but still a very young boy, stepped out of the carriage on his own accord.

The mothers in the crowd put their hands to their hearts and clucked over the poor children, surrounded by luxury but deprived of their grandfather.

Next emerged Queen Ines, wreathed in a mass of black veils that were somehow both all-consuming yet delicate enough that her face was still visible. She was shaking, and when she saw the temple for the first time as one of its widows, she collapsed into sobbing and had to be held up by her son-in-law.

The little prince ran to her and held her other hand. At this, all the mothers and grandmothers in the crowd cried with her.

The carriage then yielded up the country's next monarch. An ankle that was both shapely and feminine yet sturdy and strong appeared in the doorway, and after it came the rest of the woman. She was struggling with her enormous hoop skirt, since her hands were otherwise occupied.

Crown Princess Carolina stepped into the cold autumn sunlight, holding her father's urn in both hands.

She was a tall woman, towering above her countrywomen from at least five foot eight or nine, large and curvy, with the jet-black hair and pale skin of her people. With large brown eyes she surveyed the crowd, her every movement slow and deliberate.

The people could tell that Carolina knew what she was holding. It was also obvious that she knew that she was about to trade it in for a scepter.

The royal family of Imbrio lined up on the steps of the temple and waited.

With a blast of trumpets, the ceremony began. It started with the national anthem and continued with several speeches from various important figures of government. Most of the crowd couldn't hear them, so at this point there was a lot of excited gawking at the foreigners who had arrived to pay their respects.

Both sides of the civil war in Zembluss were there. There would no doubt be interesting analyses tomorrow in the taverns of the way each faction looked—did the royalists look like they were regaining strength, based on what they wore to today's funeral and the size of their guard complement? Why had the insurgent faction not worn appropriately dark clothing?

Certainly the most interesting foreign delegation was from their neighbors to the immediate south, Perach. Their darker skin made them easy to find among the places of honor. What a tiny woman their queen was, standing in the middle of nearly a dozen guards! Not only short but slender. And was that her child strapped to her chest? Did she not have a nurse?

Some of the less cosmopolitan mothers in the crowd had to be reminded by their friends that Perach had different customs.

There was a very beautiful woman with heavy hips and a large bosom standing next to Perach's queen. Her presence confused some of the Imbrian celebrity-watchers. They knew she wasn't the queen's sister, but neither could she be a servant in those clothes.

Anyone in the crowd who had the queen's proclivities understood, and many were pleasantly surprised.

What attracted even more attention than Perach's queen and royal mistress, however, were the two guards closest to Queen Shulamit. One of them was a blond man with bulging arm muscles. He was taller than all the other guards and seemed to be in charge of them. The other one was an enormous dragon, dark green-black like the way the Imbrians painted their shutters. He curled himself around the Perachi royal family like a resting cat and watched the crowd with enormous gold eyes.

There was a blast from the trumpets. The teary-eyed Imbrian nobles had stopped droning, and Princess Carolina stepped forward. In all this time, she had never taken her hands off her father's urn.

Absolute quiet fell over the mourners. Not even a foot stepping on a crunchy leaf split the air.

The Crown Princess bowed to the crowd, a slight nod of the head. It was to be her last acknowledgment of them as princess. Then she turned around and entered the temple.

When she emerged, the urn was gone from her hands, and on her brow a sparkling crowd of diamonds rested.

The crowd rose up in an enormous thundering cheer.

Queen Carolina nodded back at them somberly.

Chapter 4. Queen Carolina

Visitors floated through the palace in puffs of finery and etiquette. These were the people whom fate had set apart from the teeming masses outside; they were the elite, the nobility, the wealthy merchants, and the foreign monarchs. It was time for them to pay their personal respects to the royal family in their time of mourning.

Isaac waited with the Perachi delegation just outside the royal family's private parlor while the Imbrian guards checked the basket of fruits and other edible gifts that Shulamit had brought. He was human again, or an approximation thereof—the past few nights he and Rivka had been on the night watch and sleeping by day in one of the carriages, so at the moment he was keeping himself awake with a combination of wakeful magic and seven cups of tea.

Shulamit used the downtime to breastfeed. Isaac could tell she was doing it as much for herself as she was for Naomi; these past few days she'd been anxious and distracted, and now that she was here in the Imbrian palace, there was a practically visible tension radiating from her tiny body.

Isaac wanted to help, but he knew she'd come to him for help when she was ready—if she needed him. He wondered how much of it had to do with her teenaged crush on Princess Carolina, now Queen, and how much was the funeral itself. Queen Shulamit was never close to King Fernando, but surely the funeral of another king, a king who had left behind a daughter to rule in his place, was triggering memories of her own sorrowful coronation.

That couldn't be pleasant.

Isaac didn't want Shulamit to feel stared at, so he looked away at random. His eyes fell idly on a nearby servant as she hurried past. The woman started like a hunted animal when she noticed him, and he heard water sloshing in the basin she carried. He smiled at her and hoped it was enough, then looked somewhere else.

As he stood idle, his mind wandered back to Home City and the Frangipani Table. How troublesome that Ezra had not shown up that morning! It would have been such a graceful opportunity to catch him in the act. Now, with the palace's only shapeshifter out of the country, Yael had no choice but to hold him off for another week or two. Or call the whole thing quits—it was within her right.

Isaac growled slightly in his throat at the thought of prey lost due to the vagaries of fate.

The Imbrian guards returned with Rivka and the fruit baskets. "All good, Your Majesty," said a guard in broken Perachi.

"*Obrigada*," said Shulamit in Imbrian.

Isaac noted surprise and approval on the faces of the guards and enjoyed the moment. His little queenling wasn't a brainiac for nothing.

The doors were pulled open for them, and in a cluster they filed into the salon with Rivka at the lead.

❖ ❖ ❖

There were about a dozen other mourners there already, some speaking with each other quietly in the corners, some orbiting the royal family. At the center of the room was Queen Carolina, her enormous skirts spread out over a small, curving sofa. Her little boy and girl were playing

26

under the furniture, and her husband stood to one side holding a glass of port. He was speaking with the man who stood on her other side, a tall gentleman wearing a vest, whose hands were busily cracking nuts open with a metal implement. He had a full beard that went all the way around his face—unlike Isaac's own graceful afterthought.

"Here, I've finally gotten one of the damned things open," Isaac heard the man with the beard say in Imbrian. He was surprised at how much he understood, given that the last time he'd been up this way he'd been under a curse and stuck in the body of a horse—with an intellect to match.

The bearded man tried to hand the nut to Queen Carolina, but she waved it away. "I can't; I'm not hungry." Her voice was a flat murmur.

"Oh, but Caro, you must eat!" her husband protested.

Isaac watched her ashen face, saw her pain, almost smelled her tears.

"I really—" she began.

The bearded man lifted her hand, the one closest to him, in his own. "Here," he said, pressing the nut into it with his other hand. "Don't eat for hunger. Eat for life. The country needs life and you are the country now."

Carolina turned to look at him, and Isaac saw things in her face he didn't expect. It was as if night was reaching out to pull its own dawn closer.

Instinctively, he looked at Rivka, the blazing sunlight to his own gray dusk. She was scanning the room for possible hostiles, and his heart leapt a little with admiration and love. *She* wasn't about to get distracted from her life's work by gossip fodder.

Queen Shulamit stepped closer to the other queen's sorrowful bower. "Carolina," she said in a cracking voice, in Imbrian. "I'm so sorry."

Carolina's attention shifted abruptly as she turned her head at the sound. "Shulamit! Thank you, thank you for coming." The words poured out in voluble fluent but accented Perachi. "Oh, Shulamit, Shulamit, tell me... how long does it hurt? How long do I feel like screaming? Like... breaking? There is something *breaking*."

Carolina's husband rubbed her shoulder soothingly. On her other side, the bearded man squeezed her hand, then let it drop and wandered off.

Shulamit smiled wistfully. "I wish I had the answer you want to hear. It's just going to take a lot of time."

"How long with you?" There was an intensity about Carolina.

Shulamit sighed. "Couple of years? You never really stop being sad, not all the way. But you'll go longer and longer without the really hard bits. And eventually you'll just be sad that he's not there, not sad that he died. If that makes any sense."

Isaac noticed her shrinking back into Aviva, who was waiting supportively just behind her with entirely non-platonic closeness. Ever since they'd entered the Imbrian capital city but especially here in the palace, Shulamit had been physically clingy with her sweetheart. Had she been a different type of woman, Isaac would have wondered if she was trying to show off to Carolina, her old crush, that she had a pretty girlfriend. With Shulamit, it seemed to be more about Aviva being a security blanket.

He understood the feeling, a little. On the rare occasions women who weren't Rivka piqued his interest, it disturbed him and made him immediately want to seek her out, to recalibrate his settings back to normal.

"I'm glad you came," said Carolina, "and I'm sorry I couldn't be there, you know, five years ago. I had just given birth to this little one, you see…" She gestured to her daughter, who had gotten bored of sitting quietly and was lying on the floor clapping her hands.

"But your father was there," said Shulamit, "and I never forgot that. So now, I am here for him. And, well, to see if there's anything I can do to help you."

"Just that you came means something."

"Um." Shulamit licked her lips. "This is Aviva." Then came the awkward, grimacing grin she usually kept hidden, because, as Isaac knew, she thought it looked like the face of an angry ape.

"Pleased to meet you, Your Majesty," said Aviva.

A light of understanding came into Carolina's eyes. "Ahh, I remember those things you said! When you visited, what was it, nine years ago?"

"Think so." Shulamit bounced Naomi in her wrap, burning off spare energy.

"I'm glad things worked out for you the way you wanted, that way," said Carolina.

"We've brought you…" Shulamit turned around, motioning to her guards. "We've brought all kinds of food. I don't know very much about your mourning customs, but in my culture, when somebody dies, we have days where people come and bring us food, and take care of us, and let us… you know, tell stories, or just cry, or whatever we want. And we cover the mirrors so we don't have to see ourselves ugly-crying."

Carolina let out a smirking sniff, the closest thing to laughter her grief would allow. "I don't need a mirror. I have to see my little ones crying."

Shulamit looked down at Naomi protectively as the guards set the gift baskets in front of Carolina. "A sampling of Perach's agricultural riches, hand-picked just for you."

"Thank you."

The children playing on the floor started to pick through the basket. "Ooh! Papaya!" said the tiny princess. "Mamae, can I have it? Can I have it?" It was so large compared to her tiny, roly-poly frame that she could barely lift it.

"Go see if Papai will call a servant to cut it up for you." Carolina patted her on the head affectionately.

Really? thought Isaac. *He needs a servant to slice open a papaya?*

"What's this?" asked the little prince in Imbrian, half holding a bottle that was much too heavy for him.

"Fernando, no! Put that down," said Carolina.

"Extra pure olive oil," said Shulamit. "First press."

"How wonderful," said the bearded man, returning with a glass of port. "We will finally have the chance to do a blind taste test of our two country's oils."

"Nothing tastes of food right now," said Carolina.

30

"Perhaps the Prince-Consort will try his hand at it, then?" Then, turning his head toward Shulamit and her family, he bowed deeply. "Your Majesty. I have not yet had the honor."

Carolina looked from him to Shulamit, then back again. "Yes, you have, nine years ago! Shulamit, I don't know if you remember João—Visconde João Carneiro de Façanha?"

"He was the one playing the guitar, right?"

"When I sang! Yes, that was him. Wow." Carolina shook her head. "Nine years. How long it's been."

Isaac eyed the glasses of port that were being passed around. He didn't want alcohol muddying his thoughts and his reflexes, but the foreign wine appealed to his sweet tooth and there were constant reminders that it was available on the other side of the room.

Arms folded across his chest, he remained with the other guards and distracted himself by continuing to cavesdrop.

"Such beautiful baskets you brought us," said the Prince-Consort as he examined its further contents.

"Representing the very best of Perach's wealth—her farms and her groves," said Shulamit, adding, "Well, everything that would make the week's journey without spoiling, anyway."

"Oh, wow, coconuts!" exclaimed the little prince as he continued to rummage in the basket.

"Imbrio, too, is proud of the riches she grows," said the Prince-Consort. "I'm sorry, where are my manners? Let me get you something to eat from that beautiful spread over there. I'll call a servant."

Shulamit, wide-eyed and speaking far too quickly, blurted out, "No, that's fine. I'm not hungry."

Isaac's eyes narrowed. From his position with the other guards, he could see her knuckles standing out from her hands—sharp, pointy bones that spoke of stress. What was going on? She'd been brushing off offers of food for years, ever since finding out about her sensitivity to wheat and fowl. That's how one falls in love with a cook. Why was today different?

"Are you sure?"

"Oh, Shulamit, you must try a Rissol de Frango, a chicken pastry pocket," said Carolina warmly. "Since eating gives me nothing right now, you go enjoy it for me."

"No, thank you," Shulamit repeated.

Isaac stepped in and rescued her with a blatant lie. "The queen is fasting for Simchat Torah." Now he had to hope the Imbrians were as uneducated about their customs as he was about theirs!

Shulamit lifted Naomi up to kiss her on the forehead, but from Isaac's angle it was obvious that she was using her daughter's curly hair to mask her smirk.

"Ah, then I wish you an easy fast," said Carolina with sympathy.

"Thank you." Shulamit managed to get the words out with a straight face.

"Some other time, then," the Prince-Consort continued, "you must return and sample our bounty. We have so much that is known all over! And not just food. There is indigo, there is cotton—" He paused. "Queen Shulamit, I think your... er... wife would like to say something. She looks quite distressed."

Aviva's eyelashes fluttered as everyone turned to stare at her. "I... it's not a good topic for a room of tears."

"What is it?" Carolina pressed. "*Querida*, it's not like I can get any sadder."

Aviva looked at Shulamit. Taking the queen's slight nod as approval, she said, "There are many in our country who find Imbrian cotton and rice to cost something we can't pay—that of human misery."

Carolina's mouth opened slightly. Said the Prince-Consort, "Oh, but you have been listening to rumors!"

Shulamit shook her head. "Too many of our brokers have come back and told us the same thing. Plus, there are a few who have escaped, and we listen to them too."

"Ungrateful." Carolina looked hurt. "We gave them food and steady employment. What more does the lower class need?"

"Jobs where they have a chance to improve their lives," said Shulamit. "And where they aren't forced to stay... anyway, I wasn't going to bring this up, but surely you know I've been in negotiations for months with representatives from your father's trade ministry about these issues."

"I did know, yes," Carolina admitted.

"Some Perachis don't want to buy Imbrian when they hear about these things."

"Yes, my father mentioned it."

"I'm very sorry, Carolina," Shulamit added hastily. "Please don't hate me. And don't think about any of this today."

"I could never hate you." Carolina looked up at her with a placidly sad, pale full moon of a face. "Who else do I have so much in common with, now?"

"And she's right, you know, Caro," João interjected.

"What?" The Imbrian queen turned sharply to look at him.

"If it's our farms that make us strong as a nation, why can't we all share in those riches as one united people?" His voice was smooth and frank.

"We do share," said Carolina. "But people are not all the same. Some people work the fields, and some have to lead them."

"I don't see any 'have to' about it," said João. "A country belongs to its people, not its rulers."

"You have interesting philosophies, sir! You will have to tell me all about them when I have awoken from my sorrows." Carolina looked at her husband. "I don't know. Maybe I am hungry after all. Those *Rissóis*, I kept talking about them…"

"I will get it for you." The Prince-Consort stood up straight to his full height, a thin, gangly shape dripping with ceremonial medals, and snapped his fingers in the air.

Almost instantly a quaking servant in a crisp, white apron appeared before him and bowed. *"Sim, sua Alteza Real?"*

"Bring the Queen a chicken pastry and a glass of port," the Prince-Consort told her in Imbrian.

"Sim, sua Alteza Real." The servant bustled away toward the food table on the far side of the room away from the windows.

"Did you see that wrinkled apron?" the Prince-Consort commented to Carolina under his breath.

Isaac heard, and wanted to smack him like the silly boy he was. On what planet did "I will get it for you" mean "I will summon a servant, whose clothing I will then criticize despite her impeccably efficient performance?"

The wizard drew up to his full height of seventy-seven inches. He had the bad habit of relishing the feeling of superiority, and right now, he was very happy to be Perachi.

Chapter 5. The Map

Four days after the queen and her party had bid farewell to
the mourners in Imbrio, the royal procession stopped at a
roadside inn in the north of Perach. Its back kitchen door
opened up to a lake thick with cattails and lily pads, and
there were pink wading birds with beaks shaped like
wooden spoons poking around between them for water
bugs.

Inside, Aviva worked her knife diligently against the hard
winter squash. Rind collected in her wake, beautiful
streaked rind that reminded her of the unevenly streaky
sunset she could see through the doorway. The squash was
badly bred and difficult to peel, but she enjoyed feeling her
muscles burn. After her days of idleness in Riachinho de
Estrela, she felt power rushing back into her soul as she
resumed the work that meant so much to her. She
understood why Shulamit had insisted that she dress up and
refrain from any behavior too productive in a land as class-
conscious as Imbrio, but oh, the relief to *make things* again.

She forced her knife down harder into the almost-rocky,
orange flesh. *There*. There was the soft spot. "Oh, so you
have feelings after all, you little—"

"Are you sure I can't help you with any of that?" the
innkeeper called to her from the other side of the kitchen
and then started to walk closer. Her arms were covered in
flour and raw dough up to the elbows. "I don't want anyone
thinking I wasn't a good host to the queen."

Instinctively, Aviva placed her padded body between the
dangerous flour and Shulamit's dinner. She smiled warmly.
"Thank you, really, but I've got it. And you are a *terrific*
host. Trust me."

36

"You sure?" The other woman was bright-eyed and wanted to help.

"I am golden," said Aviva with a toss of her head. A strand of black hair worked itself loose from her hairsticks, and she tucked it behind her ear. "As long as all the guards are fed, I can take care of the queen."

"Those squash can be pretty hard."

"I was noticing that!" Aviva grunted as she pressed the knife down into the orange impossibleness again. "I'm used to the ones we get down in Home City, I guess. But as long as it softens up when it's cooked..."

The innkeeper was nodding. "Oh, yes, yes, don't worry."

A noise of boots at the door made both women look up. Rivka was standing in the doorway holding a basket of raw meat. She was masked as usual, but from the way the corners of her eyes were turned up, Aviva could tell she was grinning. "All ready for you!"

"Perfect timing—I already cut up all the onions and garlic." Aviva peered into the basket. "Oh, you're such a sweetheart. I thought you were just going to butcher it!"

"I guess I got maybe carried away?" Rivka chuckled. "You're already cutting up enough things with your onions and garlic and, what is that? Squash?"

"Squash that wants to be a brick when it grows up," quipped Aviva. "I feel like my arms got ripped off at the elbow."

"But it feels better than hanging around Imbrio pretending to be a woman of luxury, right? I know you."

"Mmmm," Aviva purred as she began to toast some chopped garlic. "My hands smell like spices again." *I don't know who I am when my hands don't smell like spices.*

She cast the thought into the pan along with the pieces of onion and let it cook away.

❖ ❖ ❖

Between the guards and carriage drivers, Shulamit's royal party completely filled the inn's dining room. The guards were happily eating chicken and couscous prepared by the innkeeper. The queen herself had staked out a pleasant little table in the corner so she could lean back against the wall while she nursed the little princess. Rivka and Isaac were sitting on either side of her playing checkers with green and black olives when Aviva appeared carrying her pot of food.

"Smells a lot better than it did when I caught it," Isaac quipped, his arms folded across his chest.

"Three hours in the school of flavors makes the deer learn all kinds of new things." Aviva placed the steaming vessel between all of them on the table, narrowly missing several olives.

"You should write these down," said Rivka as she eagerly dished herself out a portion of the venison stew.

"Huh? What did I say?" Aviva blinked.

Shulamit chuckled and adjusted her tunic. "You are one of a kind. You are…" she trailed off, her face peaceful and happily lovesick. Tears sprang into Aviva's eyes. It was such a welcome contrast from the tightly wound, fearful bundle of twigs she'd held in her arms these past few days in Imbrio.

"Oh… I just feel so lucky right now," Shulamit added, hugging Naomi gently. "Lucky to have all of you. My dragon-*tateh* caught the deer, Riv cut it up, and you cooked it. Just so I could have food without…" Words paused as her face crumpled into tears. "Oh, I'm sorry."

Aviva darted into the bench and sat down, pulling her into a sideways embrace. "We love you."

"I know," Shulamit sobbed into Aviva's shoulder. "And I love all of you. I'm sorry. Okay, I guess I needed that. Screw Imbrio."

Aviva giggled.

"I don't even really mean that." Shulamit sighed. "And you really are one of a kind. So many people would be scared of me seeing someone I'd loved as much as I loved Carolina, back when I was younger."

"I believe in us," said Aviva. "Besides, you always said she didn't like women the way you do or something would have happened back then."

"Right. Exactly. I mean, I didn't realize it at the time, but I must have been so obvious!" Shulamit finally began to eat her food.

"I've been wondering ever since we left," said Isaac. "Who's that minor nobleman—João?"

"He was around back when we were teenagers," Shulamit said through mouthfuls of venison and squash. "He and Carolina were in love with each other—"

Isaac looked extremely pleased with himself. "I guessed as much!"

"Yeah, I guess he's still hanging around," said Shulamit. "They couldn't get married because of how much she outranks him. I don't know what the situation is now. Who knows—maybe she has the Prince-Consort and then João on the side, and everybody knows about it. Or maybe not. I have no idea."

"Her husband certainly didn't look jealous," said Isaac, "so he's either completely aware and fine with it, or in denial."

"He used to accompany her on the guitar," said Shulamit, "when she sang. She has a great voice."

"I hope they're not hurting her husband," said Aviva, "because I liked João. He was sticking up for the working class."

"If she listens to him," said Shulamit with great seriousness, "if she's actually paying attention to what he says instead of just focusing on his eyes or whatever, then maybe we can get this Imbrio boycott problem solved. I don't want to sound like I'm glad King Fernando died, but if João can influence the throne—" she took a drink of the inn's sweet, rustic wine "—it's a whole new market. I have to say, I'm proud of our culture and our people that they think about things like this, even if it means diplomatic headaches for me."

"What's that you've got there?" Rivka was peering into Isaac's hand.

"Oh, it's the last of Yael's rugelach." Isaac offered it toward her.

"Now I *really* know you love me."

"You know, that whole thing is so *weird*!" Shulamit commented. "I wonder if we'll ever find out why Ezra never showed up?"

❖ ❖ ❖

"*Dead?*" Shulamit, who had arrived back to her home palace thirty minutes ago, stood in the sunny courtyard with her mouth hanging open like a broken door. "Ezra. Dead."

"Yes, Majesty." Tivon, Rivka's second-in-command in the Royal Guard, scratched his beard. "Knifed in the back down at the docks, the night before you all left for Imbrio."

"Wow."

"The body wasn't found until after you were gone."

"Wow," said the queen again, rather stupidly.

"Whoever killed him dressed him up like a foreign sailor," added another guard, "hoping we'd assume it was just someone who'd come in from the river and gotten killed in a tavern brawl."

"But because of the report from that woman at the Frangipani Table, we got suspicious," said Tivon.

"And rightfully so!" Shulamit exclaimed.

"We thought maybe she did it—" said the second guard, but stopped talking when he saw the queen's face.

"Don't worry," Tivon reassured her. "I know that doesn't make sense with everything in the report on her, and besides, she takes in boarders and they swear she was inside the whole night until she left for work in the morning."

"Right…" said Shulamit. "She wouldn't come and report him and *then* kill him. Not after telling *us* everything he had on her anyway!"

"Still, we sent a patrol youth to watch her restaurant," said the second guard.

Shulamit rolled her eyes. "So what else do you have?"

"We went to his house and collected all his papers," Tivon answered, "figuring that if he's blackmailing one woman, maybe he's blackmailing another? Or more than another. Could be many victims."

"I'll look at them on my throne." Shulamit shook her head as she walked out of the sun. She was surprised as anything, but her blood raced in anticipation of launching herself full speed at this new puzzle.

❖ ❖ ❖

"I'll tell you one thing," said Shulamit from her throne to Rivka, who was standing beside her. "Ezra definitely knew how to keep himself entertained." There was a look on her face somewhere between unimpressed and withering.

"Why, what's that one?" Rivka peered over at the paper on top of the pile on Shulamit's lap. Tivon, as requested, had delivered all the papers the guards investigating Ezra's murder had retrieved from his rented room.

"A list of all the women Avi the cheese man was visiting on the sly."

Rivka lifted an eyebrow. "Are they suspects? Or just Avi himself?"

"You look it over. You're head of the police, right?" Shulamit passed her the paper.

The captain scanned it briefly. "More than half of these women are married."

"How many?"

Rivka counted to herself in her native language. "Five?"

Shulamit chuckled bitterly. "Wow. I had no idea cheese was so popular with married women." Rivka made an odd sound, and Shulamit looked over to her quickly. "What?"

"Isaac has made a joke you don't want to hear," said Rivka dismissively.

"Never mind," said Shulamit archly. She was smart enough to put two and two together. "Do you see any of those women going down to the river docks late at night and stabbing Ezra?"

Rivka considered each possibility. "No, not really, but if pushed to desperation…"

"So we have six suspects just from this one paper alone."

"At least he kept very good notes. What's that one?"

"Oh, this?" Shulamit held up another paper. "Ezra threatened to tell this man's rich wife that he had a young mistress over in Ir Ilan. He got a lot of money out of him before the wife died and he didn't have a reason to pay anymore."

"That one is then probably not involved," mused Rivka.

"We don't even know that Avi and the Cheesettes are involved, not necessarily," Shulamit pointed out. "These look like starter notes."

"Oh, like he maybe hadn't approached any of them yet?"

"Right," said Shulamit. "Look, here's what I think happened. I think he was on the take from the man with the mistress. Then, when the wife died, Ezra lost his main source of income. So he had to find someone else to blackmail."

"And that's why he was taking notes on Avi," said Rivka.

"Exactly. Meanwhile, he found out about Yael and bothered her too."

"Does it say how he found out about her?"

Shulamit shook her head. "I haven't gotten to that part yet. Did you see this one?"

"What is it?" asked Rivka.

"It's notes from the Marquis' servants. He was trying to figure out definitively if Liora and the Marquis are a couple."

Rivka snorted. "Is he kidding? Liora would pay him *to* talk about her."

"Anyway, we know they had nothing to do with the murder," Shulamit pointed out. "They left on tour right after Yom Kippur." That was a week before Yael's audience with the queen in her sukkah.

"What's that one? It looks like a map."

Shulamit shifted papers around. "Mmm," she agreed, turning the paper slightly and studying it more closely. "It's a map of Perach. But I don't know what all this mess is." She squinted and shook her head. "I don't know; it looks familiar, somehow."

"Well, you do run the country."

"This line… these patterns…"

With one arm folded across her midsection and the other arm upright so that her fist rested against her nose, Shulamit raked her memories. Those swirly bits. That pair of streaks. Why did they look so familiar? Why did she feel like she'd seen it before, what seemed like ages ago before the emotional upheaval of visiting Imbrio again and seeing Carolina?

"Oh my God!" Heat flared in Shulamit's cheeks. "Rivka, this makes *no* sense, but—Guard! Who's out there?"

One of the guards appeared at the doorway. "Majesty?"

Shulamit held out one pointing finger. "Can you please bring me my latest notes on our agricultural pests?"

"Absolutely, Majesty." He disappeared into the sunlight.

Rivka squinted at her. "I don't get it."

"You think *I* do?" Shulamit skin tingled as she waited for the papers to show up and either prove her wrong or show that she was absolutely right, thus opening up nothing but a cartload of further questions. Both hands fidgeted with the ends of her filmy, yellow scarf.

Shulamit felt like every second was bloated and lazy until the guard reappeared. Where was he? Finally, the requested

45

papers arrived, and she tore into them with such ferocity that several fell onto the floor and had to be retrieved.

"There!" she finally exclaimed triumphantly.

"What?" Rivka leaned over her shoulder eagerly, and Shulamit heard a soft thud as Isaac leapt off Riv's shoulder onto the back of her throne to get a better view.

"The olive blight," said Shulamit, her lips barely moving as she tried to make sense of the completely unexpected connection. "Ezra drew a map of the olive blight and put it in the middle of his blackmail notes."

"Is there anything else on the paper?" said Isaac in his normal voice.

Shulamit turned it over. "Oh, I'm so nervous, I'm not thinking straight. This is the map I already had."

She flipped over the correct parchment. In Ezra's lazy scrawl, it said,

*Imbrian man (Name: Rui?) *possibly leader*
Imbrian man with missing tooth. Drinks like a fish
Perachi woman (from Lovely Valley?) Money-minded
Unknown man (Light skinned. Imbrian?)
Unknown woman (Perachi?)
Who is "André"?

"There is *no way* this means anything good." Thoughts whirled through Shulamit's mind, thoughts that she was afraid to put to words. What did Imbrio have to do with agricultural pests? What about—what about *Carolina*?

46

"*Malkeleh*," said Isaac, interrupting her mental maelstrom. "Let me see Ezra's map again."

Shulamit flipped the paper back over.

"Look," said Isaac. "His map—the infestation goes down the river straight into the Lovely Valley."

Shulamit shook her head slowly and groped around for Rivka's hand. She clung to her friend's arm with both hands like it was a bellpull, then hugged it tightly to her chest. "Whatever this is, we have to stop it. We have to stop *them*."

Chapter 6. Agent of the Crown

Rivka headed over to the Frangipani Table, her own hastily scribbled copy of Ezra's list tucked into her belt. While Shulamit pored over the farm maps she'd spread all over the floor of the throne room, Rivka wanted to get cracking on tracing the criminals. She had years of practice at this, both as Shulamit's Captain of the Guard but also before that, on the road as an independent bounty hunter and mercenary, and all her instincts told her that the list was the key to everything.

After all, it made the most sense—if Ezra had stumbled onto some kind of international conspiracy, its perpetrators would have every reason to silence him—even without his likely threat of blackmail. His chosen "profession" just made it worse.

There was no reason for the Imbrians to have been at the Frangipani Table specifically, other than its popularity, but she figured it was a good place to start. After all, he *had* been there often enough to figure out that Yael warranted further scrutiny, so maybe he spent enough time there for such lucky guesses to be reasonable.

Men from the Royal Guard were milling around in front of the restaurant when Rivka arrived. She heard "Look, the Captain's back!" and both of them stood up slightly straighter.

Rivka, too, felt her posture straighten, and the rest of her approach was a fluid swagger. "Peace." She waved to them. "You can go back to the palace now."

"Oh, but what about—?"

She shook her head dismissively. "She's not the one who knifed Ezra."

The guards looked at each other, then back at Rivka. "Yes, sir," said one of them.

"Just in case, I can stay if you—"

"No," Rivka said simply. "You're relieved. Thank you!"

They treaded off down the road, and Rivka entered the restaurant.

Patrons eating their lunch swiveled their heads when they saw her. Since she knew they couldn't see her smile at them from behind her cloth mask, she waved slightly. After Lord knew how many days of the place being under guard, she wanted them to know this was a friendly visit. Questions only.

Yael was arm-deep inside a duck when Rivka broached the kitchen. Her eyes widened when she saw the captain, and she froze slightly.

Rivka showed both palms in reassurance. "It's fine, I sent them away."

Yael exhaled, and her arm began moving around inside the bird's cavity once again. "They weren't *that* bad, but..."

"I know," said Rivka sympathetically. "Bad for business."

"It's hard enough trying to live up to my husband's memory without rumors flying around." Yael found a small handful of salt and rubbed it over the duck's naked skin. "I have to be twice as good as we were together, just to make sure they think it's the same. Those guards tried their best to be nice, but..."

"They thought you carved up Ezra like one of your ducks."

Yael nodded. "And the worst part was, I could have… I mean, someone else in my situation might have. I couldn't kill a man, but another woman might."

"We're looking into that," said Rivka, pulling the rolled-up copy of *the list* from her belt as if unsheathing her sword. "When was the last time you had any Imbrian customers?"

Yael's brows descended. "Do you mean *anyone* from Imbrio or new people I didn't recognize?"

"I'm not talking about people like the chair-maker's wife who've been here for years," said Rivka. "Not one Imbrian at a table full of Perachis either. Imbrians eating together."

"I did have… these men… it was during the holidays." Yael frowned in thought. "I remember because I was still taking reservations for breaking the fast."

So sometime between Rosh Hashanah and Yom Kippur, Rivka recorded mentally. *Maybe a week or so before he bothered Yael.* "How many men?"

"Two. No, three," Yael corrected herself. "I forgot about the third one because he wasn't speaking much. They had a Perachi woman with them, but I don't think she was from here. She didn't say much either, except to help them order their food if they didn't know a Perachi word."

"But the two men who spoke, they were Imbrian?"

Yael nodded. "All three men were light-skinned like you, except with black hair, and the two who were talking spoke in Imbrian. They were a pretty profitable table. Went through a lot of wine."

Drinks like a fish, Rivka read off the paper. "Was one of the men missing a tooth?"

"I didn't notice," said Yael, "but maybe one of the waitresses did."

"You probably want me to wait to talk to them until there's a lull."

Yael's face softened. "I like that you're willing to do that." She cut a piece of twine and stitched up the duck cavity. "Should I be ashamed that I only really care about this so much as it clears my name? I mean… *Ezra*."

"Maybe it helps to think that Home City is a place where even people like him are not allowed to be killed in the street." Rivka's eyebrows went up slightly as she talked. She meant what she said, very solemnly.

Of course, she had her own motives for pursuing the strangers, motives that were secret palace business at this point, but Rivka took her position seriously and meant what she said. Perach, especially with Shulamit at its helm, was a fair land.

❖ ❖ ❖

Rivka was gone for several hours. When she returned to the palace, she headed straight for the queen. The afternoon had been productive, and she was a vessel eager to dock and deliver.

Reminding herself that there might be a sleeping baby inside, she altered her pounding step as she approached. With a nod to the guard standing at the door, Rivka entered the throne room.

The floor was completely covered in parchments and other papers, spread out in what Rivka took for a haphazard disarray that definitely didn't resemble straight lines. She was surprised to see fine sand beneath them in some places—where had that come from?

In the center of the paper explosion sat Queen Shulamit, kneeling, and crouched over in a position that made Rivka subconsciously stand up straighter to protect her own back. She was holding something that looked like a flat gray stone, staring at it intently.

Isaac paced in the back of the room. His right arm held Princess Naomi against his right shoulder. In his left hand, he held a piece of parchment, and he looked like he was studying it intently while he walked and bounced the fussy little girl. He'd stripped down to something short-sleeved, and Rivka felt an unexpected jolt of sensuality at the sight of his formidable forearms.

Shulamit looked up when she saw Rivka. Lifting the hand that held the rock, she greeted her. "I hope you found your enemy because I found mine."

Rivka drew her brows down. "Rocks, they're using to kill the olive trees?"

Shulamit shook her head, beckoning with her other hand.

The captain squinted down at the rock when she'd come close enough to see. In the center of the polished stone, fixed with resin, sat a fat little insect that reminded Rivka of a locust. It had a long, segmented stomach, and its shining, red wings were flecked with hints of blue. "Oh."

"Someone in the Division of Agriculture was kind enough to fetch me one while we were up in Imbrio," Shulamit was busily working at the end of her filmy, yellow scarf with her thumb and forefinger.

Rivka blinked at the bug. "You want I should interrogate it? Ask maybe where the Imbrian conspirators are?"

"Nahh, we can leave that to His Lizardhood over there." Smirking, Shulamit nodded to Isaac.

Still bouncing the baby, he walked over and joined them. Rivka hadn't noticed it before because he'd been singing so quietly, but there was a rumbly lullaby being murmured into Naomi's ear.

"All princesses in need of guard should have such a strapping dragon." Rivka knew that, even masked, he could see her eyes of conquest.

He flashed her an impish half smile that was all the more magnetic for its subtlety. "Captain Riv did battle today with a tavern?"

"What? Oh." Rivka looked down at her stained tunic. "I guess that means you can see it."

"I can *smell* it," said Isaac.

"I'm glad for it," Rivka countered. "The man who spilled it on me by accident was so desperate not to be in trouble with Captain Riv that he spilled a lot of other things."

"Was that at the Frangipani Table?" asked the queen.

Rivka shook her head. "No, after, when I went down to the river docks. There were no witnesses to the murder, but our clumsy beer-drinking friend was sleeping it off in a dark corner one night and overheard a key interchange. They must not have noticed him or thought he was just a knocked-out *schnorrer*."

"What'd he hear?"

"He said there were two Imbrians and a Perachi woman meeting in the shadows, and that the woman seemed to be giving them directions on a map. He thought they were looking for bawdy houses."

Shulamit chuckled, then collapsed back into a frown. "Do you think that's our Lovely Valley traitor, then? I mean, it would make sense, if she was sharing a map of the farms with the Imbrians."

Rivka nodded. "That works with what I found out from Yael and the waitresses. I don't think everyone on Ezra's list was actually at the table that night. There was only one woman, for example, and I think that's the one he labeled 'unknown.'"

"And this André probably wasn't there either." Shulamit studied the original list.

"The waitresses said they were speaking mostly in Imbrian," said Rivka. "They probably thought they wouldn't be understood, but Ezra must have spoken enough Imbrian to figure out what they were up to."

Shulamit rolled her eyes. "That's their own fault. What a silly assumption!"

"Does Aviva speak Imbrian?"

Shulamit sputtered a little. "That's not the point. They were taking a pretty big chance that *nobody* would speak it."

"Maybe they still kept their voices down," Isaac pointed out, "but Ezra, being a career eavesdropper, had his tricks."

"You don't mean magic, do you?" Shulamit narrowed her eyes and did not look pleased.

Isaac shook his head. "No, just ordinary cunning. Oh, *shayne maydeleh*, you must be in such pain, little one!" he added to the infant in his arms. "Here. Maybe this helps." He handed the paper in his left hand to Rivka and then placed its index finger in Naomi's mouth.

Rivka noticed as she took the paper from him that his hand was startlingly cold, colder than a corpse. It was like ice. It was unexpected and startled her, but it seemed to soothe the poor teething baby. "That's clever," she blurted, staring.

With calculatingly sultry eyes he accepted her compliment and began to sing again.

"Oh, now, that's just not fair," she murmured in their native language.

That just made him sing slightly louder, his lips moving sensually and deliberately in her direction.

Rolling her eyes, mostly at herself, she looked back at the queen, and at the floor beneath them all. "Wait! I just figured out why all these papers are everywhere."

Shulamit grinned. "Yes, Isaac made me a map! He cast a spell on the sand outside and drew it in here, in the shape of all Perach. That way I could place the papers down on the map in the right place."

Rivka shook her head slowly, smiling at the effectiveness of the idea. "Nice."

"Each one is a report of an infestation," the queen continued. "They're not all the same as the olive blight, which is apparently carried by these little brats"—she gestured to the stone—"but I wanted to have all the information in front of me so I could think."

"And so what do you think?"

Shulamit pointed to one of the farms and looked up at her captain. "I want to go here tomorrow and see, on the ground, what this really looks like. Who knows—maybe Zayde Lizard really can eat all the bugs himself."

"I'm a growing boy," said the forty-eight-year-old, stocky wizard.

Aviva appeared in the doorway, and as usual, Shulamit lit up on cue. "Look, I'm more queen than I've ever been," she called out, gesturing to the map. "I'm literally sitting inside my country."

"You're a pretty little spider in a web of parchment," said Aviva, looking around the room.

Shulamit's face hardened into determined lines, and her head rose resolutely. "Then I hope my webbing is strong, 'cause I've got a *lot* of bugs to catch."

Chapter 7. The Kiss of Your Land

When Aviva walked into the throne room and saw
Shulamit sitting on the floor, immersing herself in the study
of how she might better her country, she fell in love all
over again. The feelings swelling in her chest made her
think of what it was like to hold a jug beneath a merry
stream as it splashed over the rocks of a tiny waterfall,
watching it fill up and overflow and the cool sweetness
washing over her hands. There was water everywhere, and
Aviva bathed in it, submerged up to her broadly smiling
face.

It was late now, some time after dinner, and the baby was
asleep with Rivka's mother, Mitzi. Shulamit sat in the
center of her bed in her sleeping robes, braiding and
unbraiding the fringes of one of the decorative blankets.
Her fingers, like her mind, refused to lay still. "Rivka's
beggar witness said the traitor from Lovely Valley was
shedding chicken down."

"Looks like she has more than one reason to make you
sick."

"I know, right? I'd be laughing if I wasn't so worried."
She looked down at the blanket. "Rivka's sworn to hunt her
down, as well as all the Imbrians involved—so I'm glad we
have at least that lead."

"What about the invasion?"

"The latest report showed the infestation reaching down as
far as a big family farm owned by a man named Gil, but no
farther—not yet," said Shulamit. "I told the guards to ride
on ahead at sunrise and wait for me there."

"And you'll catch up to them with Rivka on Isaac's back?"
Aviva was used to such practices.

Shulamit nodded. "Bring Naomi over to the main kitchen when she wants to nurse. One of the scullery maids is nursing right now. She knows you might need her."

"Naomi and I will see if we can't have ourselves some adventures with sweet potatoes while you're off in battle."

Shulamit looked up sharply. "Battle? Right..."

Aviva lowered her eyelids seductively. "I should anoint the general before her campaign."

"Anoint?" Shulamit's eyelashes fluttered in confusion.

Walking over to a corner of the room, Aviva retrieved a small vessel she'd smuggled in when they retired for the night. "You carry all the hopes of the country with you tomorrow," she said as she returned to the bed. "You should also feel the hope of the olives themselves."

She revealed what was in her hand.

"Is that olive oil?" asked the queen.

Aviva nodded.

Shulamit's face twisted. "But what if it—what if there's—should we be wasting it like that?"

"I used less in dinner."

The corner of Shulamit's mouth twitched upward in smirking admiration. "You were planning this."

"Of course I was planning this. I might *talk* rubbish, but there's more in here than just carrot scrapings." Aviva grinned and knocked on her head with her finger.

"C'mere."

Aviva climbed onto the bed carefully, holding the vessel at a safe angle. She took up a position behind Shulamit, kneeling so that the queen's small backside was nestled in between Aviva's comfortably padded thighs.

Shulamit sat perfectly still as Aviva pushed her robe off her shoulders and down to her waist. With gentle fingers, Aviva flicked the straps of Shulamit's nightie one at a time downward, letting the silky material collapse in weightless folds around her tiny waist.

Aviva poured a rarified amount of olive oil from the vessel into one of her hands and began to work its slick softness into the queen's skin.

"This is what you fight for," Aviva murmured as she massaged. "This is precious. It needs you; it loves you. This is the kiss of your land."

Shulamit let out a voiced breath, an indistinct rose petal.

"You should remember this touch when you're out there, in the fields," Aviva continued. "You fight for our food. You fight for our fuel. You fight for the lights we see by in the dark, and for our country's prosperity."

Her lips were close to Shulamit's ear now, and she purposely exhaled into it. Shulamit's warm body let out a quaking shudder, and Aviva nuzzled her face against the side of her head.

❖ ❖ ❖

The olive groves lined the far side of the mountain ridge parallel to the great river that Perachi ships used to take their cargo south to the Sugar Coast or north to Imbrio. Here, on the Home City side, the mountains trapped both clouds and warmth, and more tropical crops such as banana and litchi fruit flourished. But over on the other side of the mountains, the air was drier and the soil more poor. This made perfect conditions to grow the hundreds of thousands of olive trees that gave Perach its cooking oil, light, and snacking olives, with plenty left over to export and grow rich.

If one followed the river south, of course, the mountain range flattened completely into the rich, dark soil of the Lovely Valley. This was the true source of Perach's wealth.

Shulamit's primary goal was to do whatever she could to keep the insects, and their rotting blight, from reaching the Valley.

Her guards were riding on horseback through a pass in the mountains, and they'd most likely reach Gil's farm by lunchtime. Since Isaac's dragon flight was faster than a horse on land, she and Rivka could leave after breakfast and still get there at the same time.

The mountains were as beautiful as always, but at first Shulamit couldn't enjoy it. She kept peering down among the trees, wondering where the horrid little creatures lurked.

But the sky was like a clear blue bolt of silk, and the wind rushing past Shulamit's face and ruffling the filmier parts of her clothing soon improved her spirits. With Rivka's sturdy body behind her and strong, reassuring grip on her waist, Shulamit reveled in the wonder that was dragon flight.

It took the sight of a field of brown trees to wipe the smile from her face.

"Oh, Rivka." Shulamit, wide-eyed, pointed to the grove as Isaac began his descent.

"Looks pretty ugly, doesn't it," Rivka agreed in a flat voice.

Shulamit narrowed her eyes. There was so much famine in the world already—how could someone cause it purposely?

"I see people," said Rivka.

"That's where I'm headed," said Isaac, his magnificent wings sparkling in the sunlight as he altered his course.

There were more than a dozen people waiting for them on the ground, right in front of a building Shulamit took to be the farmhouse.

First, there were four of the Royal Guard who had ridden
on ahead this morning through the pass through the
mountains, so that the queen wouldn't be traveling through
the countryside with only Rivka and the dragon protecting
her. Shulamit had done things like that in her youth, but
that was over five years ago and she knew better now.

The rest of the crowd looked like they might be Gil and his
family, the farmers who lived there, and perhaps some of
his neighbors. These were the people who stared up at Isaac
as he descended, mouths unselfconsciously open in
wonder. It was possible this was their first view of a
dragon. The wild ones, the beasts without reason, preferred
the unpopulated wilderness, and trained shapeshifters like
Isaac weren't terribly common either.

Isaac landed, and Shulamit, conscious of the dead foliage
and broken trees all around her, tried her best to smile
anyway as she waved at the farmers.

Rivka hopped unceremoniously off the dragon and then, as
usual, helped the dainty queen get down to the ground
without too much damage to her stylish, light pink clothing.

Out of the corner of her eye, Shulamit saw Isaac transform
into his lizard form and scamper up to his perch on Rivka's
shoulder as the two women approached the company.
"Good morning!"

A tall, broad man in his middle age stepped out from the
group of farmers. "Good morning, Majesty!" he said, his
voice almost swallowed up as he faced the ground in a
respectful bow. "Thank you for coming."

Shulamit nodded. "You must be Gil."

He nodded back at her. "Yes, Majesty. These are my sons
and daughters, my younger brother, and that's my eldest

62

daughter's husband over there." A braying noise attracted Shulamit's attention, and she turned to see a couple of donkeys grazing near a large stone. Gil chuckled. "They're part of the family too. But they've been idle lately, I'm sad to say."

"They power the wheel that crushes the olives for oil?"

"So it's true that the queen is well learned!" Gil beamed, but even through his flattery Shulamit could see the stress lines in his face and the fire of nervousness in his eyes.

"Tell me about the flies."

Gil sighed and nodded slowly. "Walk, and I'll show you."

Followed closely by Rivka and the rest of the guards, Shulamit let Gil lead her over to the trees.

"These trees are our oil crop, so they have smaller leaves," he explained, his hand thrust into a cluster of brown strips. "If they were healthy, they'd all look like these." He gestured over to the few plants here and there that still carried the silvery gray-green leaves of a healthy olive tree.

He didn't have to point out the bugs to the queen. She saw them everywhere—in the air, on the branches, on the leaves themselves. They glittered in the air as if they were literally making off with the queen's jewels instead of her country's economic prosperity. "Ew."

"They're not the worst of it. If only they were," Gil continued sadly. "First, there's this." He pointed out how some of the leaves that hadn't turned brown still carried a strange black smear that reminded Shulamit of soot or even eye kohl, which was what Aviva would have said. "They carry *that*," said Gil, "and what's worse, they carry an invisible blight that moves with them from tree to tree."

63

"The perfect weapon," Shulamit murmured. This was all horrible, and unthinkable.

"That was a long flight," Isaac spoke up from Riv's shoulder, startling Gil, "and I think I deserve a nosh."

Rivka chuckled low in her throat. "You certainly have your pick of them." She approached one of the trees so that Isaac could crawl into their infested branches, then stepped back and watched as he prowled.

Shulamit watched with amusement as Isaac caught one, then another of the insects, wolfing them down in two or three gulps with no chewing.

"He can have as many as he wants," said Gil, smiling bitterly. "I wish he could eat them all."

There was a rustle in the midst of the olive tree as all six feet five inches of a transformed, human Isaac stepped out of it. On his face was a sly smirk that Shulamit knew meant he was feeling extremely full of himself right now. He brushed dead olive leaves from the sleeves of his black *sherwani*, commenting, "Let's see what I can come up with."

All of Gil's family filtered over to observe curiously as Isaac began to wave his hands in the air. As magical energy flowed through the wizard's massive body, his gaze traveled slowly and deliberately over the grove. He was targeting his prey.

Shulamit watched with admiration as the insects began to pop. One by one, here and there, they disappeared in tiny bursts of light. She noticed that with each fizzling insect, whichever of Isaac's hands was nearest its tree twitched slightly.

The farmers began to applaud and hoot, and Rivka smiled widely enough that it was obvious even through the mask because her cheeks were sticking up.

But the process was too slow, and with each insect that was killed, two more appeared from other trees to take its place. Isaac's eyes blazed with determination, and his hands twitched faster. The miniature explosions continued, more at a time now, so that the trees nearest them were glittering as if sunlight sparkled on a rippling sea.

The film of lights expanded to cover more trees as Isaac widened his influence, and Shulamit was startled to hear him breathing heavily, almost panting. His skin had grown alarmingly pink, with the sweat rolling off his face in drops.

"Isaac..." Shulamit called out to him with alarm.

Pop, pop, pop, the insects went off all around them. Isaac was shaking.

With a gasping noise that felt like a knife in Shulamit's stomach, Isaac went limp. It was only thanks to Rivka's great strength that she was able to cushion his body as he fell to the ground, motionless and unconscious.

Chapter 8. Mi Shebeirach

Isaac awoke drowning in pain. His skull squeezed at its tender contents until he felt sure he would throw up if he moved. Even the scant amount of light filtering in through a window was enough to make him clamp his eyes shut again in revulsion.

The indistinct murmur of voices from another room also felt like torture. He tried to get purchase with his lips to talk, but the first thing that came out was just a breathy groan.

Somebody clutched his left hand. Hoping his guess was right, Isaac clutched back and muttered, in his native tongue and Rivka's, "My head."

"What do you need?"

Beautiful, radiant battle-goddess. He pulled her hand to his head and plopped it across his face. The pressure from without helped somehow with the pressure within.

"My head hurts. Breathing hurts. The light hurts, the sound—"

"Shh…" She massaged his temples with both hands. "I'll get you a cloth of hot water."

"Maybe also ginger?" He wished the sound of his own voice wasn't part of the problem.

"I'll see," Rivka answered. "Before I go—are you too hot, too cold? I opened your jacket in case you needed air."

"I wish I could take off the jacket. Everything is…" Isaac looked for a word. "Unpleasant."

"I'll try when I get back with the cloth," said Rivka, "but you might have to roll over."

"I don't know if I can without throwing up."

"Oh, Isaac…" Rivka's fingers dug into his scalp as if she were trying to dig out the source of his distress. He felt long hair splash across his face and then her kiss on his forehead. "You brave, generous idiot."

"Tell Aviva when she plans her menus that I'm off bugs for a while."

An unexpected wetness on his hairline told him just how worried his wife had been.

❖ ❖ ❖

Moderating her usually heavy step as if she were tracking a criminal, so that her footfalls wouldn't disturb her husband, Rivka quickly found the communal room of Gil's farmhouse. The murmur of several conversations between guards and farmers ceased instantly when they saw her.

Shulamit, who was sitting in the center of the room nursing Gil's youngest, looked up sharply and met Rivka's eyes with a face of deep anxiety.

"He's awake. He's alive. I need hot water and a cloth," Rivka barked. "And ginger tea."

Shulamit let out a long, slow breath, her chest heaving. She hugged the strange baby absentmindedly. "What happened?"

Rivka shook her head. "He… just overdid it. He'll be fine."

"But the bugs…?"

"I don't think the bugs have some kind of magical anti-Isaac warfare properties, if that's what you're asking."

Shulamit shrugged. "This is a nightmare. I don't know *how* far it goes."

A woman had appeared at Riv's side. "If you come with me, I can help you with those things you needed."

"This is Gil's wife, Eliana," said the queen. "She came back from the neighbor's while you were in there holding vigil."

Rivka nodded at Eliana respectfully and followed her into the farmhouse kitchen.

There was already a fire going, so it was simple for Eliana to pour water from a nearby bucket into a kettle and hang it over the healthy flames. She was talkative as she worked, the words spilling out in enthusiastic, breathless bursts. "The queen is as generous as the rumors said. I've been having trouble making enough milk for my little one, and that's why I was at the neighbor's. But she's sick right now, so she sent me home. It was a miracle that the queen was here. She offered right away. She said she would have had to express anyway, since it had been hours since the princess last nursed, but still—the queen! And us just simple farmers!"

"She may be young, but she's wise enough not to look at the world that way," answered Rivka as she watched the water simmer. She didn't want to talk too much about the queen's personal business, but Shulamit already behaved as if the entire population of Perach nursed at her breast. She took her queenship very seriously, seeing herself more as an overpaid public servant with a responsibility to earn all her pretty dresses and jeweled earrings, than someone whose will should control her people simply by virtue of an accident of birth.

"Will this cloth work?" Eliana held up a clumsily woven piece of undyed linen. "One of my daughters made it for practice when I was teaching her to weave. She was so proud of it and gave it to me as a present. In a way, it's almost more useful than something perfectly made, because then you're not as afraid to ruin it with the things you're cleaning up, right?"

Rivka nodded. "This is fine. Thank you. What about—"

"Ginger? Yes, now where did I put that? I'm sure if you want me to peel it first... I'll just... can you use the ginger tea to wet his cloth too?" Not waiting for Rivka to answer, she continued volubly, "Because that way, I can put the pieces in as soon as I get them peeled, and you won't have to wait for a second kettle—"

"Yes, that's fine." Rivka loved how helpful Eliana was, but she also desperately hoped her voice wasn't loud enough for Isaac to hear.

When the water boiled, the air was full of spicy steam from the ginger. Rivka dipped a mug down into it and then a bowl. With the cloth draped over her arm, she carried both mug and bowl back to Isaac's sickroom.

His face still looked bloated, pale, and sweaty, but she wasn't scared anymore now that he was awake. He'd managed to push the black *sherwani* jacket off his shoulders, but his arms were still stuck in the sleeves. The sleeveless, white shirt he wore underneath was soaked through and clung to the curves of his chest and stomach. He looked imprisoned. For a moment, Rivka was tempted to unsheathe the dagger in her right boot and cut him out of his clothes, but they were stranded out here several hours from home and most native Perachi men were nowhere near his size.

Blue glints appeared between barely open eyelids. "When did I inhale a sword point?" Weakly, he ran a couple of his fingers across the place between his eyes where his nose joined his face.

Rivka sat down beside him on the bed. "I hope this works." She dipped the cloth into the bowl of hot water, squeezed out the extra, and placed it across his forehead. "Not just the heat, but the steam."

Isaac relaxed slightly. For a few moments he simply lay there, breathing steadily. Rivka imagined the pain in his head as an enemy she could soundly trounce, either with her sword or her fists. She would force it to the ground, her boot on its face, and roughly wrestle its hands behind its back to be tied together in submission. It was a satisfying image, but ultimately useless.

"Can you sit up and drink the tea?"

"I'll try."

"I'll get your jacket off."

With great effort, Isaac struggled to hoist himself up with his elbows. When he was upright, Rivka quickly shucked the jacket the rest of the way down his arms. She handed him the mug of ginger tea, and he accepted it with both hands.

He sipped at it slowly, carefully. "What's going on out there?"

"Shulamit sent two of the guards back to the palace so people wouldn't worry." Rivka folded the *sherwani* over the back of a nearby chair. "They'll go off duty, and two more guards are coming back with a carriage and extra horses."

"Sorry your, uh, ride conked out on you." Isaac's features drooped slightly. "She didn't want to buy horses from the farmers to ride back?"

Rivka squeezed his shoulder affectionately. "You are not 'our ride.' You're our Isaac."

"But still, I let you dow—"

"Stop!" She wasn't loud, just firm.

"So we're going back in the carriage?"

"Well, actually," Rivka answered, "if you think you're feeling well enough, Shulamit wanted to stay the night and continue to the next farm south in the morning."

Isaac nodded slightly. "I think I can do that. If only the men in my head would stop kicking my skull, I could get some rest and be normal again."

"For dragon-transforming, wisecracking definitions of normal."

"Yes, Mighty One, but that's what you like."

"I like you healthy, but I like you alive too." Rivka gave him a significant look, reminding him with her eyes that she'd known for three years what it was like to live in a world where she thought him dead.

Isaac drank more tea. "Have the bugs reached the next farm?"

Rivka nodded. "Gil thinks so. They haven't done too much damage yet, but this morning while Gil's wife was passing by with her baby, she saw that there were bugs in some of the trees on the edge of the property."

There was more silent eye-conversation as new worry crept into his face. "We'll lick this," Rivka reassured him. "That little girl out there will never let the country be eaten alive."

"Perach is in good hands."

"Is the tea helping?"

"I think so. With the nausea only though. Not with the pain." Isaac took a last drink, then handed the mug back to Rivka. "Do the farmers have any other herbs they can put in it, anything to take away the pain so I can sleep?"

"I'm sure they have something. I'll go ask." Rivka stood again.

Eliana was happy to provide a mixture of leaves selected as a pain reliever, and it wasn't too long after Rivka brought Isaac his second cup of tea that he was able to lay his head back down on the pillow and drift off. Tenderly, she drew a thin linen sheet over his body, one that would shelter him but still keep him cool. Then, after a few minutes of watching him breathe with the slowness of slumber, she left him in peace.

Outside, with stones in her hands, she exercised her muscles. She worked out regularly, but now it was done to flood her body with the cheering chemicals of physicality. Rivka craved that humming in her blood. Isaac's collapse and unconsciousness this morning had strained her heart to the point of snapping.

This way she could finally see to her own mental health while letting him have the quiet he needed to heal.

Some of the farmers were watching her, from a safe distance—especially the teenaged boys. Well, that was fine—it was good for the reputation of the famous Captain Riv, which also indirectly enhanced the power of the throne. It also inspired the younger ones to consider the Royal Guard in their future.

Rivka was happy to notice that some of the women were watching her too. She had decided only recently to start scouting for the Guard's first female members, so that when she unmasked, some day, she'd be one of many, instead of a freakish exception proving nothing by herself. Maybe some of this farming lot were good prospects. After all, they certainly knew how to work.

Also watching Rivka, from their perches on every damaged tree, were the insects at the center of all this drama. In a frivolous way, she wanted them to watch her working. Let them see how easily she lifted this boulder. Let them see the flexibility of her immense yet perfectly agile legs. If only they could fear the power of her fists. If only they knew the unstoppable force that Perach's human population already respected.

The insects only knew how to eat and reproduce. But there were people behind these evil deeds—people who could definitely be taught to fear Rivka and her fists and weapons.

She vowed to hunt them down and bring them to every bit of justice they deserved—for Isaac, for the olive trees, and for Shulamit and her beautiful, generous, afflicted country.

Chapter 9. Hadar and Halleli

Shulamit slept awkwardly that night. Gil and his family did their best to put up their unexpected guests, with offspring who usually didn't share beds squeezing in together to make room, and they were amply rewarded with gold from the treasury. Still, the best they could provide was stiff and rough to a queen's pampered skin, and even more importantly, Aviva was miles away. Shulamit woke up several times in the middle of the night panicking at her absence before she remembered.

There was also the little matter of the stealth flour that had crept into last night's sauce…

It would have been nice to wander outside, among the olive trees, as she would have done if she were back home in the palace. But that would have required waking up guards—which it didn't back home—and the idea felt ridiculous and selfish.

She awoke at the sun's light with a false alertness she knew would only last a few hours if she didn't drink serious tea. A spare pillow made a lousy stand-in for her beloved, and her breasts felt uncomfortably full. More food for Eliana's little one, then.

After washing her face in a basin of water provided by one of the farm daughters and fixing her braids, Shulamit stepped out into the crisp dawn air. It was chillier than on her side of the mountains, but that was what olives liked.

Her guards were already up and milling about, preparing the horses and carriage for the short journey to the next farm. Rivka was sitting on a rock, her legs in a wide stance and her arms resting on her thighs. In front of her slithered Isaac in his buttery-yellow python form.

75

"How do you feel?" asked the captain.

"Light-headed more than anything," the snake answered. His tongue flicked out, waved around, then darted back into his mouth. "There's, you know, a kind of dizzy buzzing."

"Queen's up." Rivka had noticed her. "Hey."

Shulamit gave her a half smile. "How is he?"

"Magic's back, but he's not himself yet." Rivka looked back over at Isaac. Shulamit followed her line of sight and noticed he'd moved over to his lizard form.

"This doesn't feel so bad," said Isaac. "Maybe I'd better ride on your shoulder today."

Rivka nodded. "It's warm and waiting like always!"

"Better try this just to see... am I clear?"

Rivka shook her head. "Hey! You two. Move that way so he can test his dragon form."

The guards scattered warily as if they'd touched hot coals.

Isaac expanded into the dragon form. "Oy."

"Not good?" Rivka's brows looked concerned.

"I feel fatigued like this." He tried to flap his wings, but they wouldn't move. "That's weird."

Rivka got up from her stone and walked over to him. "You'll be all right soon," she cooed, rubbing his nose.

Just then, Eliana came out of the house, holding her baby in her arms. "Morning, Majesty!"

"Good morning." Shulamit eyed the baby. "Does she need to nurse?"

"Oh, *Majesty!*" Eliana glowed. "You're too generous. I've never heard of anyone, king or queen, like you before. I mean, they said you were just, and enthusiastic, but they also said you were really young when you ascended the throne, and—"

"Baby needs food, right?" Shulamit smiled weakly. The fussing embarrassed her and she wasn't awake enough to be gracious. "Here, let's get her taken care of."

"So sorry about last night's dinner giving you indigestion," Eliana commented as Shulamit adjusted the baby against her chest. "That mutton came from a very old sheep, and you must be used to the tenderest lamb. Plus, we don't peel our carrots way out here in the country..."

Shulamit let Eliana talk. She knew most people weren't ready to understand that it wasn't a refined palate that caused her stomach pain if not under Aviva's strict and watchful eye—it was the simple presence of wheat. Or chicken, but that was an entirely separate problem with much worse consequences. She'd been so busy making sure there was no fowl in her food that she'd missed the flour in the admittedly clear-looking sauce.

Well, anyway. Maybe the next few meals could be rice. "Who owns the farm where we're going next?"

"Well, it used to belong to the couple who taught the children's class at temple when my oldest were that age," Eliana began, talking in encyclopedias as usual, "but they've died, so their daughter takes care of the grove. Her name is Halleli. Beautiful little thing. About your height! Would have thought she'd have found a husband by now.

She hires in a lot of her farm help and some of those men—would you *look* at the muscles. Well, of course, what am I saying? You're around *that one* all the time, so you know what I mean." She pointed unobtrusively at Rivka, whose bulging biceps stood out from her sleeveless tunic.

Shulamit looked away and tried not to smirk at Eliana's admiration.

"She's got a friend there with her though, so maybe she likes it better that way."

Shulamit's ears perked up. "A friend?"

"Yes, a sturdy young woman called Hadar who dresses like a man and—"

Shulamit was unable to disguise her shimmering glee. "Oh?" It was so hard to find women like her in this world of silence and propriety. Of course, she could be wrong, but *really*.

"Her people live in the Lovely Valley, I think," Eliana mused. "Coconut farmers, I think. That's why she's so strong—had to learn to shimmy up trees."

Shulamit was practically vibrating. Then a sober truth spoke in her ear. She was about to visit these happy women, these women just like her, and probably give them bad news.

The smile broke off at the edges.

❖ ❖ ❖

Rivka loved the chill of the air this side of the mountains, having come from a place far colder than the steamy tropics of Perach. Just as during their sojourn in Imbrio, the coolness gave vigor to her muscles and made her want to jump around and use them. She felt trapped, riding in the carriage, but with Shulamit recovering from the trace flour in her dinner, and Isaac riding on her shoulder still nursing a headache, Rivka knew that they were all very lucky to have a ride even for this short way.

With the curtains pulled back, though, she could see the lovely morning walk they could have had. A perfectly clear sky domed an earth decorated by orderly rows of trees. Birds hopped on the ground and here and there fluttered out of branches; she hoped they were eating some of the *farshtinkener* insects.

"Riv?"

"Hm?" She turned to face the queen.

Shulamit looked pensive. "You don't think Queen Carolina's mixed up in this bug thing, do you?"

"How'd you get there?"

"The timing, partially." Shulamit twisted one edge of her scarf into a tight coil, then let it relax in her hands. "This wasn't happening before King Fernando got sick."

"You think she's capable of this kind of malice?" Rivka asked. "Because of... the way they are over there about human rights?"

"That's probably part of it," said Shulamit. "Plus, I mean—she doesn't seem mean, and she thinks she's my friend, but since she's not down here she'd be sheltered from all this." She gestured out the window at the brown and sickly trees. "She might just think she was taking us down a peg to make things easier for Imbrian economic interests."

79

"Or going along with someone else's plan to take us down a peg," suggested Rivka, thinking of the other queen's husband. She remembered him saying something competitive when he saw the Perachi olive oil in the shivah basket.

"Or she could just be lashing out emotionally as a reaction to all those proposed boycotts," Shulamit continued. "That might have hurt her feelings deeper than she was showing, especially since when we saw her she was more preoccupied with grief than anything else."

"If she even knows."

"Right. But do *you* think she does?" Shulamit studied Rivka's face intently.

"I have an open mind," said Rivka. "Right now, I'm just tracking my chicken farmer."

There was a silence, and Shulamit stared at her hands in her lap. "When I was about sixteen I wanted to marry her and combine the two countries."

Rivka smiled to herself. "What do you feel now?"

"I-I'm afraid of her."

Moving carefully so as not to dislodge Isaac, Rivka scooted closer and put her arm around Shulamit's shoulder. "She's probably harmless. And even if she's not, remember—I'm always here."

The carriage stopped, and both women looked up to see an older but tidy little farmhouse with a large, well-planted property behind it. "Guess we're here already," said Shulamit, adjusting her hair and scarf.

"I think I can hold my human body up for this," said Isaac. He crawled down Rivka's arm and transformed, ending up lying down on the seats across from Rivka and Shulamit. "Oof."

"Can you get up?" Rivka looked him over.

"Yes, yes," he muttered, moving slowly. Finally, he swung his great weight upright and took a deep breath. "At least the air smells good."

Rivka was first out of the carriage and held out her arm to help the queen down. With other guards leading the way, they walked toward the farmhouse.

The two young farmers and their workers had been prepped for the royal appearance, no doubt by a dawn visit from one of Gil and Eliana's numerous offspring or in-laws. They stood outside the farmhouse, nervously watching the party's approach.

It was easy to pick out the women Eliana had been speaking about. One of them was very short and very pretty, with a curvy figure and long hair tied back under a scarf. The other was a little taller and made of wiry muscle, with short, wavy hair that was parted on one side. Their body language hinted that Shulamit's glee had been on point; they hovered in each other's space, most likely feeding off each other to create a more confident being together than they would have each been separately.

Shulamit approached them with Rivka close behind. "Peace, everyone. Thank you so much for welcoming us to your grove."

The two farmers exchanged a brief, unspoken conversation with their eyes, and then the shorter, curvier woman stepped forward. "It's such an honor to have you here,

Your Majesty." She bowed daintily, with her companion and her workers following suit. "I'm Halleli, and this is Hadar."

Hadar bowed from the neck. Rivka found herself looking over the woman's muscles. She wondered if Hadar knew anything about fighting, even in sport, or if her strength was of yet simply the task-taught type.

"It's so wonderful to meet you," said Shulamit, brimming over with sincerity. "I know our people have a hard time talking about these things, but..." She took a deep breath. Rivka smiled at her beneath her mask, hoping the good vibes helped. "I have a female companion too. Her name is Aviva. She's back home at the palace with the princess."

Rivka was proud of her, but looking at that pained yet exalted face, she wondered if that conversation would ever get any easier.

The couple in front of them were clearly happily surprised. Halleli's eyes widened, and Hadar broke into a huge grin. "See, didn't I tell you? There are rumors, Your Majesty," she explained.

"I hoped there were," said Shulamit sheepishly, but Rivka was pleased to see that she was relaxed now. The bottle was uncorked and flowed freely. "That makes things easier! Besides, I'd want everyone like us to know I was out there."

"People talk about *them* more." Hadar nodded toward Rivka and Isaac. "Does he really... the dragon?"

"Oh, I would *love* to see a dragon... I love dragons! When my parents were alive, they used to take me high up in the mountains and we'd watch the wild ones," Halleli gushed and dreamed.

"I'm sorry to say I am not feeling well," said Isaac gravely, "but I will give you a little show." With those words, he grew into his full, gigantic, green-black dragon shape. Rivka watched him, a little stirred, a little worried.

He must have noticed her concerned eyes, because he looked over at her and winked. She smiled involuntarily and wiped sweat off her face beneath her mask, her heart full of affection.

"Oh, he's so beautiful!" Halleli's face looked like that of a child in wonderment.

Hadar chuckled at her. "She draws a lot of dragons. She's always drawing when we get some downtime."

"She can draw me if she likes," said Isaac. "I may not have much energy today, but it doesn't take energy to pose." He struck a dramatic posture, and Rivka snorted with laughter.

"What about Captain Riv?" Hadar asked brightly. "I mean, I know that *obviously* some of those stories can't be true—"

"I guarantee you I did not perform my own bris," Rivka barked.

Shulamit burst into giggles.

"—but you're still a giant!" Hadar finished.

"He's *our* giant," Shulamit interjected.

"I've been working on my own form, a little." Hadar flexed, and Rivka noticed a look of delight cross Halleli's face. "She draws that too," Hadar added. "Anyway, while you're here... if it's not too much trouble... uh..." She scratched her head. "Maybe you could give me some tips?"

Rivka swelled not only with pride, but also enthusiasm. Suddenly this young and energetic woman seemed like a fantastic prospect for the female guard she'd been planning.

"I would *really* like that," she said emphatically.

Chapter 10. Abscheid und Feuerzauber

"Here, you have to try this one next." Halleli opened another jug and fished out a handful of olives, eating one herself, as she had been all morning, to show Shulamit's guards they were safe.

Shulamit and Isaac each took a couple of the tiny, purple fruits from her offering palm. "Oh, that's almost *floral*!" exclaimed the queen. "How'd you do that? It's really nice and mild."

"It's a secret." Halleli grinned. "My mother learned it from her father. We've been on this land for generations."

Shulamit chewed thoughtfully, concentrating on the pleasure of the brine slipping down her throat so that her face wouldn't betray the guilt Halleli's words produced.

There were other things on her mind too. "I would have given anything at sixteen to have known you were out there." Shulamit wiped oil from her lips. "Even just as a friend. I felt so alone, so strange. What was it like for you?"

"I didn't know." Halleli's smile was self-conscious. "You're gonna laugh at me… maybe… I thought everyone felt like this. When I was that young, I mean."

"You mean you thought that all women…"

Halleli eyed Isaac and the guards, then leaned in closer to Shulamit so the men couldn't hear. "Girls are so pretty and smell good, and men are… something else, and I just figured that every woman just found a man she felt friendly enough with to marry and that was it."

Shulamit grinned. "No, many women actually *like* lying down with men."

"You're teasing me. I know that *now*." Halleli ate another olive, then replaced the lid on the jug. "How did you know?"

"My father had this… adult stuff I wasn't supposed to be looking at. The really shameful part is that I think it was made for men." Shulamit wished they could have this conversation in private, without the male guards—even Isaac—but since she was queen, she couldn't very well be alone, and Rivka was off sparring with Hadar on the hillside. It was a good thing Rivka was planning to introduce more female guards, in case this sort of thing happened again. "They weren't always looking at each other in the drawings—they were looking out at the audience. It made me feel, you know… radiantly happy and then also shameful at the same time, like I didn't belong to myself, somehow."

"I bet I could make better drawings," said Halleli. Then her face brightened. "Hey, do you think I could do a study of your face?"

"That might be fun!"

Halleli disappeared into another room to get her drawing supplies. While she was gone, Shulamit looked at Isaac, her face grim.

"I saw them too, *Malkeleh*."

"I can't do this."

He looked down at her with compassion swimming in his hooded eyes. "Because she's like you?"

"I don't know…" Shulamit looked down at the table. "Even if she wasn't, they've been on this farm for generations."

86

"This farm lies between the infestation and the Lovely Valley," Isaac reminded her. "Your country's breadbasket. Or breadfruit-basket." He made a sickly grin at his own joke. "And the insects have already begun to feed, spreading their plague."

"Look, Isaac, I know your magic wasn't the right spell, but what about Aafsaneh?" Shulamit looked up at him intensely. "She ran a vineyard since before I was born, all those years before she became Queen of the City of Red Clay. I bet she'd have some way of wiping out the insects, or at least the blight they're spreading."

"That's a great idea, but—"

Just then, Halleli came back with pencils and paper. "I brought you some of my drawings, in case you wanted to see." She handed them over, her face glowing but shy.

"You're really good at these!" Shulamit turned pages and saw dragons, olive trees, and some of Hadar. "I like the way you captured the way her muscles stand out. It looks like she's really moving."

"Thanks," said Halleli, shifting papers around. "She doesn't like to sit still for them; she's got too much energy for that. So I try to do quick sketches of what I can see in a moment, and then combine them later when I have more time to work."

With a blank paper in front of her on the table, the pretty, young woman moved her pencil in a circle as she studied the queen's face. Shulamit noted that only after making several rounds did she touch its point to the page.

"Sometimes if I do that, I can see the picture start to appear before I even draw it," Halleli explained.

"Am I in a good pose?"

Halleli nodded, then jumped up. "Wait! I'll be right back."

She bounded outside, the door swinging behind her.

Shulamit looked over at Isaac. "Anyway, I think we should send for Aafsaneh."

"Do you think we can wait that long? Even if I were well enough to fly over there and get her?"

"We can send our fastest horse and rider."

Halleli came back inside carrying a couple of inflorescences of four-lobed pink ixora flowers. "Here, I just got these from the bush in the front garden. That way I'll remember that you were really here, in our little kitchen!"

As Shulamit accepted the flowers into her arms, she grew even more determined to save the women's grove, somehow. There *had* to be a way. If Isaac wasn't well enough to fly over to the City of Red Clay, they'd just have to find a horse and rider fast enough. Rivka would know which of the Royal Guard was the most renowned for speed. Or perhaps one of the farmers could help. Was anyone around here breeding racing horses?

Three days. *Four* days, actually, since they were farther east than Home City. Could the farm hold out for four days? How fast did the bugs move? Oh, and yes, then there was the journey back... Queen Aafsaneh could probably do it in two days, flying in her swan form.

A week, then. Did they have a week?

"You have your father's thick eyebrows," Halleli commented.

Shulamit's eyes stung a little, but it was just a reflex, and she didn't cry. "Yes," she agreed. "You've seen him?"

Halleli nodded. "My parents took me to Home City for Purim one year. I dressed as a carrot."

Shulamit giggled. "That must have been adorable!"

"I looked hideous, but I had so much fun." Halleli's pencil moved across the paper in slow, fluid lines. "It was really just an old orange dress, and I used papyrus to make myself a hat, to be my greens on top."

"I remember being a fairy," said Shulamit. "I had great big wings made of silk with a frame of cane inside." *And the whole of the country's treasury to pay for it. I should probably stop talking.* She fought the grimace that threatened to mar Halleli's portrait.

How can I take this from her? When I have the whole palace, and this is her whole family history?

Aafsaneh. It all boiled down to Aafsaneh. She *had* to know a way.

❖ ❖ ❖

After the portrait was finished, Halleli offered to show the queen around the farm. They walked out into the sunlight, guards and Isaac following at a respectful distance. "This is the tree where my father proposed to my mother." Her hand traced the bark, then drew back sharply. "Ew."

"Do you know what those are?" Shulamit found herself asking.

"Yeah." Halleli looked at the ground. "They got Gil's farm pretty good." With pleading eyes, she faced Shulamit. "That's why you're here, right? To help with the bugs?"

Shulamit gave her a weak smile.

Thumps on the dirt heralded the approach of Rivka and Hadar. "That's some great woman you got there, Halleli!" Rivka bellowed.

Hadar laughed. "Whew! You sure gave me a workout!" She was shining all over with sweat and smiling like seven birthdays.

"Wish I had her on my guard." Rivka eyed Shulamit significantly, speaking with her eyebrows.

Shulamit lifted her own in response, then nodded.

"What's going on? What are we doing?" Hadar bounded up to Halleli and caught her in an embrace from behind, closing her arms around her waist.

"I was showing the queen around the farm," Halleli explained. "We got interrupted by some bugs."

"Those things from Gil's farm made their way over here?" Hadar wrinkled her nose. "Ugh."

"They weren't here yesterday?" asked Shulamit.

Hadar shook her head. "Nah, we were totally clean yesterday morning. I've been spraying soapy water on the trees, and I thought that would keep them away. It does sometimes, with other bugs."

"They moved this fast overnight," Shulamit murmured to Rivka, who had drawn close.

"And could be on the other side of the farmhouse by tomorrow." Rivka's voice was grim.

"I thought that if we could get Aafsaneh here, she'd know what to do, how to fight them."

"Who's that?" asked Halleli.

"My stepmother-in-law," explained Shulamit. "Well, legally, anyway. I only have a husband so I could have a legal heir. He lives on a vineyard with the man he loves— he's like us." She gestured, indicating that she was including her audience. "But, technically, it's *her* vineyard, and she lived there for twenty-five years before she married the king of her country."

"Plus, she's a witch who can turn into a swan," piped up Rivka.

"She sounds wonderful." Halleli had stars in her eyes. "You think she can help us?"

Shulamit scratched her wrist. "Well, if anyone would know magic that would get rid of agricultural pests, she seems like the one…"

"They're on those trees there, now." Hadar was pointing at another row, farther to the south.

Shulamit looked at the ground. Under the soil, in the roots, the blight spread by the insects was no doubt already taking hold. When she looked up, she faced south. Past the farmhouse, she saw the mountains melting away into rolling foothills, and rows of other people's trees evening out into other types of plantations. Rice, oranges, mangoes. Vineyards and orchards, fields and furrows.

She didn't have to see the detail to know what was there—she'd been there before with her father as a young girl and then as a teenager, and more recently as a queen. There were scores of people down there growing the food that made her country rich and well-nourished, each of them with families and memories and needs.

In her imagination, she saw the bugs sailing in with each southward breeze, seeking new succulent plants to devour. She saw the blight spreading into every root in the Valley, the mold over every leaf. She saw farmhouse after farmhouse grow dark as their residents were forced into poverty, her cities teeming with the displaced and hungry.

She saw Perach forced to buy more food from its neighbors, instead of selling so much as they'd done in any life she'd known. From Zembluss, from the city-states, and yes, from cruel Imbrio, who worked its peasants into the ground to keep pretty Carolina in diamond tiaras.

This was what they wanted.

No.

"I wish she was here," Shulamit found herself saying, "but we can't get her here in time. Not with four days' journey there and back."

"So now what?" asked Halleli. Hadar stepped in front of her slightly, a move that seemed protective.

Shulamit looked at Isaac. In a choked, broken voice, she said to Halleli, "I'm afraid I'm going to make you hate dragons."

It took her a few moments to understand. "What are you saying?"

"I want you to understand," said Shulamit somberly, her hands clasped together, "that I understand if you hate me too. *I* hate me right now." She took a deep breath. "I have to stop them. I have to stop the flies." She closed her eyes, not able to bear seeing Halleli's face at her next words. "We have to burn the farm down."

She felt an arm she knew was Rivka's descend around her shoulder, and she leaned into the familiar, stiff leather, wishing she was somewhere else and wanting to cry.

When she opened her eyes, the faces of the women were pretty much what she'd been expecting. Halleli's eyes were wide, her mouth small and open slightly. Hadar had lifted both brows and was frowning intensely. "How can you just come in here with your wizards and horsemen and take our farm away?" she demanded. Halleli began to cry softly, so Hadar put both her arms around her, glaring around her at everyone.

"I'm so sorry," said Shulamit. "I don't want to. It's the last thing I wanted to do."

"What about him?" Hadar lifted her hand to Isaac. "Can't he do something?"

"He tried yesterday and it nearly killed him." Shulamit's fingers closed around one edge of her scarf, massaging the soft fabric to soothe herself. "He's got a lifetime of experience on the battlefield and in courts of at least five different countries I can think of, but this, he couldn't do."

"I wish that I could," Isaac verified.

"With this much bare earth, we could hold the bugs off for several weeks," said Shulamit, "long enough for Aafsaneh to get here and destroy them completely, if she knows how."

93

"But why *us?*" Halleli pleaded.

"This is how far they've gotten. The bugs just got here, right?"

With a frantic little motion, Halleli nodded. "But what will we *do?* We have nothing."

Rivka stepped forward, her hand out to Hadar. "Come to Home City and let me train you for the

Guard."

"Me?" Hadar jutted her face forward in astonishment. "You were serious about that? But I'm a woman!"

Rivka's response was to draw herself up to her full height, fold her arms in front of her chest, and toss her head so that her hair rippled golden in the sunlight.

Suddenly, Hadar's face changed. Her eyes widened in shock, the rest of her face frozen. Then, slowly, the corners of her mouth twitched, and the tiniest smile appeared, just for a moment.

Shulamit figured she'd just witnessed Rivka wordlessly out herself to her new prospect, and flushed with feminist zeal.

"You're young and you have a lot of energy," said Rivka calmly. "Your body is cut out for it, and so is your mind. And you wouldn't be the only woman in the Royal Guard. I've started looking for more."

"I like the idea," said Hadar, "but it's all up to her. She's my other heart." She stepped back and took Halleli's hand.

Halleli turned to look at her. "This is really hard."

"I know, love."

Bugs flew over their heads. Halleli gazed all around herself, at everything she'd grown, at everything her parents had planted, and her parents' parents.

Finally, she spoke, in a voice that was barely audible. "I won't hate dragons."

It was consent. Shulamit stepped forward and took her hands. "You're a national hero. I promise."

"I'm a national basket case." Halleli squeezed her hands, then dropped them and laid her head on Hadar's shoulder.

"My guards will help you pack up your house." Shulamit's voice was gentle. She was consciously mimicking the tone Aviva used to sing their daughter to sleep. "I'll even do what I can, myself. Do you have a wagon we can hitch to my royal carriage? Or have the horses pull?"

Hadar nodded. "We have a wagon and there's a donkey who can help, if we need him. He crushes the olives when we make oil. I guess we can sell him in the city."

"Not yet," Halleli whispered.

"Okay, we can keep him as a pet." Hadar hugged her, then pulled away. "What about her? Can she work in the palace?"

"We'll find something for her," said Shulamit.

"I can help in the palace kitchen or if anyone needs help planting things." Halleli's voice was barely audible now.

Shulamit nodded. "While we find a place you'll be happiest, you can draw pictures for me. In any case, there's plenty of work in Home City." *That's part of what I'm trying to preserve here…*

They worked quickly over the next few hours, staying one step ahead of insect invasion. Gil and Eliana showed up with some of their family, fetched by a Royal Guard and one of Hadar and Halleli's workers, and they did what they could to help pack while saying good-bye. Putting so much energy into a task distracted everyone from the sorrow of the moment, and Shulamit was able to avoid her guilt by carrying bundles from the house to the wagon.

It was late afternoon by the time the house lay empty enough to satisfy its owners. "I think that's all we really need." Halleli's face looked like she'd aged ten years in a morning. She put her hands on her hips and looked around the empty house. One hand reached out and caressed a wall.

"You are a brave and beautiful woman," said Shulamit.

Halleli answered with a half smile. "Guess I'd better go outside."

They found Isaac transformed in the front garden. "Everybody secure?"

"We'd better do a roll call," said Shulamit.

The guards all counted off, and Shulamit verified that Hadar, Halleli, Rivka, and of course Isaac were all safe.

"The horses and donkey with the wagon and carriage are up on that hill where Hadar and I were wrestling earlier." Rivka pointed. "I think that is a good place for us to wait, out of the range of the fire."

Just in case, each of the guards carried buckets of water, including Rivka. Everyone followed her to the peak of the hill—everyone except Isaac.

As she trudged up the hill with her guards, Shulamit heard a strange puff of noise behind her. She turned around to see Isaac testing his flames in the air. Black smoke and tiny, glowing sparks, like little orange jewels, flew from his mouth.

He noticed her watching "I'll wait for your command," he called out.

She nodded in response, then kept hiking.

Once atop the hill, she stood gazing out over the land. The farm was a healthy size, and hopefully its absence would create a barrier the bugs would be too confused to cross for a while. She knew it wouldn't last forever though. They'd smell food on the other side, and then they'd come.

But this was their best hope—for now.

Halleli stood beside her. "I want to remember it. I'm so scared I'll forget and then it won't exist anymore."

"You should draw it when we get back to the palace."

Halleli was silent, tears streaking her cheeks.

Rivka busied herself checking the horses, making sure they were ready for the journey that would take them back to the palace in time to sleep tonight. Hadar joined her, already instinctively treating her as her commander.

The air was so still and so peaceful, Shulamit almost couldn't believe what they were about to do to it.

Well, there was no reason not to start now. "Isaac, go ahead." She was surprised at how confident she sounded.

Down in the grove, the great dragon nodded, then reared back on his haunches.

Brilliant yellow flame shot from between his jaws. It consumed the tree in his immediate path and began to move down the row to the next.

His wings were starting to work again, but they were frail like a chicken's. He was able to get about his own height into the air again before he was forced to land. Here he set another tree ablaze.

Soon, more trees were on fire. Everything was orange, and the air was full of the scent of burning wood.

Halleli was crying. Shulamit hugged her, and then she was crying too. Her shoulder was sticky from the other woman's tears, but she ignored it and held her closer.

Hadar stood on the top of the hill, her hands on her hips as she watched the inferno consume the grove.

Finally, as if she'd seen enough, she walked over and joined the other two women, putting her arms around both of them.

Shulamit's breaths were deep and even. The decision had been made, and it was all over. Hadar and Halleli would come to Home City and rebuild.

But the danger was only halted, not stopped.

Shulamit watched the fires leap into the air, licking the blue sky. If only there were a way to surround all her country's farmlands with such fire, benevolent fire, protective fire, that would keep out all who threatened them. She imagined them, guarded like a sleeping goddess on a hilltop, protected from harm.

Chapter 11. A Night for Heroes

Shulamit and her found family did their best to make the ride back to Home City as cozy and rejuvenating as possible. Isaac rode on Rivka's shoulder as a lizard so that Hadar and Halleli would have the other cushioned seat to themselves, and he and Rivka entertained and distracted the two women with stories about their days on the battlefield together.

In between, Shulamit told them all about Aviva and how they'd met because as the palace's Second Cook, she was the only person to figure out that the queen—well, Princess Shulamit at the time—was sensitive to certain foods.

"I can't eat chicken or any other fowl," said Shulamit, "and wheat gives me stomach cramps."

"Wheat?" exclaimed Halleli with surprise. "But it's in everything!"

"Tell me about it!" the queen agreed. "No pita, no challah, no sufganiyot at Chanukah, she has to make me my own separate batch of tabouleh without the bulghur…"

"What about beer?" asked Hadar. "Does the fermentation get rid of… whatever it is?"

Shulamit shook her head. "No, but I mean, that's not something I miss."

"What about the princess?" Halleli shifted against the cushions to get more comfortable. "Can she eat any of this?"

"She's really too young for us to know," said Shulamit, "but we're being careful."

Isaac sang for them to pass more of the time; his voice was deep and luscious and he knew it. Shulamit could tell he was deliberately choosing cheery or exciting songs that wouldn't send Halleli into fits of tearful nostalgia, and she was grateful for his foresight.

The sky was already a rich lapis-blue deepening into black by the time the royal carriage and its guards on horseback arrived at the palace with their wagon and donkey cargo in tow. Members of the palace staff were gathered to meet them, and Shulamit was glad to see their happy faces in the light of the hanging lanterns when she stepped out of the carriage.

Especially two faces in particular. "I missed you guys *sooo much*." Shulamit enveloped Aviva and the baby in a meaningful hug. Aviva felt warm and squishy, and Naomi smelled like bananas. Shulamit sighed, happy to be reunited.

"Wow..." A breathless voice came from the carriage. Shulamit turned around to see Hadar helping Halleli out into the courtyard. The two farmers blinked around themselves with wonder at the palace's grandeur, standing out against the black night with its white walls and red-tiled roofs.

"New friends?" Aviva inquired, handing Naomi over to her other mother.

"New friends like *us*," Shulamit replied, saying further things with her raised eyebrows.

Aviva's eyes bugged out and her mouth bloomed into a grin. "That's great! I—"

Shulamit made a face. "It's *sort of* great. I'll explain in a second." She unpeeled herself from domesticity and walked over to the guards on duty. "Please get everybody out here. Everyone who's not sleeping, I mean." Some of the guards, cooks, and cleaning workers had early morning shift, and it would be unnecessary cruelty to disturb them.

The guards nodded, and scattered.

Soon, the palace courtyard was filled with people, milling underneath the palms, confused and excited. Through the middle of the crowd emerged Mitzi, fluttering around like a confused bird in her flamboyant dressing gown, with Tivon, off duty and from whose room she'd likely emerged, in her wake. Her piercing gaze darted from person to person. "What is it? What's going on? Majesty? Riv, is the palace under attack?"

Rivka held up both hands. "Everybody's safe."

"Oh, well, *that's* good to know!" Mitzi huffed indignantly, then settled back against Tivon's chest and waited with everybody else.

Shulamit stepped out in front of her family and staff. "My friends," she began, "these past two days, I've been with the farmers up on the mountains. I'm sorry I didn't make it home last night, but we were busy doing everything we could to try to stop those bugs. I'm happy to say that we managed to buy ourselves three or four weeks, and hopefully, well before then, Queen Aafsaneh of the City of Red Clay can come to our aid. She spent literally my entire lifetime on that vineyard before she married King Jahandar, and she is a trained and excellent witch. She is, right now, our best hope."

She paused, glancing behind her at the two farmers. They were huddled together in the darkness beside a banana plant.

"Tonight, I want to recognize one of the bravest acts I've ever seen, and the two amazing women who shared it. These women are my heroes right now. They let us burn their grove to make a bare-earth barrier to hold off the bugs. Their names are Hadar and Halleli, and I invite you all to recognize the amazing sacrifice they made for their fellow farmers."

Rivka nudged the bewildered young women closer to the queen so that they stood directly in the lantern light. They approached Shulamit nervously, but she stepped in between them and nodded to each of them. "This is Perach!" shouted Shulamit, the smile of strength on her face.

Cheers rose up from the staff and royal family. Everyone from the highest-ranked guard—Rivka, who was clapping loudly and nodding along with her claps—to the girl who had just joined the cleaning crew the week before was making noises of gladness and appreciation. Aviva ran up to the impromptu royal platform and tackled both Halleli and then Hadar with big, welcoming hugs.

Shulamit wiped tears from her eyes, and smiled at her.

Aviva was looking at the newcomers with a sparkle in her eye. "I bet you two need dinner!"

❖ ❖ ❖

Rivka pushed open the door of a spare room in the guard quarters. "Here's where you'll be sleeping." She held the lantern she carried into the room so that its light could splash over the walls. "If you need help carrying in your things from the wagon, start making friends with the other guards and they'll be happy to help."

"Thank you," said Halleli as she followed Hadar into the room. Isaac and Rivka remained outside in the pleasing autumn nighttime air.

Hadar set her own lantern down on the floor beside the bed. She kept turning her head from side to side as if planning. "Halleli—how do you feel about moving the bed there, under that other window?"

"Oh, I'm fine with whatever." Halleli traced her fingers over the walls. "It's very clean."

"I'm sure you two will keep it that way." Rivka smiled behind her mask, then swatted idly at something fluttering near her shoulder. Her smile faded. That better not be one of those bugs from the mountains. She'd checked all the luggage when the trees were burning, twice, and then once on the way back to Home City.

Hopefully it was just a moth. The wings seemed rounder than the grove bugs', at any rate. "Will you be okay if Isaac and I go off duty now?"

Hadar nodded, adding, "Yes. Thank you for the room. And the job."

"Yes, thank you," Halleli agreed.

Rivka sensed the moth again, this time tickling her ear on the other side. She tossed her head like a horse, hoping her wild hair would send it fleeing.

"I may come take you on an adventure in the morning, Hadar, so be ready."

Hadar grinned at her. "Sure!" She and Halleli were already taking up positions on opposite ends of the bed so they could lift it and move it.

Rivka closed their door and turned to face Isaac, who greeted her with a smirk. "What?"

Then she saw the rose petals. Two of them, dancing in the air as if blown on the wind—of which there wasn't any. She watched them as they circled each other, then rose up again to frolic teasingly around her head. A third joined them, caressing a bare patch of her neck, then her ear, before joining the other two.

Soon, a wreath of flower petals was revolving around her face. Isaac's left hand delicately tickled the air, each finger moving independently, as he watched her from half-closed eyes.

Rivka grinned. "Where are you getting these?"

"Bush by the fountain," he replied nonchalantly. "I picked them up while you were showing those two around."

"Oh, so you planned ahead." She wiped away sweat from underneath her mask. "You trying to tell me you're all better now?"

Isaac thumped his chest with his right hand. "Try me."

"You know, I think I will. C'mon." Rivka turned and walked away from the barracks, toward the stream behind the palace.

"I like the sound of this." She heard his voice and step, and didn't need to turn around to know he was following her.

The rose petals followed her too, swarming around her head and sometimes darting down to tap her face. She snatched at them, catching a few. They felt soft and sweet in her fingers.

Behind the palace's back wall there was a patch of grass leading up to a stream. Lush foliage here and there blocked it partially from view, and here was where she led him. Here, banana trees leaned over the water, and the air was filled with the songs of chirping frogs. They were tiny, but insistent that the night belonged not only to sleep, but also those who were awake.

The moon was only three days old, but Isaac was clearly visible in the starlight when Rivka turned to face him. "Headache's all gone?"

"I feel great." His voice was confident and booming. "I'm sure Aviva's cooking helped."

"Well," said Rivka, limbering up her body, "prove it!" She leapt to one side, hoping he'd get the idea.

Isaac's creek of a smirk became a wide, grinning river, and he raised his eyebrows. With one great motion he hurled his great mass at his wife.

Rivka, however, trained every day in one or more of the various fighting styles she'd learned, and it was easy for her to feint away from him. Hopping around with a limberness that would have surprised someone who'd seen her muscular, five-foot-eleven frame at rest, she chuckled ribaldly as she avoided his grasp.

"You know, I could just start unlacing your trousers with my mind." Isaac reached for her and then quickly shifted in another direction, a direction he clearly thought would anticipate her next move.

But *ha*, Rivka was already on his other side. "You can try anything you want—I'll fight naked if I have to!"

"I bet you would."

"You'd like that."

"I could make you finish while you're still fighting."

"You were the one who taught me not to get distracted," she retorted. She was ready though. His words only fanned the flames that burned between her legs. This theater did have a purpose—she wanted to be truly sure of him before she straddled him on the grass, without that nagging worry that he would overtax himself and have a relapse.

Plus, she knew he liked it. As if reading her mind—which he couldn't do, but one of his tricks was good guessing—he answered, "If I were your age, *I'd* probably finish while you're still fighting."

That was enough. Time to find the earth.

Changing tactics, Rivka barreled toward him and seized his massive upper arms. She tried to force him to the ground, but he used the weight of his torso to wrestle her down with him on top. With one final burst of technique that spoke to why she was a legend instead of just a hired thug, Rivka flipped him over.

He lay panting on the grass, reached out his arms, and pulled her down to him.

She had time to say, "I love you," before their mouths met.

Chapter 12. Turning the Tabletop

Rivka's hair rippled behind her like a flag as Isaac flew through the morning sky. She gripped him tightly with her thighs to keep her hands free in case Hadar needed any help feeling safe on her first dragon ride.

She needn't have worried; the young woman was handling it like a pro. All that practice climbing up and down coconut trees in her youth, Rivka figured. "This is great!" Hadar shouted into the wind.

"And I get to do it whenever I want," bragged Rivka.

"I can't even see Home City anymore. How far are we going? I thought you just meant *this*, when you said adventure."

"Nah, I thought I'd take you on a little tracking mission," Rivka said. "Plus, it's your home turf."

"Hmm?"

"Lovely Valley. I need to find a traitor."

"What? Wow! Really?" Hadar faced forward, away from Rivka, but her back and shoulders looked tense.

"You got sold out. All of you olive growers got sold out," said Rivka. "By a chicken farmer."

"A chicken farmer? Gosh… I don't… from Lovely Valley?"

"A woman."

"What do you mean, 'sold out'?"

"A woman shedding chicken feathers sold a man from Imbrio a map of the olive groves leading down into the Valley," Rivka explained. "They planted the bugs and spread the infection on purpose."

"*What?*" Every muscle in Hadar's body tensed as if she'd been stretched and pulled by unseen hands. "Someone. Did. That. On. Purpose? I will find them. I will—"

"Yes, yes, that's the idea," Isaac piped up soothingly, his great, rumbly dragon voice sounding like it echoed inside a great hall. "Only, let the captain do the hard part. The queen needs her in custody so she can tell us what she knows."

"She hurt my Halleli. She ruined everything we were working toward."

"She's hurting everyone," Rivka reminded her.

Hadar nodded slowly. "I promise. I'll obey your orders. I'm a guard now, right?"

"That's right."

"How come you took me along, anyway? I mean, I know I'm from there and all, but aren't you worried I'll be a liability if there's violence?"

"I saw how you fight yesterday," Rivka reminded her. "You can handle yourself pretty well. Besides, today might only be hunting, information, tracking. Sniffing out the scent. And we'll have the local police to help us if we get as far as an arrest."

"Thanks!" Hadar took a deep breath. "Wow. I'm—I'm glad I didn't know any of this yesterday."

"Can you think of anyone it might be?" Rivka inquired. "The witness seemed to think she was older."

"Chickens... older... not really." Hadar was silent for a moment. "I mean, there are some men I can think of... and I can definitely think of women who have chickens too, but they're not... none of *them* could be... This is all just so fucked up."

"I know," said Rivka.

"Are you sure it was chickens? Not, like, limes? Lime juice?"

"Not unless limes shed chicken feathers," Rivka quipped. "Why?"

"Nothing." Hadar stared off into space.

"You gonna want to see your family for a few minutes while we're there?" asked Rivka. "I think we're making good time."

"Maybe my sister, if she won't tell my parents I was there," said Hadar. "I don't need my father making up this week's reason why I'm a big disappointment."

"If that's how he feels, he doesn't know anything," said Rivka. "If it helps, Halleli's very proud of you."

"Yeah, it does." Hadar didn't look all that concerned about what she'd just said, but Rivka couldn't tell whether she was looking at a healed scar or a pain buried too deep to discuss.

Given that she had grown up with the uncle who'd filled in for her absent father treating *her* like she couldn't do anything right, she sympathized either way.

110

❖ ❖ ❖

The built-up part of the Lovely Valley consisted of a single long street that snaked between the endless mango groves and avocado plantations. Numerous side streets ran out in both directions to more remote farms, growing a wide variety of crops Rivka had never dreamed of during her childhood in the colder north. Even the names had once been completely unfamiliar to her—litchi, sapodilla, canistel, jackfruit.

Now they were as ordinary to her as apples once were. Litchis were Queen Shulamit's favorite food, so there were always some around in the palace; sapodilla were satisfying and sweet. Canistel was soft and mild, and Princess Naomi had been enjoying it lately, and jackfruit—Rivka would have loved jackfruit even if it didn't have such a wonderful taste, simply because of its ridiculous size. If someone had told her as a teenager that fruit came in a twenty-pound variety, she'd have laughed them out of her uncle's castle.

She was here to protect all this. The richness and prosperity of Perach was bound up in her agriculture; nowhere was that more obvious than here in the midst of a living fruit salad.

"Why aren't we sneaking in?" Hadar asked. "Word's gonna get around the Royal Guard's here. I was still here when you first came to Perach, and I remember people running from farm to farm, saying, 'Everyone, go watch the sky to see the dragon!'"

"What makes you think they can see us?" Rivka grinned and patted Isaac's scales affectionately.

"Wait, what?"

"It's my new trick. We look like a cloud," Isaac explained. "I can only keep it up for a few seconds though."

"Land here," said Rivka. "We'll walk."

Isaac landed slowly, carefully having to maneuver his wings and his other magic at the same time. Rivka jumped off and helped Hadar down, then let Isaac place his great clawed paw in her hand. Within seconds, he'd dwindled down into his lizard form and crawled up her arm to sit on her shoulder.

"Wow, that's… wow." Hadar nodded, impressed. "He's something else. Where'd you find him?"

"He taught me to use a sword."

"Oh yeah?"

Rivka threw a hooded cloak over her head and arms so her noticeably light skin and blonde hair wouldn't alert anyone they passed that Captain Riv was in town, and then the two women set out for the main drag.

They passed block after block of one-story buildings, modest but shining clean and white in the bright sunlight, before reaching the more formally built ones belonging to the local government. There was a man outside, a guard from his uniform, but he was leaning against the wall eating what looked like a pita stuffed with raw vegetables instead of standing at attention.

When he saw the travelers approaching, he held up his free hand. Without moving his butt from the wall, he called out to them, "Hey! This is official headquarters. What's your business here?"

Rivka flipped back her hood. "It's me. That looks like a good sandwich."

The guard scrambled to attention, straightening as if a rat had crawled up his pants and nearly dropping his sandwich. "Captain! Oh. Sorry. Wow." Then he squinted. "Is that—is that *Hadar*? You look so different with short hair!"

"Yeah, it's me." Hadar looked pleased with herself. "I joined the guard!"

"What?"

"Just yesterday," she added.

"The *Royal* Guard?"

"We need to come inside and talk business," Rivka interrupted.

"Oh, right, sure. Just in there."

"Business and national security," added a voice from Rivka's shoulder.

"Oh, you brought the dragon man?" The guard peered around.

"When do I not bring Isaac?"

The guard shrugged. "I have to stay out here and keep watch, but the Sheriff's in there with his deputy. Go on in."

The Sheriff of Lovely Valley was sitting at his desk trying to scratch dirt off a dagger. He looked up at the sound of footsteps, then stood to greet the newcomers. "Captain Riv! Down here checking on us?"

"I'm actually here about something serious," said Rivka.

"Here, sit down," said the deputy, pulling over a chair. To Hadar, he added, "Do you want my seat?"

"I can sit on the floor," said Hadar brightly, folding herself into a pretzel.

"Hadar?"

"Yup!"

"You cut your hair!"

"Nope, my wife did."

"Your—"

Rivka clapped her hands together. "Mr. Sheriff. Deputy."

"Yes, sir."

"Sorry, sir."

"You've heard of the insects and the blight up north in the mountains." Rivka noticed Isaac scampering down her arm as she talked.

"Yes," said the Sheriff, suddenly looking more sober.

"The insects and the blight they carry were spread deliberately by foreign agents." Rivka watched the two men's faces freeze in shock at her words. Out of the corner of her eye, she noticed Isaac spring up from the ground in human form and lean against the wall, his arms folded across his chest.

The Sheriff lifted one hand in greeting to Isaac as he replied to Rivka. "Foreign agents? Like—spies? Saboteurs?"

Rivka nodded. "'Fraid so."

"Someone would want to hurt Perach that badly?" said the deputy in disbelief.

"It may not even be about Perach, really," said Isaac from the back of the room. "Just greedy people wanting their own crops to do better on the international market."

"Or back home," Rivka added.

The Sheriff and the deputy looked at each other. "So, what can we do?" said the Sheriff.

"Right now there's a barrier of burned earth between the infestation and Lovely Valley," said Rivka. "That buys us a few weeks. This morning, the queen sent a man on horseback to the City of Red Clay. Their queen is a witch who spent half her life managing a vineyard, so we hope she'll have a good plan."

The Sheriff snorted. "I hope so too!"

"The reason I'm here," Rivka continued, "is that we have evidence that a traitor from Lovely Valley sold a map of the farms to the Imbrians."

The Sheriff's eyes narrowed and he rubbed his beard. "Great," he muttered. "Well, what have you got?"

"We're looking for a woman, at least thirty-five but probably older," answered Rivka. "who owns a chicken farm or works with chickens."

The two men's reaction was utterly unexpected. It was almost comical the way they looked at each other with dropped jaws, as if on cue.

Rivka leaned in. "What?"

"Tabletop Tova," said the deputy at the same time the Sheriff was saying, "My God, what's Tova gone and done now?"

Hadar scrambled to her feet. "Tova? Seriously? Wait, since when does she have chickens? What happened to the lime trees?"

"They all died, and she turned into a mean old cuss," said the deputy.

"No," the Sheriff interjected, "she was a mean old cuss before that. When her son moved away to marry that Sugar Coast woman."

"Well, I mean—" The deputy scratched his head. "Maybe even before that. She got kinda difficult after her husband died."

"Captain Riv, Tova was the woman I was thinking of on the way here." Hadar was practically jumping up and down with nervous energy. "She can be really hateful."

"She's gotten worse," said the deputy. "And you've been gone for a few years—you haven't even heard the tabletop story."

"That's where she got that silly name," said the Sheriff.

"Yeah," said the deputy. "Everyone calls her Tabletop Tova now."

Rivka sat back as the story poured out, both men competing for the gold medal in the interruption prizefight thanks to their morbid glee.

Apparently, this Tova had bought a new kitchen table from a respected Lovely Valley carpenter. The next day, she came hauling the table back into the shop, claiming that he'd sold it to her with a scratched top. Now, he knew the table had been pristine when she bought it, and so did a couple of other customers who'd been in the shop at the time. It was obvious to everyone that the scratches had come from her chickens, which she was ill-equipped to control because she was so new to the chicken game.

However, Tova was the type who could never be persuaded that she was wrong, or that anything could be her fault. She'd started an argument with the carpenter that escalated into a scene witnessed by at least four or five other people—other customers, and farmers in the street who were just passing by—and ultimately ended with her scratching the top again, herself. She grabbed the heavy key to her own house off her belt loop and left violent furrows in the brand-new top, spat on it, then left the furniture shop in a huff.

"And this is why nobody wants to buy eggs from her," the deputy concluded.

"She didn't used to be like this," said the Sheriff sadly. "Back in the day, when her husband was alive, she was a lot of fun—even funny!"

"She always did have a temper though," the deputy reminded him.

"It's a shame she turned into what she turned into." The Sheriff sighed.

"To me it sounds like she pushes people away to keep them from leaving first," Isaac commented laconically, "since it all started when she lost her husband and her son."

117

"She didn't have to *lose* her son," groused the deputy. "He just moved away! She could have even gone to join him when the lime trees failed."

"She probably thought she was gonna *show him*, or something." Hadar picked at her shoe.

Rivka clapped her hands down on her knees, then stood up. "If you don't have other suggestions, then let's get down to Tova's farm as soon as we can. I want to know who in Imbrio paid for this insult."

❖ ❖ ❖

The grove that had once made Tova and her husband rich on limes now lay overgrown and half-neglected around the farmhouse. The stench of chickens was in the air; they ran around everywhere within the fence, leaving a trail of feathers and droppings. The one bit of ground that still looked well-loved was a plot of vegetables. Rivka noticed that the vines sprawling across the ground were covered with a healthy amount of zucchini. If nobody bought her eggs, maybe she was living on her own plantings.

"Sergeant, you lead," Rivka ordered. "Don't want her to know what we know, and if I'm first at the door—"

The sergeant nodded. With his deputy close at his heels, he rapped his knuckles on Tova's front door.

"Just a minute, hang on!" called a voice from inside. Rivka heard footsteps, and then the door swung open to reveal a scrawny older woman with her hair in a knot at the base of her neck. She peered around at all the visitors, clearly surprised to see so many people on her threshold. "Oh, it's you, Sergeant. Thank you so much for coming. Don't know what took you so long," she added sourly. "Guess they're keeping you busy, huh?"

"Well, I, er," the sergeant stammered.

"Mangy little brat yaps all hours of the day, nips at my heels when I get outside the fence..." Tova leaned on her doorframe. "Makes me feel like a prisoner in my own home, I tell you."

"You complained about the... neighbor's dog," the deputy suddenly remembered.

"That's *right*, I did." Tova puffed herself up like one of her chickens. "Wouldn't be surprised if I wasn't the only one either. One of these days, it's gonna leap my fence and steal a chicken. If it hasn't already."

"Why don't we come inside, and you can tell us all about it," Isaac piped up in a voice so low and fluid that Rivka was glad her mask hid the grin on her face.

His charm clearly worked on Tova, and she swung the door wide open. "Come on in. Don't mind the mess."

Rivka blanched at how badly the place smelled. She thought the chicken odor of the farmyard was bad, but inside was something else... some kind of animal urine—cat, perhaps?—and the stuffiness of mold, and things she couldn't even identify. She sent a pitying look at Isaac, knowing it must be worse for him, because at least she had a mask to shield her partially.

He lifted his eyelids slightly in response, and surreptitiously snapped his left fingers beneath his nose. Rivka rolled her eyes, realizing that he was now smelling roses or raspberry rugelach or something entirely unrelated to cat piss.

119

"Don't you ever get tired of being you?" she murmured to him in their guttural native language.

He just smirked.

"Wish I had some honey-sesame bites to offer you all," said Tova, "but nobody usually comes to visit me, so I don't have anything like that in the house. You think my son would come back and visit one of these years."

"I thought he came back for Passo—" the deputy started to say.

With a quick, furtive tap to the hip, Isaac shushed him, interrupting with a comment to Tova. "It's so difficult not to be able to see your loved ones."

"I know!" she agreed. "And my nephew lives only a few orchards down, growing papayas and avocados, but well, *he* called me a piece of shit, so—"

"My dear woman, that's terrible."

"You bet it is," said Tova. "Where'd they find you, anyway? You're not from here, not with *that* coloring."

"I come from the north, but I live in the capital," said Isaac.

"Now *him* I've seen before." Tova pointed to Rivka.

"The captain and his entourage were down here for a routine visit." Oh, good, the sergeant knew how to make shit up too. Rivka was beginning to wonder. "So, about this dog…?"

While Isaac and the other men got Tova talking about her neighbor's dog, Rivka fell into the back of the group, trying to drop out of sight. Moving only her eyes, she scanned the room for clues. Anything at all might link Tova to the Imbrian conspirators—Imbrian coins, men's clothing or accessories, perhaps documents with the foreign alphabet—

Something caught Rivka's eye on a nearby table covered in papers. A cat rested across the mess, and sticking out from its gray fur she spotted a familiar shape.

Moving slowly so her migration wouldn't attract attention, she floated sideways and peered down at the cat.

It was sleeping on a copy of *the map*.

Lifting her mask slightly, Rivka pursed her lips and blew breath at the cat.

It blinked and winked, then twitched its head. She blew again, and it stood and stretched. As soon as it hopped off the table, Rivka scanned the paper carefully to be sure of herself.

It was *definitely* the map, the same map that Shulamit had found in Ezra's pile of blackmail fodder. Perhaps this was a practice copy.

Rivka spoke. "Isaac. Sergeant."

Both men looked up, and Tova with them.

"Go retrieve that paper on the top of the pile," she continued. "No, not that one—the one with the coffee stain on the corner."

Tova froze.

"Is this—" The sergeant began.

"You're all my witnesses that this was found here and not planted?" Rivka looked around the room. The deputy and Hadar nodded.

"Mistress Tova," Isaac interjected, "you've made a valuable discovery that will help the crown with some very troubling matters."

"Huh?" Tova blinked at him.

"This map is part of an international plot," said Isaac, "and we'll need your help to get us out of it."

"Yes, we need you to make the journey back to Home City with us," Rivka added. *Good work, Isaac! Now she doesn't know she's a suspect, and maybe we can actually get her to talk.*

"To Home City?" Tova looked around her at all the officers. "Well, I—"

"The queen will be pleased to hear of your arrival," said Isaac. "Maybe you can tell her about the dog too!"

Tova grinned bitterly. "Ha! Won't my neighbors like to hear about *that*! We'll see who's who around here."

And she tossed her head and glared out an open window at the world.

Chapter 13. Little Stories

Shulamit was nursing Naomi after dinner when the noise of a carriage outside heralded the return of the travelers. Rivka crashed into the kitchen-house, banging the door against the wall and collapsing into a chair with an "*Oy gevalt!*"

"No luck?" Shulamit tensed, her eyes wide with concern.

"Oh, we found her all right." Rivka smacked the table with both elbows, then rested her head in her hands. "Rode with her all the way back in the sergeant's carriage. By the way, he's spending the night here if you want to talk to him." Now she held up both hands, palms outward to Shulamit. "Kill me. Kill me now, cut my head off. If I *ever* have to sit through anything like that ever again… this relative, that relative. Her son never appreciated her. Her nephew won't give her back the oud she loaned him nine years ago. Loaned him or gave him, I don't know. She's cut off two of her sisters for reasons that are half-trivial and half-delusion. *Meshuggah!* I'm sick of it. Put her at the bottom of a well and feed her pickles."

Like a fairy godmother, Aviva appeared at her side. "Cabbage soup?" She smiled as she placed the steaming bowl in front of Rivka.

Muttering something that sounded like "I'll cabbage her soup," Rivka grabbed the spoon like a weapon and fed.

"Poor Riv. You are *so* appreciated." Shulamit absorbed Rivka's outburst. "But you found her? She's here?"

Rivka nodded between slurps.

"Good work! Great!" Shulamit ran her fingers through Naomi's soft hair.

123

"Thanks." Rivka rubbed her temple. "Oh, and thanks to Isaac, she doesn't know she's a prisoner."

Shulamit smirked. "That's our Isaac."

"He could have a fish frying in a pan convinced he was giving it a bath," Aviva piped up helpfully.

"And then feed the fish to Riv," added Shulamit.

"This fish stinks. Soup's good though!" Rivka nodded in approval to Aviva, who grinned and curtseyed. "Oh, and get this. She brought a kitten."

"The traitor… has a… kitten?"

"She has several cats," Rivka explained. "Apparently, this one can't be left alone because it still has to be fed goat's milk. Who knows what happened to the mother. The way she kept that house, a cat could get sick and die without her knowing."

Aviva cleared garlic husks off the countertop. "I feel bad for her family."

"What?" said Rivka. "Oh. I guess you're right."

"Where is she now?" Shulamit bundled her breast back into her tunic and gently rocked her sleeping daughter.

"Isaac's getting her settled into a room somewhere." Rivka accepted a plate of stuffed grape leaves from Aviva and continued between bites. "He'll have it out of her."

"You can tell him he can pick that up in the morning," Shulamit replied. "She's under guard and can't leave, right?"

Rivka nodded. "You sure?"

Shulamit nodded back. "I want to be there listening on the other side of the door if she says anything—me and other witnesses. It's just good sense, legally. I mean, you love Isaac and I love Isaac, but… you know. Let's play it safe."

Rivka smirked. "What, you're not up for a night of eavesdropping?"

Shulamit sighed wearily. "I seem to have picked up the sniffles while we were out running around the countryside these past few days. I need an early night in. Plus," she added shyly, "Aviva promised she'd tell me silly gossip from the marketplace while I soak in the bath."

"I'm glad you're looking after your health, at least." Rivka ate the last leaf roll in one bite, then stood up to go find Isaac.

"Thanks," Shulamit called after her. "Tell him we'll pick it up in the morning. Tova won't wake up any nicer than she went to sleep, right?"

❖ ❖ ❖

A thrash and a whimper roused Hadar from deep sleep. "What's the matter?"

"Wha'? Wha'?" Halleli woke up gasping.

It was still the middle of the night, and the only light was a faintness from outside, slipping in through the window high in the wall. Probably lanterns or torches for the nighttime guards; the moon was still only a scrape. Hadar saw Halleli in her mind more than with her eyes, and reached out for her. "Were you having a nightmare?"

There was a pause, and then a plaintive "Yes…"

"You're awake now, love. It's all gone." Hadar pulled Halleli's warmth against her, making sure each curve felt cared for.

"You burned up in the fire." Halleli's mouth moved against Hadar's collarbone as she talked, leaving heated moisture from her breath. "Burned up with everything else."

"Shh… of course I didn't." Hadar felt tiny and enormous at the same time, too small to take away the pain and big that she was *enough* anyway. She thought about how Halleli was older, by three years, and how she still trusted her enough to cry in her arms.

"I know, but I *saw* it. I knew it."

"Maybe I'm just hot," Hadar quipped, stroking her hair.

"Heh."

"You're shaking."

"I'm scared to go back to sleep," Halleli murmured. "Those images are waiting for me."

"Gotta put some new ones in your head, then," said Hadar. "Happy images." She traced her fingers down Halleli's back gently. "We've got plenty of happy memories to think about."

"I know… we're very lucky. Even after all this." Halleli squirmed, unpinning her arms so she could return the embrace. "Sometimes I almost can't believe we're the same people we were when we were kids… that the cute girl at the Lovely Valley general store who I used to flirt with is *you*."

"Every season you'd show up, for a few days, with your parents," said Hadar, massaging whichever tense muscles were beneath her fingertips. "They'd bargain with my dad, and you'd come find me."

The year Hadar realized what Halleli's attentions were, she told her big sister, the one who was nice, the one who *knew*. "That girl from the olive groves treats me like a boy." She knew the words were wrong, but she couldn't explain it any other way.

And her sister had smiled at her, and tucked her hair behind one ear, and told her, "Then treat her like a girl."

Hadar did just that. The next time Halleli appeared in the Valley with her parents, Hadar had asked if she'd like to take a walk around the lake behind the general store. "Back in a few minutes, Aba!" she called out, not listening for the grumbling reply.

"Do you remember those old stories we used to tell each other?" Halleli's mind ambled down the same lakeside path. "Back during those walks we took."

The two young women had amused each other by making up new versions of familiar popular legends, new versions with a simple but important change.

There was the story of the *Nobleman with Eighteen Girlfriends*. His valet colluded with the most lovestruck of all the ladies to bring his master to justice after he murdered a different girl's father. In Hadar and Halleli's version, the valet was a woman, and she and the lovestruck lady held hands and pledged eternal love at the end.

Then there was the *Story of the Singing Contest*, where a young man had to learn the rules of poetry before the strict judges would accept his genius. The girls had transformed

127

him into a bright young woman instead, and she still won the hand of one judge's daughter along with the contest prize.

Farming was hard work, and so was creating a real life together, learning to weave their disparate personalities and rough edges together into the real cloth of family. It had been years since they'd made up stories like that. "Is that what you need right now?" Hadar asked softly.

"That would be perfect."

"Which one?" Hadar shifted, brushing some of Halleli's thick hair out of her own face.

"Eighteen girlfriends."

The made-up versions were never the same twice. Sometimes the lady valet was disguised as a man until the last minute. Sometimes she was an ordinary lady in dresses. Sometimes it wasn't eighteen girlfriends but eighteen boyfriends, or a mix. The nobleman in the story was a dreadful rascal, but sometimes he was fun to watch until the inevitable downfall.

"Once upon a time on the Sugar Coast..." Hadar squeezed Halleli's rear end, and Halleli responded by opening her legs and clamping them around Hadar's thigh. Thus arranged, she listened quietly and eventually drifted back to sleep.

Hadar was getting sticky from sweat, but she didn't want to unpeel her. Maybe, even in sleep, she still needed to feel that Hadar was there.

Better to live and be a bit sweaty than die in your sweetheart's dreams, after all.

❖ ❖ ❖

"You cannot *possibly* imagine how annoying it was." Tova rolled her eyes and rested her hands in her lap.

"I understand," Isaac lied, his face kindly. "It sounds terrible."

"No, you don't understand," Tova insisted.

"May I refill your tea?"

"Thank you." Tova handed him her cup, and he accepted it with his left hand. With his right, he gestured at the teapot until it lifted itself off the table and topped her off. "That's a neat trick."

Isaac smiled amiably. "Have to." After replacing the teapot on the table, he showed her what he meant.

"Ooh, that's a nasty scar!" she exclaimed. "You know, sometimes those doctors, they really have no idea what they're doing, any more than anyone else. There's a man down in Lovely Valley—"

Isaac was not used to meeting people who didn't ask about the scar and instead rushed headlong into their own monologue, but since the whole point of this morning's torturous exercise was to get Tova to talk, talk too much, talk about *anything* until a confession came out—he knew his ego could take the bruise.

He looked at her intently with his best imitation of a compassionate stare, and half listened, all the while worrying at her words as if they were food stuck in his teeth. He was looking for weaknesses, for likely places to introduce the Imbrians into the conversation, or perhaps the

129

map itself. To steer her there delicately was the object of the game.

"Then there was that awful animal doctor who came and saw me when one of the cats was sick," Tova continued. "Can you believe he told me I had too many cats? He said *that's* why she was doing so poorly. Judgmental assbag. I told him as much. Shouted him into the street. Other people might want to know about his lack of qualifications. Course, he had to get up an attitude about our little difference of opinion. Took it personal and badmouthed me, and now none of his clients will buy my eggs."

Only Rivka would have noticed the small blue fire that now flared from Isaac's eyes. He knew his 'in.' Inside, he was running around the room high-fiving himself. Outwardly, he took a sip of his own tea, swallowed, then inhaled its grassy, green flavor for a moment as he aimed his tongue. "That must feel awful. That's your livelihood! Don't they remember that your crop failed?"

"They remember—they just don't care." Tova set her teacup down and rubbed a nervous finger around the lip.

"Wait 'til it happens to them," Isaac said calmly. The dragon retreated farther into the cave, his glinting eyes leaving the illusion of gold coins deep within.

Tova's face brightened. "Right? I mean, it really hurts. It's not just those folks, but also my neighbors"—every one of which she'd already told Isaac some story about having antagonized—"and the farmers from the far side of the lake, and the traders' families too. Not that you can really trust those traders. One of them had a pretty little jug she'd picked up in City of Lakes, and she was holding it for me, but I didn't have the money right when she wanted it, so it went to somebody else. Told *her* which way the sky was

130

up! Told other people, too, so they'd know what kind of deals she made."

Back to the topic… Isaac's nostrils flared, and he swallowed more tea. "It wasn't your fault that you didn't have the money, because of what happened to your crop."

"Ex*actly.*" Tova punctuated the syllables with her finger. "She should have understood. They *all* should have understood." She sat back in her seat and folded her arms across her chest.

"Someone should make them understand." He said it as a flippant aside.

Tova smirked. "Well, that's coming."

Isaac's pinky finger twitched, the slightest of movements. Outside the door somewhere, the queen, who was listening in with Rivka and Tivon as witnesses, would feel her earlobe tugged slightly as his magic moved her earring. He wanted to make sure she was listening. "Someday, of course, yes," he said out loud.

"Oh, I don't mean someday," said Tova. "I mean this season. You'll see. And then we'll all be equal again."

Yes, except they would have helped you like they help everyone else if you weren't so full of meanness. "Why? What happens this season?"

"Bugs." Tova waved her fingers in the air. "Put us *all* back to point zero, *and* show them what it feels like."

Isaac put on his best skeptical face, slightly condescending. "What, you have, you have chicken eggs that out of hatch these bugs?" He made a motion with his

131

left hand like an egg cracking open, and smiled so that his words sounded like he liked her but didn't believe her.

"Of course not, silly! No, I just wound up on the good side of a deal. Got money out of it too," said Tova. "The bugs are coming down from the olive groves. I just had to show 'em how to get there."

"Oh, was that what the map was, then?" asked Isaac. "We didn't know."

Tova nodded. "Can't wait to see the looks on their faces."

"Indeed. It's good to hear you still had people who would do right by you, after so many in the Valley," said Isaac.

"They seemed nice enough, I guess."

"Local boys? Boys from the Valley?" Isaac loved getting facts by contradicting the answer he thought likely.

Tova shook her head. "No, not even Perachi. Hey—why do you want to know all this? Am I in trouble?"

Shit. "Just making conversation," he answered, but it was too late. The frantic fear response in his subject had taken over.

"Knew you'd find something to pick apart," Tova said in a puff of dismissal. "Can't just let a woman be. Bet you think I have too many cats too."

"I didn't say—"

"Let me tell you, Mr. Too Tall, I'm not saying another word about that map or those bugs. I'm being held here against my will. You brought me here under false pretenses—"

"Well, yes," Isaac admitted, "but you're a threat to the national economy, and I don't even think you realize what you did." He stood up. "Mighty One! *Malkeleh!*"

The door opened, and Shulamit appeared in the doorway with Rivka and Tivon behind her.

Said Isaac to them, "I got as far as I got. She's all yours."

Chapter 14. A Royal Pain in the Throat

The sunlight of the next morning streamed through Shulamit's throne room from the open door at the far end. She perched in the ornately carved wooden chair, sitting against more cushions than usual, her hands holding what was already her second cup of herbal tea with honey and lemon of the day. Yesterday, she'd gone through about twenty.

Naturally, it made her urinate constantly, but the concoction did wonders for her raw and aching throat, and even the steam felt like it was doing something healthy to her nose.

Isolated, out-of-context fragments of the previous day's hours of interrogation passed through her mind.

"We want to give you the benefit of the doubt, Tova."

"Maybe tell me what's hard for you to talk about here?"

"It's the right thing to do."

"Was it men who knew the traders, maybe? Since they travel, they might have gone up to Imbrio and—no?"

"How did they find you? Or did you find them?"

"You're trying to twist this around and put words in my mouth!"

"I never said that. Did you hear what he said? I never said that!"

"I don't have to talk to you."

"Then, fine! I'll just stay here. You already brought me here under false pretenses. Can't believe some people say how fair and free this country is."

"Is the Imbrian throne behind this?"

"And another thing—this pita is dried out and nasty."

Shulamit sighed into her tea. Rivka was in there again, ready for another day with Tivon at her side, trying to run down Tova's stubborn will through sheer persistence. Isaac was at his customary position behind the queen's throne, since he'd already antagonized Tova too much to be of any use.

"Majesty, are you sure it's a good idea for me to draw you when you're not feeling well?" Halleli piped up from a small cushion on the floor. With a board beneath her paper, she was yet again sketching the queen.

"It's fine," said Shulamit. "This is just practice, anyway, right?"

"I can practice Isaac, too, while I'm in here. I'll need to get good at all five of you if you really want that portrait done."

"I do!" And Shulamit really did. Even if half the reason for the project was to keep Halleli busy and around for conversation while she found her a more permanent job. She was also helping out in the main kitchen, but the companionship was nice. None of Shulamit's ladies-in-waiting shared her attraction to women.

"You'll need taller paper," Isaac quipped, and Halleli smiled a little.

Shulamit asked Isaac who was next for royal audience, and he went to check. "Yael's here."

"Bring her in."

"Nice to see you looking so human today!" Yael's greeting was warm and mirthful, and Isaac grinned back at her. Then she bowed toward Shulamit.

"Good morning!" said the queen. "Please excuse my voice. I was running around in the mountains, and—"

"Oh, you poor thing! You have to let me make you chicken soup."

Shulamit choked down her initial response, gave Yael a weak smile, and asked, "So, what brings you to the royal sickroom today?"

"Well, Majesty." Yael drew closer so that she could speak in low tones meant only for Shulamit, "I found out how Ezra knew I'd had a male name."

"Go ahead," prompted Shulamit.

"Apparently," said Yael, "he was having a thing with one of my waitresses, and she's like me. She swears she didn't tell him that I was too, and he must have just put two and two together since I guess if you stare at me long enough, once someone puts the idea in your head… you know?"

Shulamit nodded, coughing into her hand. "That makes sense. What made her finally tell you?"

"Well," Yael sighed, "she didn't. Up and left me in the lurch, and wrote me a note. She says after Ezra got knifed and the guards set up house in the restaurant, she got skittish and didn't want to get mixed up in anything. She's got an alibi, anyway, but I don't think she cares about that."

"At least now you know."

"I'm glad I know, although at this point it would be more useful just to have my waitress back."

Shulamit lifted an eyebrow. "So you're looking to replace her, then?"

"I have some ideas, but nobody I know who's a sure bet to leave what they're doing now."

"What if I had somebody for you?"

"How do you mean?" Yael cocked her head to one side.

"Halleli!" Shulamit called out.

Startled, the girl dropped her pencil and scrambled to her feet. "Yes, Majesty?"

"Can you wait tables?"

"I'm a hard worker, Majesty," Halleli said. "I can do anything someone teaches me to do."

"She grew up on a farm. And I know she knows her way around a kitchen. Yael, she helped out in the main kitchen here yesterday and I heard only good things," Shulamit explained.

Yael looked Halleli up and down. "Your name's Halleli?"

"Yes, ma'am."

"And you're from a farm?"

"Yes, ma'am. We had an olive grove, but we had to burn it to stop the—"

Yael clapped her hands together. "You're one of those little girls everyone's been talking about in the marketplace! I heard about you. The heroes! Yes, okay, I'm *definitely* giving you a job. Plus, I need a waitress. Just don't tell me too loudly what I'm doing wrong with my olives!"

Halleli's eyes were wide in shock. "Thank you," she sputtered.

"Maybe you can make some sense out of our kitchen garden too," Yael continued. "My husband was really the one who looked after it, so with him gone it's just a complete mess."

Hope spread across Halleli's face. "I'd really like that! Uh, Majesty, should I stay and finish the sketch or...?"

"We can do that later, at leisure." Shulamit waved her hand. "I mean, you live here now. Hadar's got guard's quarters. So there will be time." She coughed again.

"Thank you." Halleli looked like she was getting happier by the moment. "I'll go tell Hadar."

"I think she's lifting weights with the rest of the afternoon detail," Isaac contributed helpfully.

❖ ❖ ❖

The atmosphere at the Shabbat table that evening was reassuring and even festive. Shulamit, taking her cue from the way the twin lights of the Shabbat candles danced defiantly against the darkness, felt hopeful about the problems with which she'd been wrestling. Her two little displaced farmers now both had employment, and since tomorrow would be four days since she'd dispatched the messenger to the City of Red Clay, it wouldn't be long now before Queen Aafsaneh would come and share her magic. Plus, there were cold cooked carrots in herbed vinaigrette on the table, and lentils fragrant with spice.

Even Rivka was in good spirits, which surprised the queen after Rivka's reaction to her first few hours with Tova's conversation. "I left her in there with candles and challah and a glass of wine," she explained after the blessings. "She seemed to appreciate it. To be honest, I don't think it's long now. She's very flattered that I listen so much."

"I don't think anybody's been listening to that woman in months," Tivon commented, "but they're smart not to. If you take her seriously, everyone she meets has done her dirty three times over."

Rivka served herself a quarter of a chicken from the main dish by spearing it with her fork. "But having us there spending two days on her, it makes her feel important. She is *almost there*."

"Such a long time, two days," said Mitzi breathily. "It's a shame you can't, you know, threaten her or something."

"We *have* been threatening her," Rivka told her mother. "She's an accessory to international sabotage, which counts as treason. She could lose her farm or go to prison."

"No, but I mean, you know, *threaten her*." Mitzi slashed at the air with a dainty fist, which looked far less threatening than she meant it to. Shulamit had to hold back a laugh so she wouldn't spew lentils all over the table.

"That's not how we do things, Mammeh…"

"Do you think these carrots are soft enough for her to try one?" Shulamit turned to Aviva, who was holding Naomi on her lap.

"Let's put one on the table in front of her and see what happens." Aviva shifted the baby around so she could pat the table with her little hands.

It was a good dinner with loved ones, and prayers that were designed to set the night apart for contemplation did their work on Shulamit's heart. She slept well, head tucked up against Aviva's fleshy shoulder, her other arm around Naomi.

Queen Shulamit woke up to find Aviva already gone, probably in the kitchen working. She held Naomi to her breast and roused herself slowly, blinking into the bright sunlight coming in through the window curtains. In her half-awake stupor, she didn't even register the chatter outside until a guard's voice called, "Majesty, are you awake?"

"Yes, I'm just nursing."

"A message just arrived for you from the royal house of the City of the Red Clay."

Languor fell from her shoulders like a robe, and she sat bolt upright. "Yes! Please. Come in."

The guard entered and approached her, a paper in his hand. It was folded over and sealed with wax. "Their messenger just arrived. He's refilling his water vessels while he waits for a response."

Shulamit took the paper in her free hand and looked at the seal. It was definitely from Queen Aafsaneh. Holding it against the bed with the heel of her hand, she pried apart the two halves of the paper and then held it up to read it.

Greetings to Queen Shulamit, and best of wishes for her health and happiness. Her Royal Majesty Queen Aafsaneh is recovering from a broken foot and therefore must regretfully delay her aid to the farms of Perach while she heals. She will arrive when it is safe for her to do so. Until then, much love and all blessings. —A.

There was a feeling like being stuck in time. Setting the paper down on the bed, Shulamit bit her lower lip. She'd never anticipated this; Aafsaneh's visit seemed so certain that it somehow felt as if she were still arriving today, or tomorrow, even though that was obviously not happening. Shulamit had the curious sensation of existing in two timelines at once—the one that she was expecting and the real one.

So the Swan Lady wasn't coming. At least, not until later. How much later? Would she heal faster than the bugs would make their way across the barrier of bare earth?

Besides, her injured foot! Shulamit wondered what had happened and felt sorry for the poor woman. If they were in the same place, Shulamit would have rushed to put pillows behind her and under her, and order her decadent cold drinks made with rosewater and strawberries. But she was far away, and it was hard to dote on somebody in the abstract.

"I guess I should send her something nice," Shulamit murmured into Naomi's curly, black hair. "Since the messenger is waiting for a reply anyway."

141

Still, she felt deeply selfish and guilty, because she knew that her "get well soon" came with a heavy dose of "because you're my only way out of this mess."

❖ ❖ ❖

Isaac sat beside Shulamit in her salon as she lounged on a sofa playing with fabric samples. The little queen kept shifting and fidgeting on the cushions, her fingers nearly shredding the delicate silks and weavings. He placed his book of magic spells down carefully on a small mosaic-topped table beside the sofa and tried his best to calm her. "I'm sure she'll heal quickly. Aafsaneh is a healthy woman, and her magic is strong."

"I believe you," said Shulamit, "but I wish I had at least *one other idea*. It feels so dangerous to be hanging everything on this one hope."

"I read books every night, you know, to see if I can find a different spell." Isaac sighed. He was frustrated by what had happened at Gil and Eliana's farm.

"Thank you," said Shulamit. "I wish I could help!"

"You have your own responsibilities, without adding to them to learn magic," Isaac chuckled. Then he unconsciously straightened in his seat, hearing a familiar confident step just outside.

In a burst of brown and gold as usual, Rivka thumped into the salon.

Shulamit craned her head to follow Rivka's progress around the sofa toward them. "It's not even lunchtime. Does that mean she cracked? Where are they?"

"I don't have it, not yet, I don't have much. *But*"—Rivka stood before them proudly—"I know this now—the men who paid Tova are being bankrolled by someone who's been inside the Imbrian palace."

Shulamit froze. Pieces of gauzy, pink silk floated to the floor. "You don't mean—you *can't* mean—"

"I don't," said Rivka bluntly. "Well, I don't know. Maybe I do. I don't know who it was yet. She didn't say the Imbrian queen. It was just her way of trying to insist to me that they were classy people, not common street ruffians. She heard one of them saying to the other something about the cookies they make in the palace, how they even have the Imbrian royal crest imprinted on them before baking, and she asked them, 'Wait, you've been to the palace in Home City?' and he said no, that their boss had sent them cookies from the palace in Imbrio. It was some kind of holiday gift, but she's too caught up in her own drama to remember Imbrian holidays."

"That still could be Carolina that gave it to them." Shulamit was mumbling and Isaac barely heard her. "Oh, please, please, please don't let it be her."

"Why does it matter?" Rivka scratched the back of her neck. "Anyway, I'm going back there while she's still ready to talk. Like I said, I'm almost there." And she bounded away without another word.

Shulamit looked at Isaac, and he saw sadness shimmering in her eyes. "*Malkeleh*! Why these tears?"

"Isaac, she's so terrible and so beautiful." The tears squeezed out and slid down her cheeks. "I hate myself for loving her when I was younger. Doesn't that make me just as bad, somehow?"

"Why do you say she's terrible?" Isaac petted her head gently, being careful to caress in one direction only, knowing how fussy she was about her precious braids. "Her airs are only natural for someone born to such high office. She is only a little spoiled, like you were once."

"But, no, it's not like that! Wait—don't you know?"

"What is it that I don't know?"

"I thought Rivka would have told you."

"Rivka doesn't tell me your secrets, *kindeleh*," said Isaac. "But if it will upset you to talk about it—"

"No, I need you to know," said Shulamit. "I didn't know you didn't know already."

"Then tell me a story." Isaac put his arm around her shoulder protectively.

She leaned her head against him. He felt her dry her eyes on his sleeve, and then she began her tale.

Chapter 15. Six Weeks Shy of Seventeen

Crown Princess Shulamit, six weeks shy of seventeen, pushed aside the curtain on her side of the royal carriage and gazed out across the marsh. The light of sunrise illuminated the green-gold spikes, knee-deep in a vast sea until they ended at the high ridge of the road. Wading birds scattered when they heard the hoofbeats and the rattle of wheels, their search for this morning's crabs and snails interrupted. She could see some of the crabs if she squinted, scurrying sideways with their one swollen claw. Why were they like that? What was its purpose?

"Sweetheart, close that curtain."

Shulamit turned to face her father. King Noach was a man of average height, lithely built but with a broad chest. His head was bald to the back of his crown, but the black-but-graying hair that started there flowed down in thick waves to his shoulders. "You should look," she told him. "The marshes look really pretty in the morning."

"I already told you," he countered. "You shouldn't let people out there see who's riding in this carriage. Knowing there's a wealthy young woman here could put you in danger."

"There's nobody out there," Shulamit insisted. "It's just birds and crabs."

"I'm just trying to keep you safe," said Noach solemnly. "You never know."

Shulamit thought he was being silly, especially because they were traveling with such a huge component of the Royal Guard. But it was a little too easy to imagine villains popping out from the mud, so she returned the curtain to its original position.

145

Looking down at her clothing, she rearranged her filmy, pink scarf and straightened out the ribbons that decorated the end of her long braids. She ran her fingers over the smooth silk of her dress and adjusted the trousers she wore beneath. "Aba, can I have your shaving glass?"

"What, again?" Noach's tone was teasing. "Don't worry— you look lovely, and your clothing is perfect. You'll definitely impress Crown Princess Carolina. Maybe even make her jealous of such an outfit."

Princess Shulamit didn't want to make Princess Carolina jealous. What she wanted was for Carolina to feel the same way when she looked at Shulamit that Shulamit did when she looked at Carolina—that she wanted to lie down at her feet and die, or grab her around the waist and stare into her eyes, or kiss her until they both forgot to breathe.

"Sweetheart?"

"Huh? What?" Shulamit turned to see Noach offering the mirror. "Oh. Thanks."

She looked into the glass and saw a little female replica of her father's bushy eyebrows staring back at her. The braids, however, were perfect, which was what she wanted to check. Nothing stuck out at the top or had unraveled from the braids themselves. She was satisfied with the rest of the ensemble as well; from her ears sparkled tiny jewels of pink in the same shade, and the white lace on her collar evoked elegance and refinery.

Let's hope I live up to my clothes, the little princess told God.

❖ ❖ ❖

Shulamit and her father stood before the great royal palace
in Imbrio's capital, Riachinho de Estrela. It rose to the sky
in towers of columned marble, striking and cold in contrast
to the comfortable, homey, winding palace network of one-
story chambers and courtyards that Shulamit knew from
home. There was a courtyard here too, with orderly,
manicured gardens and artistic patterns of pavement
reaching out to the stone wall that surrounded the whole
affair. But it all seemed grand and imposing, like a great
chord played by every instrument in the band at once.

She drew closer to her father and clung to the arm he
offered as they started their way up the palace stairs.

King Fernando III of Imbrio came into view just beyond
the palace's front pillars as the little princess summited her
climb. His hair was black but his skin strangely pale, and
he wore his beard bushy and long. Beside him was his wife,
Queen Ines, a folded fan in her hands. And beside the
queen—*there she was*, the most beautiful girl in the world,
Princess Carolina. Dark eyes with long lashes shone out
from a pale face ringed with waves of thick, black hair. She
was tall, curvy, and broadly built, her wide hips accented
by what seemed like hundreds of petticoats that broadened
her skirt until she looked like a human flower. She smiled
at Shulamit when she saw her, and Shulamit, to her own
embarrassment, responded by grinning so hard she was
practically laughing.

Shulamit's legs wobbled beneath her, and she was
convinced that if she wasn't holding on to her father like
his arm was a rope swing on a tree, they'd turn into noodles
and she'd go sliding back down the stairs and land with a
crash back in the courtyard.

"Fernando!" Noach dropped Shulamit's arm and stalked
forward to clasp the other king's hand in his.

"Oi! Tudo bem?" said the other king, which was *Hello, how are you?*

They hugged quickly, and then Noach stepped to the side to nod respectfully to Queen Ines. "Good morning! You look beautiful today." He spoke in Imbrian, which Shulamit found easy to understand, at least as slow and booming as he was.

"Thank you," said Ines, beaming. "We're so glad to welcome you both! This is your first time here, isn't it, Shulamit?"

Her mind racing to catch up with the faster and less enunciated speech, Shulamit nodded as she found her practiced words. "Yes. It's beautiful."

Carolina stepped forward, and Shulamit's heart flew upward and banged into her brain. She realized she was gaping at her open-mouthed. It didn't get any easier to think when Carolina reached out her hand and took hold of one of Shulamit's. "You're here! Come on—I have so many wonderful things to show you."

Warmth spread across her face as Shulamit let herself be dragged away after her. It was so easy to imagine that the minute they were out of sight of the parents, Carolina would pull her closer by that hand she held, spiral her inward, wrap her other arm around her back, and kiss her against the marble columns. Lord knows, she'd daydreamed about it enough times that it seemed completely plausible.

Naturally, it didn't happen, and the daydream poured out and evaporated, replaced by a tugging ache. But at least she was still holding her hand. Shulamit reveled in the contrast of softness with confidence, and hoped her own hand wasn't too wimpy, or too grippy, or too clammy. "Where are we going?"

"It's a surprise!"

What if the surprise is that she loves me back? Shulamit sighed. She needed to calm down and stop thinking about this and just enjoy the moment. Maybe, *maybe*, things would happen later on in the visit. After all, she had *plans*. It was silly to expect anything this early.

Hallways that she was too lovestruck to notice whizzed by; she had the vague impression of gilded portraits and statuary, and rooms hung all over with embroidered drapery. Finally, they reached the outside again. Carolina pulled her into the sun, then dropped her hand and pointed.

"Look!"

Shulamit's mouth fell open in an appreciative gasp as she gazed all around herself at the person-high wall of flowers. The bushes went on for quite some ways, down into a garden path, thick and fluffy, green foliage covered with a generous layer of brilliant pink flowers. They reminded Shulamit a little of the hibiscuses from back home, but they were smaller and darker.

"They grow so high!" she exclaimed. "And they're everywhere!"

"They're azaleas," said Carolina. "And it looks like they match you. We'd better be careful as we walk the path, or you might get lost in them!"

Shulamit looked down at her dress, then back at the blossoms. She grinned awkwardly at the similarity.

They rounded a corner and began to sink into the rhythm of a comfortable stroll. "I am not walking you too fast, am I, Shulamit?" Carolina asked suddenly, her face earnest as she turned toward the other princess.

"No, I'm good!" Shulamit could feel herself answering too quickly, too enthusiastically, but never mind that. She was in too deep to care. "It's all so beautiful."

"Because I remember that you sometimes feel ill," Carolina continued. "How is your—" And here, she said a word in Imbrian that Shulamit didn't understand.

"I am—what?" Shulamit bit her lip, her mind racing over her language lessons.

"Your—*here*." Carolina patted her own stomach delicately through the layers of ribbons and petticoats. "When my family visited your palace, you were sometimes ill."

"Oh." Shulamit twiddled the end of one of her braids absently. "I've been good during the trip so far." Her face flushed at the idea that her mysterious stomach upsets had made such a big impression on Carolina that she was still thinking about them, months later. She found reassurance in her relative health of the past few days, when she'd mostly been sticking to a diet of rice and fish because that's what they grew and caught and served around here.

Maybe that was the key to her misery—simple foods. When she got home she vowed to shut herself away in the palace library with a piece of pita and a mug of chicken broth.

"All this sun will be good for you, I hope!" Carolina looked around herself at the garden. "Oh, I am foolish. You come from such a sunny place. I forgot. Our winters are so bleak and dull. The sky is white. Can you imagine it? White as cotton, and some of the trees become bare as—"

Shulamit couldn't place the Imbrian word. "I'm sorry, what is that?"

Carolina ran her fingers down her own arm, then tapped herself, hard. "Bones. All the bones in the body, together."

Skeleton, thought Shulamit in Perachi. "Maybe you should spend the winter with us every year," she found herself blurting out, then wanted to hide behind her scarf and blend in with the flowers in horror at her own forwardness.

"Our winter makes us love our spring," said Carolina. "Here, I will show you more beauty." She gestured to a group of bushes of a different type than the walls of azaleas all around. Instead of flimsy, their leaves were sturdy and glossy, larger, and of a darker green. The blooms that decorated their branches were the same brilliant pink, but they looked more like roses. "This is a camellia."

Shulamit smiled and nodded appreciatively, and trotted along after Carolina as she floated from flower to flower. Not all of the azaleas were pink; they reached a corridor where they were all white, and then a pale and watery lilac. Hyacinths of purple and yellow rose out of the earth in cheerful clusters.

Carolina pointed out a tiny blossom of white-and-cream tendrils. "This one is very special, because you can drink it." She carefully picked one and used her fingernail to remove the stem, then lifted it to her lips. "Here, I will fix one for you."

Transfixed, Shulamit watched as she retrieved another flower and prepared it. Drinking flowers. That was practically a metaphor for... wasn't it?

151

She realized Carolina wasn't going to literally feed it to her, so she accepted it in her trembling hand and mimicked what she'd seen Carolina do with it. The drop of nectar was sweet and fragrant and only contributed to the swirling clouds of hormones in her mind.

"It's called honeysuckle," said Carolina. "One day, when I was very small, Papai and I were riding in a carriage, and we reached a bridge that men were fixing. We would not have taken that road, but nobody knew the bridge was down. So we got out of the carriage while we waited and ate all the honeysuckles on the side of the road."

"Sometimes when Aba tours our farms back home, he takes me with him and the farmers always give me things they've grown." It wasn't a *great* story and not really the same thing, but Shulamit felt like she had to respond and it was the first thing that came out.

"The landowners give me cookies we call cat's tongue," Caroline replied, "because so many of the things we grow you can't give someone just to eat. Like cotton, or rice, or indigo."

"Can't really eat fluffs of cotton!" Shulamit wanted to hide in the roots of the camellia bush. That was possibly the stupidest thing she'd ever said. Ugh. Were boys this dumb when trying to talk to girls?

She wished she could ask her father for help with this sort of thing. He was *fabulous* with women and usually had more than one girlfriend at a time. But when she tried to tell him how she felt about women—how she felt about Princess Carolina, and how she was a little bit in love with Queen Esther from the Purim story—he just dismissed it as something she didn't understand and would grow out of. The good part was that he'd promised her he'd never choose a husband for her. But he definitely thought her heartfelt, honest feelings were something she was misstating and exaggerating.

"Where are we going now?" Deep in her fretful reverie, Shulamit had missed the transition of their walk from walls of flowers to walls of plain and thorny hedge, a hedge that was cultivated and trimmed within an inch of its life and rose several heads above them.

"This is our garden maze," explained Carolina, "but I know the way to the middle."

"Then I'll feel safe with you because we won't get lost." Shulamit then spent the next several steps worrying that her comment had been too forward, too flirtatious, too obviously something that ordinary girls said to boys, not to other girls. See, this was why she wished she could have her father's help!

Maybe she didn't need it. After all, Carolina was a girl, just like her, so why not just speak to her the way she, Shulamit, would wish to be spoken to herself?

Eyes wide open with admiration for Carolina's beauty and elegance, the little princess realized this wasn't much help. They might both be women, but they weren't the same people. Carolina was tall and broad and gorgeous; Shulamit, an awkward waif with a body, she thought with a grimace, that didn't seem any different from the way she'd looked at eleven.

What she could bring to the table was her brains. She wondered if she could impress Carolina with them, and tried to think of something relevant to say.

Luckily, Carolina didn't seem to mind the silence as Shulamit frantically scrubbed her brain for interesting trivia.

"Here—we've found it!" Carolina stepped into the clearing, her arms outstretched. Delicate lace drooped from the edges of her sleeves and floated in her wake.

There was a small stone tower at the core of the maze's center. "Wow, this looks really old." Shulamit's eyes were wide with admiration as she ran her hand over the cool, gray rock.

"Good eye!" said Carolina. "It has been here almost a thousand years. It was part of the castle that stood here long before my family's dynasty. Now it is all that remains, so we have built a maze around it to help protect it."

"That's great!" Shulamit was happy that she could stop feeling so self-conscious about smiling all the time, because now there was an excuse to smile that wasn't an eighteen-year-old goddess with big hips.

"Do you want to go to the top?"

"Oh, can we, still?"

"Yes, we make sure to keep it free of damage and debris." Carolina turned and led her into the narrow, winding staircase. "And since it rises over the maze, you will love the view."

When Shulamit slipped into the crevice in the rock tower, she found herself pressed close against Carolina's fragrant warmth. A throbbing awoke between her legs, and she ached to be held. She followed her up to the top, wanting nothing more than for Carolina to turn around suddenly on the stairs and kiss her.

I'd better get it together or I'm going to fall off the top of the tower if I'm not careful, Shulamit told herself angrily.

Still, when Carolina reached the top and reached out for Shulamit's hand to help her up, Shulamit took her hand into her own with as much sensuality and reverence as if they had been lying betwixt each other's thighs.

The gardens, however, provided a welcome distraction. "This is beautiful!" Shulamit gaped at the view of the walls of azaleas through which they'd walked, and the camellia garden, and on the other side, pools of water lilies and neat, orderly rows of blossoming peach trees, and loquat trees in full fruit like little plums of yellow velvet. Workers maintained the tidiness of the grounds, picking up dead leaves and trimming hedges. Beyond, she saw the palace where Carolina lived, and the high walls shielding it from the world outside. "If I lived here I'd come up here to read, and between pages I'd take a break and pick a different flower to stare at each time."

Carolina was looking down at the loquat trees, her brow furrowed. "Do you see that? What impudence!"

"What?" Shulamit looked down into the grove. There were workers harvesting some of the fruit, placing them into small boxes on the ground. Everyone looked like they were taking great care with them.

"That man has eaten two of the loquats he picked," Carolina said in a huff, "instead of putting them in the boxes as they belong."

"Those fruit are for the palace kitchen, right?"

Carolina nodded vigorously. "Yes, they are. They are not his to eat. I will tell my father. It scares me that they do not fear the whip more, and still persist on—"

"Whip?" Shulamit exclaimed. "They're going to whip him for eating two loquats?"

"It is not the first time," said Carolina. "He says he is hungry, but he has the same rice in the morning as the rest of them. And don't we pay them? If he does not like what he earns, he should leave, instead of sneaking our fruit like a thief."

"Oh, Carolina, please don't tell anyone." Shulamit's cheeks were burning, and she shook a little. "Just let it go, just this once."

"Why?"

"Because it's just fruit, and because I feel sorry for him. Rice doesn't really sound like enough food. I mean, I've been eating a lot of rice on the way here, and I know I feel better when I have more than that."

"But he is only a worker. You are… Crown Princess of Perach."

"*Please*. Don't make my first memory of Imbrio be like this." Shulamit didn't know what else to say. "And if you want, I'll pay you for the loquats." She looked down at the grove. "I'll give you my earrings."

"Oh, funny Shulamit with her big heart!" Carolina squeezed her upper arm, and Shulamit melted in a wave of confusion as she thrilled at the touch. "All right, I won't say anything, and you don't have to give me your earrings."

"Thank you." Shulamit tried to smile and felt the muscles of her mouth moving too awkwardly to be attractive.

"The sun is getting lower. Is it time for us to head back to get changed for dinner?"

"Already?" Shulamit looked westward and saddened slightly. Even with the unpleasant bits, she was enjoying being up here in this beautiful place in such close quarters with the girl she loved.

"We can go back the other way, so you can see the water lilies up close."

She headed back down, holding her skirts close to her so their vastness wouldn't scrape against the sides of the staircase, with Shulamit following close behind.

Chapter 16. En Bateau

Princess Shulamit looked around the grand dining hall at the Imbrian royal family and their guests, admiring their exotic, ornate clothing and wondering what the next course would be. It was so nice to have varied food again, after all the rice she'd eaten on the way here. The vegetable soup was simple but flavorful, with a base of pureed potato, and the simple green salad that followed was so fresh and crisp that it almost looked too perfect to eat. The olive oil provided to pour on it with the vinegar and salt tasted different from the oil back home, but still very good. Shulamit knew there were people who could tell whether an oil was Perachi or Imbrian just by the taste, but she was far from being one of them.

Princess Carolina was seated across from her, but the pleasure Shulamit took in her food took some of the pressure off the infatuation. It was almost easier to enjoy Carolina's presence when she had something else to think about at the same time.

Still, she ate *impeccably*—at any moment, those large, dark eyes might be on her, and she didn't want to have lettuce leaves poking out of her mouth or vinegar dribbling down her chin.

Her heart sank a little when she realized the next course was *more rice*, accompanied by a strange, gray meat she didn't recognize. She reached out her hand for the serving spoon to take some anyway, but her father stopped her with a gentle touch to the wrist. "That's not for us, sweetheart."

She looked at him curiously. "What animal…?"

"It is wild boar," said Queen Ines, "from our royal forests. Don't worry! There is also fish and potatoes on the way."

158

"Thank you." Shulamit moved her braids so that they hung down her back instead of over her shoulders, out of the way of her food.

The fish was saltier than she was used to, but it was still delicious. Dessert was made of little custards, overwhelmingly sweet and drenched in a brown syrup that Shulamit thought was going to be honey but was thinner and runnier. She found herself licking the spoon as she studied the novel flavor, peering at Carolina across the table. Wouldn't it be wonderful to kiss her after they'd eaten something like that? She imagined a moment alone with her—just two girls pressing together their sugared mouths, kissing each other spotless.

"I think your daughter is enjoying the flan," said King Fernando to King Noach with amusement. "Is this the first time she's had it?"

"Maybe so," said Noach. "It's good to see her eating like this. She ate so timidly during our travels."

"You can have a second, if you like," said Queen Ines warmly.

"Mmmm." Shulamit put the spoon down with embarrassment.

King Fernando pushed back his chair and stood. "Now that dinner is over, we can all take our coffee in the salon. I think my daughter has prepared something to entertain us."

"Oh?" Shulamit turned to Carolina with interest as she followed everyone away from the table.

"Yes, I have improved in my singing lessons." Carolina grinned, her face radiant.

159

"I love your voice," said Shulamit. She was excited about the informal recital; at last, an excuse to stare at Carolina for minutes at a time!

She accepted her coffee cup and curled up next to her father on one of the sofas, wrapping her pink, filmy scarf around her shoulders like the embrace she wanted from Her Lady.

Carolina was standing at the far end of the room talking to a tall man with a beard that went all the way around his face. He was a little older than they were—maybe in his early or midtwenties, and his broad shoulders and trim waist made him seem vaguely triangular. He held a guitar that was also strapped around his neck and back with a piece of leather.

"Good evening, Visconde!" called King Fernando to the stranger.

"Good evening, Majesty!" the man replied jovially.

"Give us some good music tonight," said the king.

"I always try, Majesty." The man bowed, then took a place behind Carolina.

She folded her hands across her stomach and waited for his opening chords.

Shulamit's head lolled backward with unexpected delight as Carolina's glorious soprano voice filled the room. Several moments later she realized her own mouth was hanging open, so she closed it and swallowed delicately. Gripping her cup, she let the sound fill her body, until every hair on her head, every inch of skin, every drop of blood was Carolina's song.

The words were sad, some kind of lament over unreturned love. Shulamit pretended they were for her. Then they became her own words, in her heart, and she saddened as she realized for not the first time that if one of them had been a boy, it was likely their fathers would be arranging their marriage. Why did things have to be so unfair? Shulamit didn't want to be a boy. And she *definitely* didn't want Carolina to be a boy. The thought of being touched by boys made her tense up even more.

When her father looked at her, puzzled, she realized she was showing her emotions too much. Settling back into the cushions with false calm, she applauded at the end of Carolina's first air and listened as she began a second, more jaunty performance.

Since their fathers wouldn't be able to help things along via the obvious political alliance, Shulamit would clearly have to fend for herself in matters of love. She cast her mind back to the racy books she'd found in her father's library. What she wanted with Carolina was far more wholesome and poetic than the salacious little stories, but they had given her some ideas that might prove useful. Her *plans* would work best if she and Carolina had a chance to spend some quiet time alone together indoors.

Carolina's vocal acrobatics tore Shulamit from her schemes. How was it possible that she hit all those far-apart notes with such precision? What a woman!

❖ ❖ ❖

It was morning, and Princess Shulamit bounded out of bed ready to have adventures. She'd planned out her outfits for every day of the visit with excruciating care, down to the last earring, but now that she was in Carolina Central itself,

161

she rearranged her clothing, fretted and posed, second-guessing every decision.

Her only guide to what Carolina might find pretty in another woman lay in the way Carolina herself dressed. She'd been wearing blue yesterday, but Shulamit usually disliked the color and owned nothing suitable. Her next best clue was "finery," so she selected her lilac dress with the fuchsia shoulders and trim, for its extensive embroidery and ribbons. The matching fuchsia trousers she wore underneath were made of something reflective that shimmered, and the scarf was a work of art—starting at fuchsia and working its way to lilac, it had been hand-painted by a Perachi palace artisan.

Thus arrayed, she made short work of the pastry, coffee, and cheese the Imbrian servants brought her for breakfast. Her stomach cramped painfully as she left her room for the gardens, where she and Carolina had agreed to meet. She tried to ignore the squeezing and figured it was just nerves from her crush. Then she remembered the coffee and decided to slow it down a little bit. After all, she was more used to tea.

Princess Carolina was sitting by one of the water lily ponds when Shulamit found her. She wore gray like a big beautiful storm cloud, and was all over ribbons and fine white lace as the day before. "Good morning! You match the flowers again today."

Shulamit smiled awkwardly. "I always seem to do that."

"Are you all right?"

"What? Oh yes," Shulamit stammered. "I think I drank too much coffee. I'll be fine." She wondered if being in love felt less queasy once the other person loved you back. Taking a deep breath, she rallied herself against the pain.

"Let's go out on the river in a rowboat," said Carolina animatedly. "The weather is perfect."

That sounded safe and "sitting down," so Shulamit agreed. "Is that the 'little river of stars' your capital city is named for?" she asked as they made for the riverbank. Everything was safely within the palace's outer walls, so there was no need to worry about taking along the guards.

"Ah, no," said Carolina. She swept one hand toward the sky. "At night, when there is no moon… you know, the river of stars in the sky?"

"Oh! The Milky Way," Shulamit answered. "I guess it's special for us, too—we start our month on the nights with no moon."

"We have a legend that the founder of our city followed the river of stars to this place, led by the Gods." Carolina surveyed the boats, choosing the one that seemed in the best condition. "Remind me later and I will show you a painting of the story in my mother's salon."

I want to row with you on the river of stars… Shulamit daydreamed, thinking about how there were no beautiful paintings of women like that, only vulgar ones.

Soon, Shulamit was alone with Carolina on the peaceful water, and she desperately wished there wasn't this need for subterfuge and strategy. If only she could be sure her feelings wouldn't be met with amusement, confusion, disgust—if only she could just speak openly. *Being around you just makes me want to get to know you better*, she pretended she could say. *You're beautiful and elegant and gracious, and I know that if you just held me I'd be happier than I've ever been in my whole life.*

Carolina's hand dipped into the water, and Shulamit followed the curving, subtle line of her arm with yearning eyes. She was going to go crazy if she didn't say something *else*, even if she couldn't talk about how she felt—not here, not so openly. Time to start impressing her with trivia again, as she had back in Home City.

But Carolina spoke before she could think of anything. "I am so glad that you came with your father on this trip." She moved the oars through the water, and beside them, the riverbanks floated by. "It is hard for me to find friends of high enough rank to be appropriate companions."

"I get lonely too," Shulamit admitted. She did have companions, ladies-in-waiting, but even though things were far more informal in Perach than in Imbrio, she felt cut off from them by her plainness, and her nerdiness, but most of all her attraction to other women—which none of them seemed to share.

"There were some older girls, the daughters of Counts, when I was younger, but they are all grown and married now and it is not the same with those much younger," Carolina continued. "And there is João, of course, but he is a special case."

"Who's that?"

"Visconde João Carneiro de Façanha," replied Carolina. "You remember him from last night? The man with the guitar."

"Oh," said Shulamit. "Is he your music teacher?"

Carolina chuckled. "No, no. My music teacher is a strict old lady who yells at me until I am perfect. João is the son of a landowner who gave his life to save my father's. In gratitude, he allowed João to spend time in the palace, so we are friends. For example, he is invited to the ball tonight, even though he is under the rank of the other guests."

Sunlight glinted off the water and spilled into Shulamit's eye. Behind it, she thought she saw in Carolina's face a mirror of her own troubles.

Carolina must have sensed her scrutiny. "If he were a Count's son I would marry him," she said simply. "Instead, he must remain behind me and play the guitar while I sing. These things are upsetting, but they are the way of the world. Otherwise I am sure you would notice all those handsome guards who look after your father. You are so sensible to ignore them."

Shulamit let the misunderstanding of her obliviousness toward the Perachi guardsmen go without comment as she digested this news. She had a rival, but he was a disqualified and defanged rival. And here she was, a crown princess in her own right.

Unconsciously, she fiddled with one of her dangling amethyst earrings. "So…"

Answering the wrong question, Carolina continued, "I will make my choice next year, perhaps. A widowed Duke has been paying me court, but he is older than I'd imagined. There is a young Count who makes me laugh. He is perhaps a bit frivolous for a royal consort, but I can always balance him. They say I have a cool head."

Shulamit listened patiently, the squeezing in her stomach making her glad that Carolina was the one rowing.

"Then, of course, Zembluss has two princes my age, but with the political situation over there being what it is... I suppose you have also rejected them for the same reason."

"I'm not marrying any princes from Zembluss." Shulamit frowned at the idea.

Carolina smirked. "Poor men! They have far more to worry about than finding wives, I imagine."

"My father says there will be civil war soon, over there."

"Soon, yes." Carolina looked out over the water. "I agree."

"Which side do you—"

Carolina tossed her head. "Imbrio will not get involved."

A splashing sound and then rustling in the plants on the riverbank made both girls turn their heads. On the shore, a group of bare-chested men gathered strawberries from a field, placing them in wooden crates as they worked. A fully dressed foreman was standing over one of them brandishing a wooden stick. He raised it high in the air and brought it down on the worker's shoulder. Shulamit realized the initial noise had been the picker trying to get away.

She whipped back around to face Carolina, eyes wide. "What...? Why...?"

Carolina lifted her chin a little, studying the scene carefully. "Do you see that crate there?" A wooden box lay on its side, a few layers of rich, red berries spilling out into the dirt. "He must have broken it, and all the berries inside

166

fell into the river," she explained finally. "It can be taken out of his pay, yes, but when things like that happen, it also wastes time and shows a lack of care."

Shulamit's mouth dropped open. "But he's a *person*, and it's… just… fruit." She massaged her cramping stomach and felt spoiled; the beaten man was probably in more pain than she was.

She craned her head as the boat drifted past the scene, unable to take her eyes off the man on the shore as he returned to work.

Carolina's voice filtered into her thoughts as if coming from the next room. "I'm sorry if it upset you."

Shulamit didn't know what to say to that.

"You've pulled out one of your braids," Carolina remarked.

"Oh. Oops." Shulamit looked down and realized her nervous fingers had made short work of her hairdo. What's more, the cord holding the braid closed had vanished. She bit her lip.

"I'll fix it." Carolina beckoned to her. "Here, lean close."

Shulamit inched forward on her seat and leaned forward as much as she could.

Carolina, too, angled her body in Shulamit's direction. She pulled a silver ribbon from the bodice of her dress. "There are so many! Most of them are just for show." Shulamit was held by the command of her eyes, now rapturously close to Carolina's curvy bosom. Her breasts were captivating as she leaned, beautiful hills against the gray storm clouds of the stately dress.

With deft fingers, Carolina rebraided Shulamit's thick hair. As she began, her fingers brushed more than once against Shulamit's cheek, and the other princess' lips parted slightly as she patiently waited for more of this unexpected pleasure. There were a few moments of tension as Shulamit felt torn in two between the argument they'd almost had and the simple, silent pleasure of closeness, and then she simply gave up and enjoyed it.

"Have you ever—" But no. She stopped. Not here. She was too scared, and besides, what if it worked? Here they were in a rowboat, where any contact even more intimate would result in capsizing.

Carolina, looking over her handiwork with satisfaction in her eyes, raised them to Shulamit's. "Worn my hair in braids? When I was a girl, of course. Now I prefer it down."

"It's lovely." Shulamit looked away over the water, squinting to keep out the reflection of the sun.

Chapter 17. Sabbath Blessings

Layers of delicate lilac surrounded Princess Shulamit's
tiny body, flowing down to the floor. She twirled in front of
the glass, stretching out her arms. A ball! She'd practiced
the foreign dances with her father, back home, but she
knew that one look at Carolina and she'd manage to put her
foot down in three places all at once.

"Princess Brainy!" Her father's voice boomed from out in
the hallway. "You're beautiful already. Let's go."

"Just a minute!" She rotated sideways, checking the glass
again. Her braids were staying in place where she'd tied
them, together behind her back. Carolina's silver ribbon
was still there from this morning; she hoped the Imbrian
Infanta would forget to ask for it back.

"Come back to my room," Noach called to her. "We're
going to do the candle blessing before we go downstairs."

It felt right in Shulamit's heart that there should be a ball
on Shabbat. What better way to segregate the ordinary days
of the week from the special night than by dressing up and
turning the palace magical?

When she got to her father's room, she found every single
guard they'd brought standing there waiting for her. They
were the only other people in the palace of their faith, so
here they all were, ready to share the ritual.

The candles were there, waiting, as well. King Noach lit a
fire stick against one of the lamps burning on the wall and
handed it to Shulamit. She lit the candles, *one, two*, then
covered her eyes.

"Bless you, our Lord, King of the Universe..." Noach
intoned.

Shulamit felt the specialness of Shabbat close in around her, almost like the mother she'd hardly known. *I want…*

She didn't have words to complete her prayer, but she didn't need them. A comforting peace infused her anyway.

Confident and excited on her father's arm, Princess Shulamit left the room and headed toward the festivities.

❖ ❖ ❖

Lights twinkled everywhere, and the room was filled with happy people in lavish dress. A troupe of musicians gave song in a corner, and efficient servants circulated holding trays of treats. Shulamit noted with delight that the air smelled of orange blossoms.

"Noach, my friend!" King Fernando was upon them, his queen at his side. "I am so eager for you to meet—" And he whisked Shulamit's father away. She stood by herself for a moment, peering round for Carolina.

"Shulamit! Over here!"

Princess Carolina was standing over by a great marble column, holding a little crystal goblet of dark red wine. She waved her other hand, beckoning Shulamit over.

"Your dress is—"

"What a marvelous—"

Both girls paused and giggled. "You first," said Carolina.

"That's a beautiful dress." Shulamit was dazzled by the array of pink and white lace, and the skirt that bloomed from Carolina's waist in such an enormous froth that

Shulamit wondered if she had trouble walking through single doorways.

"Yours as well, dear Shulamit."

Shulamit grinned, half-ecstatic, half-self-conscious about her strange smile. "Lilac's my favorite."

"You wear it well."

Something over Shulamit's shoulder attracted Carolina's attention, and a bright light flared into her eyes. "João! I can introduce you to the Crown Princess of Perach."

Shulamit turned to see the guitar player from the previous night standing beside her. He had a frank and friendly face, and his hands were full of party snacks. "Can't let our beautiful Infanta go hungry."

"Here, I will give my port to Shulamit so that I can give this my full attention." Carolina held her glass out, and Shulamit accepted it automatically.

She looked down at the glass. *I guess I'll get to say the wine blessing anyway...* The words were easily mumbled out of earshot, and then she took a tiny sip. The heat of a more intense alcohol than her people's fare burned through her throat, followed by deep sweetness and a complexity that reminded her of raisins.

"João, may I present the Crown Princess Shulamit, daughter of Noach, of Perach, heir to the throne and great lover of books." Carolina gestured grandly. "Shulamit, Visconde João Carneiro de Façanha. My friend," she added, with a face that Shulamit would later recall as "complicated."

171

João bowed deep, then restored himself and smiled as he took Shulamit's free hand. "I am honored." As he lifted Shulamit's hand to his lips in a dry kiss, she noticed a large ring on his hand. She narrowed her eyes and thought maybe she could make out the figure of a ram's head, or at least something with curling horns.

"João thinks as you do, Shulamit." Carolina daintily ate the food he'd brought her. "He wants to take away the beating sticks from the men who watch over the workers."

"Positive rewards, Caro—not punishments!" João looked at Shulamit. "So you agree with me that the workers should not be beaten?"

"Of course they shouldn't!" Shulamit exclaimed, happily surprised that her... rival... or whatever he was... was also her unexpected ally, and confused about what that meant. "We wouldn't do that kind of thing back home. It's cruel!"

"We'll have to work together to convince our Caro, then." João looked at Carolina affectionately. "Just think, lovely princess, how terrible it would be if someone ever were to hit you like that."

"I think I should have them thrown from the window," Carolina said casually.

"Those men don't deserve it any more than you do."

"Yes, but I am the Infanta."

"Your pride in that is built on their pain, dear one."

"I should make you get me another glass of port if you're going to scold me all night." Carolina finished off whatever little burst of bread she'd been eating. "Or take little Shulamit for a dance."

172

"I'll do both. But first, the dance. Then we can all find more food." João held out his hand to Shulamit, and with a shrug, she abandoned her glass and accepted it.

Thankfully, Imbrian court dances didn't require too much intimate contact between partners, so the dance with a strange man didn't feel too threatening. João was even relatively skilled at buffeting her around the dance floor to make up for each time she lost track of the steps. "I hope you're enjoying your time here in Riachinho de Estrela!"

"I am," said Shulamit. "I haven't been outside the palace grounds, but even just inside the wall, Carolina's shown me so many beautiful things."

"I'm sorry you had to see some ugly things too. Here, no, this way." He guided her to spin the other direction, his limbs remaining at a safe distance.

"I'm not used to the class difference being so..."

"I am, and I don't like it. Things can be different."

"I hope you're right," Shulamit replied.

"She'll understand, some day. I won't give up," said João, his eyes far away on the beautiful Infanta. "Some day."

❖ ❖ ❖

The hour had grown late, and the other landowners with whom João had been conversing in a men's smoking room begged his leave and departed. Returning to the ballroom, he scanned the swirling finery for Princess Carolina. The guests were thinning out, necessitating smaller dances for those still with energy, and he noticed that the other king and princess were among those who had already departed. He surmised they must be upstairs and asleep somewhere.

173

Carolina, however, did not look sleepy. Instead, she looked radiant and relaxed, stretching one arm over her head over in a corner by the curtains and potted orange trees in full blossom.

João loved the look that sprang into her eyes when she saw him. It made him feel twice as alive, like he'd never grow tired of it, like it called out to its brother spark within his own heart. "Be careful, princess, someone might see how perfect you look in that unusual pose and paint or draw you like that."

"You can if you like," she tossed off, clearly pleased.

"Ah, but we've been over this," said João, drawing closer so they could speak intimately. "I have no hand for drawing."

"But you could take lessons!" She was enthusiastic and flushed. He wondered if she had just danced, and he'd found her just after the dismount.

"I have a farm to manage," he reminded her, imagining that he was curling one lock of her glorious, black hair around his finger as he wished he could. "When am I supposed to practice?"

"You practice your guitar."

"You would have me grow rusty at guitar just to draw you? No, I don't think so."

"Never." Carolina paused. "I wish you had it with you now."

João smiled at her and lifted her hand to his lips. This, at least, was permitted and actually quite common and understandable. If she shuddered into the contact, if an exhalation thicker than normal escaped her divine lips, he was the only one to know.

"Tell me that story you were telling my father and King Noach earlier," said Carolina. "They were laughing and I want to laugh too!"

"Oh, that?" João smirked and shook his head with disbelief, thinking of the ignorance he was about to relate. "Refugee nobles from Zembluss were at my farm looking at seed, to start over. I showed them the new strawberries we developed, the ones as big as peaches. I thought they'd love it—beautiful stock, best we have to offer. Instead, they refused to believe it was natural—actually outright accused us of witchcraft!"

Carolina giggled. "Just because they'd never heard of it before?"

"Not just witchcraft, dangerous witchcraft. As if eating it would cause sickness."

She rolled her eyes. "Don't tell me they're the type who think everyone in the clergy is corrupt." In Imbrio, sorcery was the purview solely of the clerics.

"Considering what's been going on up there, it wouldn't surprise me if they didn't trust their own mothers."

"People are already dying."

"Your father asked me to go to Zembluss."

"What?" Carolina exclaimed, her rose of a mouth going slack, drooping on the stem. "But he said Imbrio would remain neutral!"

175

"He wants me to observe and report back." João picked up her hand again, but held it low and out of sight, so that he could massage her palm with his thumb. She gripped at his hand as if drowning. "Don't worry, I'm not leaving for at least a month."

"He trusts you." Soft words, barely breathed. "Promise you'll come back safe to me."

"Of course I will."

She was an ice sculpture, he reflected, ice protecting them both from their separate fires. Imbrio had winter and he knew what would happen if his bare skin touched an ice sculpture that had only slightly begun to melt.

He imagined himself getting stuck to her, unable to leave without ripping the very skin from his body.

"Will you take your guitar?" she asked in a low voice, already sounding stronger. The ice was a castle now.

He nodded. "Of course! It's part of who I am."

"At midnight, will you play? And I—here—I will sing? Or at dawn. Whichever you prefer."

"Sunset," he decided. "It's the prettiest."

❖ ❖ ❖

The day after the ball, a warm, gray rain rolled in and made it very easy to stay in bed. The servants who brought her breakfast told Shulamit that Carolina was still sleeping off the ball, after staying up all night, so she saw no reason to get dressed in a hurry. She lounged around in her pajamas all morning, practicing her Imbrian on local books or reading those she'd brought from home, and generally lolling around in the wide, lavish bed. Shabbat morning really felt like Shabbat morning under the spell of such intense goofing off.

She also used the time to bathe in great, luxuriating detail. Perhaps today, with the wet weather, was the opportunity she'd been waiting and praying for—a day spent indoors with Carolina, socializing in her chambers. They were grand and stately, and had two wonderful, tantalizing ingredients: *privacy* and *a bed*.

In the bath, scrubbing away every trace of dead skin, she organized her thoughts. Her father's books, her only clue to what lay ahead, gave her ample strategies.

One idea was to offer to braid Carolina's hair. After yesterday in the boat, she could even pass it off as returning the favor. Then, with tender touches, she would make Carolina feel relaxed and pampered so that she might open up for more.

That's how it went in one of the stories, anyway.

Another story started with a conversation about comparing their bodies. "I wonder whose breasts are bigger!" certainly wouldn't work in this situation, because it was obvious, but maybe if Shulamit pretended she was curious about bigger breasts up close, since hers were yet so small…

She finished off her breakfast pastry in the bathtub while daydreaming that Carolina was in there with her. Her stomach began to cramp, which she put down to nervousness. Nerves were natural, of course—for today might be her first kiss. She hoped it would be more. Looking down at her body under the scented water, she realized that she might, within a few hours, be sharing it with another woman for the very first time.

With deep breaths, she tried to calm the twisting in her belly.

Dressed and reading again, she looked up when she heard the knock of a servant on her door. "Yes?"

"Your Highness." The maid bowed low and didn't meet her eyes. "Princess Carolina is awake, and invites you back to her room for lunch and board games, if is your pleasure."

Shulamit grinned and clutched her book to her chest. "Yes! I'll come with you. Thank you." She hopped out of bed. Even her nervous stomach couldn't suppress the sparks of fiery anticipation that radiated through her.

Chapter 18. A Woman Worth Daydreaming About

Carolina's bedroom was spacious and ornately decorated, with plenty of room for the table and chairs at which the two princesses now sat as they ate their salad.

"I am sorry I slept so late!" Carolina poured more oil from the tiny crystal decanter over her greens. "I stayed up until dawn. These balls can be so exhausting, but I love them."

"It was a lot of fun," Shulamit agreed. "I liked looking at all the pretty dresses. It was like a fashion show!"

"I'm glad you and João got along so well together." Carolina flung her arms out in a dramatic gesture. "I want all my friends to be good friends!"

"Even if we did gang up on you a little?" Shulamit teased.

"My father always told me that I will be queen someday, so I should learn to listen and take all things calmly." Carolina's eyes twinkled mischievously.

"I bet you get the 'queen someday' speeches all the time, like I do," Shulamit observed.

"But our fathers are right, dear Shulamit," said Carolina. "It is our wonderful and terrifying destiny."

"Makes me glad we have each other," said Shulamit boldly.

"Me as well."

What next? "Do you ever…" Shulamit felt her heart beating in her face.

"Oh, finally! Our main course is here."

Shulamit, raw so that everything was extra loud, turned to see a servant bringing in a covered dish. The woman placed it in the center of the table and removed the silver cover.

A beautiful roast chicken sat presented on a bed of rice. The fragrance of lemons and garlic brought smiles to the faces of both girls. "Wow, look at that perfectly crispy skin!" Shulamit breathed.

"I'll let you have the crispiest part, if you want." Carolina nodded at the servant, who began cutting the chicken into quarters. "White or dark?"

"Oh, anything is fine." Shulamit waited for the servant to finish carving and leave the room before she felt comfortable speaking about *the topic* again. "I love how tangy this is."

"Imbrio is proud of its food, just as Perach!" Carolina said between bites.

Something in Shulamit's innards felt like it was boiling. She *had* to get the words out. Already she could see a hint of light gleaming through the gloomy weather outside. This might be her only chance. "Carolina... have you ever heard about women who love each other?"

Carolina's face was placid. "Women should always love and support each other. The world is a terrifying place if one has no friends."

Shulamit had to fight to swallow the next bite. She felt like her nerves were strangling her. "I agree... I meant... something else. I... it's interesting that... sometimes women..." Deep breaths. She bought herself time by taking a drink of water. "Women can... be special to each other." Then she took a very large bite, to avoid having to say anything else for at least a moment.

180

Carolina paused, then broke into a smile of understanding. "Yes, of course I have heard of this! We have women like that in this country. There is a well-known Countess who lives with a companion; perhaps you saw her last night? She was wearing... oh, let's see, what *was* she wearing?"

"Have you ever been curious about what it's like? Because I wonder..." Shulamit knew she was saying all the wrong things. What's more, her insides were twisting and churning and felt like they were being braided by a very cruel hairdresser.

"No, I never thought about it for myself... are you all right?"

"I'm sorry, I'm making a mess of this." Shulamit sighed deeply. "I'm too nervous to think, and it's not your fault." She leaned sideways against the arm of the chair. "I should just calm down."

"Dear Shulamit!" Carolina refilled Shulamit's water glass. "Here. Drink some more. Poor thing."

Shulamit did as she was told, more out of weakened bewilderment than any real desire for more water. "You already know the rest; I think I'm too scared to say it." She crumpled back against the chair. "I understand if you don't feel the same way. Most women don't. It's just... you're so beautiful and elegant and honestly *perfect* and—oh God— oh no—help—"

Her breathing grew shallow and panicked. No. No. *No No No No. Not here, not now. Lord God No. No. Fuck. No.*

She tried to disappear, folding herself into the corner of the chair. What she *wanted* to do was get up and run out of the room, but it was too late and she was too weak and nauseated.

181

"Shulamit…?"

"Help, I'm—"

The chicken came back up with such force that Shulamit felt like she'd been whacked in the back of the head with a board. She heard Carolina yelp, saw out of the corner of her eye as the other princess sprang out of her seat. Holding on to the side of the chair because it was there, Shulamit continued to be sick, this time on the floor.

Tears formed in her eyes and she tried to sob, but her body wouldn't even cooperate for that. Everything was jelly and she was useless.

Strangers came into the room and tried to pry her out of the chair. It took the servants several minutes to scoop her out and carry her away, a shaking, shivering, soiled mess. Inside her confused, humiliated skull, she clung to holy words, repeating to herself, *Hear, my people, the Lord is our God; the Lord is one* and then just finally *Lord… Lord… Lord…* over and over again as a mantra to take her mind off the pain.

"Bathtub," she croaked to whoever held her when they reached her bedroom. They put her down gently inside the empty tub. One of the servants caressed her head, then pulled her braids out of the way and bundled them into a knot. "Aba. Get Aba."

"What?"

"What is 'aba'?" the servants asked each other.

"King Noach." With this final utterance, she collapsed against the side of the tub, curled in the fetal position and quaking like flowers in a storm.

182

There were more embarrassing bodily functions that she had no power to control, spaced out with unbearable pain. Finally, a familiar pair of arms encircled her tiny body, even through her filth. "Sweetheart. Oh, my poor sweetheart."

"Aba," Shulamit gasped. "Am I going to die?"

"No." He kissed the sweat away from her forehead, his nose buried in her hair.

"How do you know? I feel terrible."

"Because I'm king, and I said so."

"I hate everything."

"I know, sweetheart." He rubbed her back. "Is that better or worse?"

"I don't know," she mumbled.

"Would it feel better if you were in bed?"

"Maybe, but I'm a mess."

"We can get you cleaned up. I'll call those ladies back."

"I don't know if I'm *done* yet."

"I'll see if they have ginger anywhere around here. And maybe something to help you sleep."

She did sleep, eventually. When she woke up, her stomach still felt like she'd squeezed into a doll's belt. "Aba…"

He was right there, waiting with a chamber pot. "Princess Brainy requests her magical sick pot?"

She made a weak noise to indicate "ha-ha," then leaned into the pot.

"Now that you're up," said her father as he discreetly removed the evidence of her trauma, "you should see what Carolina sent up for you."

"Mm?" Shulamit turned where he was pointing. A huge bouquet of flowers, at least seven different types, rose from the sideboard at the foot of her bed. "Mmm." This second mumble was in appreciation.

The weather had improved and the windows were open. Noises from other parts of the palace filtered in. Was that Carolina's voice she heard?

She couldn't make out the words. A woman who sounded like the other princess, shouting, and another voice—pleading, protesting. And then—*thwack!*—and screams.

Screams and moaning. What *was* this place?

Her father must have noticed her distress, and he shut the window just as a servant walked in. As he handed her the chamber pot to take away, Shulamit heard him ask, "What's going on out there?"

"The princess is punishing the cook for what happened to your daughter." The maid disappeared with a curtsey.

The window wasn't even thick enough to keep out the screams as they grew louder, and Shulamit buried her head in her pillow. "Make her stop." The words were a whisper, and she left drool on the pillow when she opened her mouth. But she could do nothing.

❖ ❖ ❖

"You see, Isaac?" Queen Shulamit sighed. "It was all… so ruined, so *dirty*. My love for her was gross to me, gross, damaged… After that, I was too ashamed to enjoy her company. Otherwise, we would have been good friends, even if she didn't like me the same way I liked her. Who else could understand what it's like to be Crown Princess? She could have been my best friend… but… I was too horrified." After a pause, she added in a barely audible voice, "I couldn't even look at the flowers she sent me without hearing those screams, over and over."

"You already know it's not your fault that she beat the cook," Isaac pointed out.

"But she beat her because of *me*," Shulamit protested. "Because of my food problems, someone…"

"She made that choice, not you," he reminded her. "And you loving her didn't cause her to oppress her people, or hurt yours."

Shulamit's eyes widened. "You think it's her, then?"

"I don't know what to think," said Isaac, "except that I'd rather have more information before I start having ideas. I don't like to be wrong, and there's still too much chance for that right now."

"Anyway, I think the man she married might have been that 'frivolous' young Count she mentioned when we were in the rowboat." Shulamit played with the fringes she'd created on the destroyed fabric sample in her lap.

"And yet, João still has influence in her life."

Shulamit nodded slowly, then sniffled. "I still feel so tense."

"That's only because you care, which is why I'm so proud of you." Isaac kissed the top of her head. "I know why you think it's your fault."

"Because I loved her, and—"

"No, it's not just that," said Isaac. He took one of her hands in his. "I know because I'm the same way. If it's not your fault, then you have to admit to yourself that bad things, *very* bad things, can happen without anything you did or didn't do. That can be terrifying. We all want to believe we could have stopped it, we could have done something, it was all under our control. But that isn't how the world works. Sometimes, maybe even most of the time, we never had any power to stop it at all. That is hard to hear, and hard to think about, and that's why you want to make it your fault."

Shulamit blinked several times and breathed deeply.

"Let go, little one." Isaac squeezed her hand before relinquishing it. "It may be hard to forgive yourself, but sometimes it's even harder to make yourself realize the trouble was never yours to be forgiven."

Aviva walked in carrying Princess Naomi on her hip. Even just seeing them was like a hug to Shulamit's soul, exposed and exhausted as it was after her reminiscences. Delicate wisps of Aviva's hair, like always, fell down around her lovely face; she was constantly pulling out and replacing the hairsticks that held it up in its customary messy bun, but in the industry and activity of her busy life, it only took minutes for the pieces to cascade down again.

She might not wear ribbons and skirts wide enough to turn her into a human flower, and her speech was impulsive and nonsensical instead of measured words of state, but this was who deserved the queen's love: Aviva who knew the value of hard work; Aviva who knew physical labor to be worthy of respect. Aviva who would only beat someone in self-defense.

Shulamit chuckled when she noticed the orange mush down the front of Aviva's shirt, on one of her shoulders, and across both her and the baby's faces. "Now *there's* a woman worth daydreaming about!"

Aviva smiled back at her. "I don't know... today, maybe I'm a woman, but maybe I'm a sweet potato." She gestured at her trophies.

"The crown wishes to investigate further." Shulamit beckoned, and Isaac got up to make room for Aviva on the sofa.

Bootsteps announced Rivka's presence again. Shulamit spun around, her fingers already laced with Aviva's. "Anything?" Then she furrowed her brow. "Is that Tova's kitten?"

"It was!" Rivka barked, cradling the tiny, black shape with a tenderness that would have surprised strangers, although not her loved ones. "Not anymore. She can't take care of it; she's not keeping it clean. Besides, I can't deal with the urine smell in there anymore, either."

Shulamit looked at Aviva. "I bet she wasn't happy about that."

"Then we'll have to capitalize on her anger," said Isaac. "*Malkeleh*, are you feeling better?"

"I don't care how I'm feeling," said Shulamit, leaning in to hug Aviva one more time, then getting up to follow him. "I have a kingdom to save."

Chapter 19. State's Evidence

"Majesty, I'm telling you, look in the law books," Tova insisted, twisting her hands together as she glared over the queen's shoulder at Rivka. "Look in the books. He had no right to take that kitten away from me. No right at all."

Shulamit, holding her scarf over her nose in a vain attempt to block out the smell of cat urine and other unpleasant, sour odors, observed Tova with detached fascination. She really wasn't that much bigger than Shulamit was herself, but yet, so much hatred and disagreeableness emanated from her that she may as well have been Isaac's size—in his dragon form. If all the stories were true—most of them from her own mouth!—she'd disowned most of her family, harangued her son, and tormented most of her neighbors.

"I did it for the cat, you *meshugannah*—"

Tova interrupted Rivka's growling with a snarl of her own. "*Him*? What does he know about animal welfare?" She shook her finger frantically in Riv's direction, but her words were directed at Shulamit. "He imprisoned a *dragon* and is using it for transportation and *warfare*! Dragons aren't meant to be under human control. They're intelligent animals. Just—"

Shulamit's mouth dropped open and hung there. Was she even hearing this? "The dragon is—"

"Meant to be flying free, in the skies, in the mountains!" Tova's arms were outstretched, presumably to the skies and mountains.

"You do realize the dragon's just the wizard in one of his serpent forms," Shulamit blurted, rolling her eyes.

"That guard's just tricking you." Tova shook her head. "Look in the books. Look in the books."

"There's nothing in the books that say a suspected traitor is allowed to take a kitten into the cell with her in the first place," Rivka pointed out.

"Oh, sure, *he'd* say anything! This *place*." Tova sighed dramatically.

"Listen, you *shtik drek*." Rivka's eyes narrowed, and Shulamit held her breath, unable to repress a smile. "That kitten is the most innocent thing in this palace, and you are literally *the most guilty*. It's trying its best to stay as clean as it can, but you wouldn't let it go outside when it needed to, so it messed all over you, and itself, and it's going to get infected, and none of this is relevant because you're *hurting my country* and we're standing here arguing over a *kitten*. Meanwhile, nobody can breathe in here because of the cat pee smell—"

"Yes, that's right, that's just what Rui said," Shulamit interrupted suddenly.

"What?" Tova's eyes blazed, and she abruptly sat up straight as if a thorn had appeared on her seat.

"Rui," said Shulamit smoothly. "The Imbrian. He also said your house smelled of cat pee, so I suppose I should have expected the cell to get that way too." She wrapped the filmy scarf closer around her face, hoping it was opaque enough to block out her gigantic, ghoulish grin.

Rivka looked at her, and Shulamit got a kick out of watching the spark appear in her captain's blue-gray eyes when she understood. Of course, neither of them had ever spoken to Rui or knew anything about him, beyond what was written in Ezra's notes. But Tova didn't know that.

189

"It most certainly does not! He said that?" Tova slammed her hand down on the table.

"He also said you had too many cats." Shulamit's heart raced. She was praying Tova's anger would snap and she'd sell out the Imbrians before her brain caught up to her and realize that if they'd spoken to Rui, they wouldn't need to know where he was. *Maybe I can say they said this stuff in Ezra's notes… if she catches on…*

"I do no—That's a lie! What's 'too many,' anyway?" Tova was on a roll. "How does he know what's too many? Nobody has a right to say 'too many cats.' Too many for what, anyway? Like to see him run a household all by himself. Him and that André. Who says they're so clean, anyway? Pair of dirty assholes."

Shulamit caught the name and shot a glance over to Rivka. She'd caught it too. André—the other name on the list.

"Should I tell you the other thing they said?" Shulamit wished she was the one holding the kitten because she was terrified that her bluff wouldn't work and desperately wanted something to bring her calm.

"What?" Tova shouted.

"They said that must be why your son doesn't visit." Shulamit felt like a baby bird flinging itself out of a nest. Would these wings work? They were really rather terrible wings, when you thought about it. Rivka had bragged to her mother that they didn't torture prisoners here in Perach, but this… this *was* torture, sort of.

Tova exhaled slowly. "*Pieces of shit.*" She glared around the room. "They're in Ir Ilan, at the house at the back end of Grapefruit Street. And they can go fuck themselves. I don't need this shit."

Then there was silence in the room, punctuated only by Rivka's kitten, which had begun to purr loudly while massaging her leather tunic with pulsating paws as it looked for milk.

❖ ❖ ❖

Rivka and Shulamit stepped out into the sunlight and made sure they were a safe distance from Tova's cell, then chortled to each other with effervescent glee.

Shulamit shook her fists in front of her in excitement. "I can't believe that *worked*!"

"Everybody, watch out—the Queen of Perach is coming," teased Rivka.

"So can you get there tonight? It's still early."

Rivka looked up at the sun and considered the brightness and angle. "With men on horses? I'd say we'll get there when it's dark, but that's actually better. We can surprise them, and they should all be at home."

"Better send Isaac in there first, lizard-wise, to make sure Tova didn't double-cross us."

"I doubt she has the faculties for that." Rivka shifted the kitten in her arms. "Ooh, *shayneh ketzeleh*!" She leaned her face down toward it, and it batted at her mask with its paw. "Oops, no, bad idea."

"She's a warrior, like you," quipped Shulamit. "I'll go find Isaac—you get everyone else you need."

Rivka watched the queen stalk off purposefully back toward the salon, then headed for the barracks. As she passed by the room she'd given to the newcomers, she heard unmistakable noises of weeping. Was that Halleli?

"Oh! Captain. I'm sorry; I didn't see you." Halleli sniffled and wiped away her tears.

"I didn't mean to disturb you," said Rivka, peering into the doorway. "Do you like cats?"

"Sure, I—"

"Here. She's yours now if you want her."

Halleli looked surprised but accepted the tiny creature into her arms. "She's adorable!"

"I'm sorry for your loss," said Rivka.

"I'll be all right. I don't mean to seem ungrateful, after everything you and the queen did to make sure we landed on our feet. I mean, you've given Hadar this amazing opportunity, and Yael is going to let me draw the patrons in the restaurant to make extra money."

"But your feelings are real, and you shouldn't have to feel guilty about them," Rivka reminded her.

"Thanks." Halleli wiped away another tear. The kitten buried its nose in her armpit. "Awww! I…" Halleli smiled. "I think I'll call her Olive."

Chapter 20. The Conspirators

High above the cloud cover, the queen's dragon made for Ir Ilan. The air here was barely above freezing, and between the speed Isaac was flying and the ambient moisture, he felt cold inside his bones. At least here, though, he knew he wouldn't be spotted on his approach to the city. If the whole point of him riding on ahead, especially without Rivka, was espionage via lizard, hiding his flight was vital.

A wizard's life of adventure meant that he was no stranger to physical discomfort, but neither did that make this any more fun. Steeling his numbing wings against the chill, he entertained himself with thoughts of hot soup, of tea, of mineral baths, and finally, Rivka. Possibly even Rivka feeding him soup in a mineral bath, his fantasies growing more decadent as he fought to ignore his chapping snout.

The rushing, wet air bit him ferociously and brought him back to faraway times and places. He was a young wizard in a fur coat and hat, tearing through a frozen battlefield with his hands outstretched in magic spells. He was a novice, standing outside in the wizard stronghold watching his breath fog up and practicing his newfound magic by shaping it into the four letters of his name. He remembered his hands growing numb with cold as he persisted; *yud* was easy, of course, but at first he kept getting stuck on the intricacies of *tzadik*.

The dragon snorted. Now he could write an entire message in the sky with floating leaves just by thinking about it.

His mind sank even further back into memory. He was a young child hiding in the corner to get away from all the yelling. It was cold inside the house, and dangerous too— dangerous if you said the wrong thing to one of the adults, or even one of the older boys. Mammeh couldn't help; she was even more cowed than he was. He wrapped the old blanket around his shoulders and wished he was invisible. Don't tell them anything anymore. It's not safe. If they know what you're thinking, you're not safe.

Pushing this unsettling reverie aside, Isaac realized it was time to check his flight path. Dipping below the clouds, he did his best to mimic the chaotic, prey-driven behavior of a wild dragon, one that didn't have a human soul lurking inside. The sudden warm air enlivened him and jolted him back to his tropical present, rich in warmth both literal and emotional.

He scanned the grasslands for deer to pretend to chase— not that a real meal wouldn't be welcome after all that flying in cold!—but his real mission was to study the road and the rivers. Not too much longer, now.

Once he landed, Isaac had to make his way toward Ir Ilan in lizard form. He crawled methodically through the grass, inhaling the clean, alive smell of green growth and dirt. After the misery up in the clouds, he was determined to enjoy this part of the journey even if it was annoying that he couldn't do it ten times faster in human form.

The marketplace that ran down the central road of Ir Ilan was closed up for Shabbat, but there were still people strolling around taking in the late afternoon air. Isaac scurried back and forth on the road avoiding their feet. Here and there he crawled across the walls of buildings instead, when the way seemed easier.

Grapefruit Street was relatively empty compared with the activity on Orange Street and King Asher Boulevard. The houses grew farther apart as the road wound and curved between the trees, and Isaac stopped seeing people in the path. Veiled in greenery, the calm neighborhood didn't seem like it would harbor a gang of Imbrian spies nor any kind of conspiracy more serious than a chicken hiding her eggs.

When Isaac had the final house in his sight, he fixed his eyes on it and ran. He was so single-minded that he nearly ran smack into—another lizard!

They stared at each other, lizard and shapeshifter. Isaac cocked his head. The other lizard replied by unfurling his great red dewlap. A challenge.

I don't have time for this. Isaac did a couple of lizard push-ups and showed his own dewlap, never taking his eyes off the other lizard.

Convinced, the other lizard backed off. *Rivka is going to laugh at this for days*, Isaac thought as he ran toward the house. He laughed himself as he realized from a rustling behind him that the other lizard was following him into the house.

When he got there, he saw why the other lizard was so invested in keeping him away. A healthy supply of tiny ants provided ample motive to defend this modest territory. He restrained himself from sampling them, wishing to avoid further pointless conflict with his reptilian brothers.

Isaac crawled up to the ceiling so he could take a census of the room's human occupants.

The first person he noticed was a nondescript man, with the characteristic pale skin and black hair of the Imbrians, asleep on a sofa in the center of the room. Two jugs rested beside him on the floor, and one look at the man's open mouth told Isaac that this might be the heavy drinker with the missing tooth from Ezra's notes.

A woman, Perachi from her coloring and clothes, emerged from the house's back room. She ignored the sleeping man and sat down at the large table, returning to the garlic cloves she'd been shucking.

"All that and you return so quickly to your cooking?" Isaac jerked his head to follow the Imbrian-accented voice. Another pale, dark-haired man appeared, in the doorway of the back room. His shirt and hair were rumpled, and he leaned against the doorframe.

The woman looked up from her work. "But Rui will be back with André and they're both expecting dinner. You remember, like last time? They didn't stop to eat the whole way so they wouldn't get overheard like that time in the restaurant."

Isaac thought he saw fear in her large eyes.

The Imbrian approached her slowly, his movements fluid. "Talia, *minha adorada*." He laid a hand delicately on each of her shoulders and nuzzled her head from behind with his nose and mouth. "Our busy little flower."

They won Tova with hate, and this Talia with love, Isaac noted. Then he simply continued watching.

"You could help me, if you like," Talia suggested. "If I finish faster, maybe you can... I can..." The Imbrian was kissing the back of her neck now, and his hands had traveled across to clasp her bosom.

Isaac turned away. He kept to the shadows as he headed for a vase of branches at the center of the room, figuring it would be a perfect vantage point once Rui and André returned. Settling in between the leaves, he waited.

Talia somehow managed to cook while evading her Imbrian suitor's advances, and at some point the inebriate on the couch woke up, blinked stupidly for several minutes, and then demanded water.

Before long, the house was filled with the aroma of garlic and frying meat, and not a moment too soon. Horse hooves thumped outside, and there was a great jangling and clattering as the door opened to admit two large, pale-skinned men. They both had black hair and healthy beards. One was young and very thin, the other larger, older, and radiating the confidence of a leader.

"It smells wonderful in here," said the older of the two in Imbrian. Then he repeated himself in Perachi. "Thank you, Talia. I can't wait to eat."

"Did anyone see you?" asked the one who was Talia's lover.

"No, we were safe."

"What about at the border?"

"We posed as traders looking for new sources."

"That's ironic," quipped Talia's lover.

The leader laughed. "You could say that."

"Is André carrying a message?" The man with the missing tooth stood up, making a face as if standing brought him pain.

The younger of the new arrivals stepped forward and removed a folded, sealed paper from deep within his clothes. "Right here."

197

"Let's open it!" said Talia's lover.

"We should let them eat first," countered the man with the missing tooth.

They both looked at André, who shrugged. "It's up to Rui."

The older leader, the one who was called Rui, pursed his lips for a moment, then sat down at the table. "The letter can surely wait five minutes. It's been days since I've eaten anything that wasn't packed in a pouch."

As they fell upon the food, Isaac evaluated the situation. That paper was probably the most important thing in the room right now. He could think of plenty of magic-based ways he could abscond with it easily, but unfortunately, they were all untenable as all involved him revealing his presence. That would never do, because Rivka and her team planned a surprise ambush.

Well, nothing to do but wait in the vase until they finished eating and then, hopefully, they'd open up the letter and read it out loud.

"What about money?" asked the man with the missing tooth.

Rui, his hands around a stuffed pita, cracked a smile. "Don't worry. I've brought plenty."

"Plenty for you to drink your share as usual," muttered Talia's lover.

"I've done everything Rui asked of me, and more." The man with the missing tooth glared at him. "Where were you the night we took care of the snoop in Home City?"

Isaac's heart quickened. Ezra's murderer had just confessed right in front of him!

"Light another lamp," Rui commanded. "It's getting darker outside."

If night approached, Isaac realized that his wife and her troops wouldn't be far behind. Perhaps it was time to make his escape and go find them at the prearranged spot at the corner of Asher and Orange.

On the other hand, all he had so far was proof-*ish* that they'd been involved in the murder of Ezra. Other than a vague and offhand comment, nobody had as yet mentioned the plot to ruin Perach's olives.

He also *desperately* wanted to find out what was in that letter.

"Talia is a true goddess among women." Rui stood and held out his hand to her, and she nodded bashfully in appreciation. She began to clear away the dishes as the men filed into the seating area, some carrying oil lamps, which they set upon the table where Isaac was sitting in the vase.

"Is there enough light in here?" asked André, looking at Rui for approval.

"I can see." Rui was last to join them, relaxing into a chair holding a glass of something Isaac figured might be port.

"Can you see well enough to pay us?" asked the man with the missing tooth. "The plan is working. The leafhoppers have completely infested the northern groves. Talk is all over the market and the oil prices already rise. Yet, here I am low on coin. If I were to be cut loose tonight, I'd have an empty purse to show for it."

"Who told you to drink your purse?" muttered Talia's lover.

Isaac vibrated with excitement. That was *more* than a confession.

"André brought us a *generous* payment this time." Rui rummaged through his pockets, and Isaac heard the clinking noise of money. "Are they desperate enough to buy Imbrian oil yet?"

Time to get out and find Rivka. He still wanted *the letter*, but with the team on the way, it was more important to find them and confirm that yes, this was *definitely* the house.

Isaac was just about to crawl down the vase and make his exit when Talia's lover pounced on something and flicked it into the fire in one of the lamps. A horrid, choking smell filled the air.

André turned toward the drunkard in shock. "Did you just—what was that for?"

"He's crazy," said the drunkard dismissively.

"Shut up, you alcoholic idiot," said Talia's lover.

"Did he just throw a lizard into the lamp?" André squinted into the flickering glare.

"He does that every time a lizard crawls in here." The drunkard waved his hand dismissively and relaxed against the sofa.

"And for good reason!" Talia's lover shouted. "You're so drowned in drink you probably can't remember, but any one of them could be the Perachi queen's spy."

André looked at Rui, his eyes squinted in puzzlement. "What?"

"That pervert wizard," said Rui, counting out coins and seemingly nonplussed by the murdered creature or the argument it had caused. "He transforms into lizards and snakes, so that one's been killing all the lizards that run in here. And we have ants, so there's no shortage." He paused for a moment, recounting the money under his breath. "You're making me lose count."

Isaac, who had frozen in place during this entire horrifying conversation, slunk backward into the vase. Now what?

"It does make sense, I guess," said André. "Why did you call him a pervert?"

"He's sleeping his way across the Royal Guard, is what I heard," said Talia's lover.

"I thought it was just the captain," said the man with the missing tooth.

Thank you for standing up for my fidelity, Isaac grumbled inwardly. What could he do? If he turned human, he could easily subdue the men temporarily with buzzing whips of energy from his fingers and walk out of the room. If he levitated random objects—such as one of Talia's kettles— they might be distracted for a few moments. But, either plan depended on revealing the presence of a wizard, and then they'd all flee before he could get to Rivka and her men.

"There, there, and there." Rui paid each of the men. Then he raised his glass. "A toast! To our noble and beautiful Queen Carolina."

201

"Long live Queen Carolina," said the other men, each lifting his drink in respect.

Yes, but is she behind this or not? Isaac scanned the room with rotating, beady eyes. This way? That way? Across the floor? Over the ceiling? What was the best way out of here? Because he *had* to get out. That was not optional. His safety, his duty to his adopted country—there had to be a way to preserve them both.

Step one was probably a diversion, but one that was innocuous enough that it wouldn't make anyone think magic was involved. There were eggs on Talia's kitchen counter, but when he tried prodding at them with his mind, he realized they were comfortably settled enough in their basket that rolling one out to crack on the floor would be conspicuously unnatural. Same with the oranges beside them. Too bad. What he really wanted to do was send all the oranges whizzing around the room, knocking each conspirator in the head. Maybe an extra one for Talia's lover and his lizard-scorching habit.

What about the fire itself? No… that could be too dangerous. He didn't want the house going up in flames; he needed that letter to get back to Rivka—and Shulamit—intact.

He could pull a single hair on someone's head… then they'd yelp and everyone would look in that direction. But nobody was sitting with his head back against anything, so there wouldn't be the obvious answer of "it caught in the chair."

Then he remembered the ants.

Carefully, gently, his breathing steady and his body trembling with concentration, he coaxed the trail of ants by

202

the doorway farther into the room. Each time he inhaled, the energy of his breath drew them closer. *That's it, little bugs. You want bugs? We have bugs too. I'll give you bugs.*

Rui smacked his ankle. "Those stinking ants. I don't understand."

The drunkard shook his head. "It's not like this place is dirty or anything."

"They're harmless," Talia called from washing up the kitchen.

"I don't care," Rui huffed. "I don't want them *on me*."

Meanwhile, Isaac crawled gingerly out of the vase and scrambled as fast as his little legs could carry him toward the crack under the door.

"Hey!"

"What, did you find where the ants are coming in?"

"They're coming in from the door," said Rui. "We already knew that. But there's another lizard over there."

Talia's lover leapt up from his seat and was across the floor in two bounds.

"Don't encourage him," yawned the man with the missing tooth, rolling his eyes.

Isaac ran for the gap, but his pursuer beat him to it and blocked the way. He narrowly escaped the rough pair of hands that grabbed for him and leapt onto the wall. Talia's lover darted after him, but Isaac made it up to the ceiling and continued his evasion.

Scurrying to and fro across the ceiling in random squiggles, Isaac did his best to avoid the men chasing him. One of them—he couldn't tell which in the confusion—was trying to use Talia's broom to sweep him down, and another swatted at him with a fan.

"It's *just* a *lizard*," called the man with the missing tooth from the sofa, and he took another drink from his jug.

Isaac ran curlicues across the ceiling until he saw once again a clear path to the doorway. If he ran across the ceiling and down the door, they could catch him on his way down. But if he went down another wall and across the floor, they could step on him.

But stepping on him could result in a clean getaway, if he understood his training properly. He took a deep breath. Maybe it was time to find out if lizard shifters shared their mundane cousins' breakaway tail.

He allowed himself half a second for prayer and the rest of the second for Rivka's eyes, and then he ran to one edge of the ceiling. As the men pooled there in that corner, he doubled back and ran down a different wall.

Isaac's limbs burned as he scrabbled for his life across the floor. The black space under the door stood out like a dark beacon. He only had to make it *most of the way through*. Come on… for queen and country… and his own head!

Thump, thump, thump and someone was right behind him. Then, suddenly, a shock of pain rocked his backside. His tail was crushed under a boot.

But he kept running.

His center of gravity shifted wildly and he was nearly thrown off balance, but he adjusted and kept running, squeezing under the door to darkness and safety even as a pair of hands clapped against what was left of his tail. Soaked in adrenaline, he was well into the brush on the side of the road before the feeling of rawness set in. There was stinging pain as if he'd peeled a cuticle too deeply on his finger, but worse, and whatever a lizard had for exposed skin when its tail had been pulled off felt tender and angry in the night air.

He curled himself around a stick and caught his breath, evaluating his body. He'd made it out of the house, but the night had only begun and he needed to find Rivka right away. There was no time to waste by continuing in this tiny form, especially if Talia's lover managed to persuade the others that letting a lizard, *any* lizard, get away meant that the queen's forces were on to them. But what would happen, now that he'd been mangled, once he turned back into a man?

21. The Raid

Captain Riv Maror waited on horseback with the rest of her troops, in silent formation between a building and the fountain at the corner of King Asher Boulevard and Orange Street. She scanned the streets for Isaac—as a human or a lizard—her eyes also occasionally glancing upward in case he'd had reason to meet them as a dragon.

In the meantime, she also evaluated the men she'd brought with her. Each face was resolute and prepared for the mission. Each man had relatives in the Lovely Valley or otherwise employed in agriculture; nobody in Perach could survive without the hard work and luck of the farmers. They all knew what was at stake and, though they might now be smiling and joking quietly in the false calm of the night air, hands burned to grasp their weaponry for the patriotic cause.

Steps coming from farther down Asher attracted Rivka's attention. "Hey," she barked in a low tone, and her men heightened their guard.

The black shape against the charcoal-gray of the sky looked and walked like Isaac, but something was different.

Rivka hopped down off her horse to meet him. She was only able to see him clearly close up, and her eyes crinkled with puzzled laughter. "What happened to your shirt?"

For her husband was completely bare-chested, the bulky hills of his torso reflecting starlight.

He answered her with a loaded smirk. "You should be thankful that's all that happens if I lose my tail in lizard form."

Rivka's eyes widened. "What happened?"

206

"They're killing all the lizards that get into the house in case they're me." Isaac looked over the men, counting silently. "Good, we can take them with no problem."

"Then it's them? You're sure?"

"It's *definitely* them," Isaac affirmed. "I still don't know who they're working for, but I know three things. One, the man with the missing tooth killed Ezra. He admitted it. Two, they've planted the bugs on purpose so that Perach will be forced to buy Imbrian, as we thought."

Rivka noticed angry murmurings among her men. "And?"

"And three," Isaac continued, looking deep into her eyes, "there's a letter from Imbrio, a sealed letter, which we need to bring out of that house and get back to the queen."

Rivka nodded slowly. "I'm on it." Then, casting one last affectionate look at Isaac's naked torso, she slipped back into battle mode. "I don't suppose there's any way we can get you another shirt before this begins."

"Not unless anyone else here is six foot five." Isaac shrugged and smiled. "Oh, well!"

His amused eyes told her that he'd love her all the more for *not* noticing and staying focused, at least, not until the battle was well and truly won.

"Do they have guards posted outside the house? How about at the front end of Grapefruit Street?" Rivka quizzed Isaac, looking over her team. When he shook his head, she started giving orders to the rest of the men. "We'll leave the horses at Grapefruit and Asher, with you and you. Everyone else will come with me. Isaac, how many doors? What about windows? Okay, we want you and you at the two windows; you two stay at the front door and keep them from leaving except with us… and everyone else is coming inside with me."

"What about me, Mighty One?"

"I said everyone else, Shirtless." Her eyes twinkled at him, but the brows over them were furrowed and serious.

Isaac smirked. "I'm certainly going to live up to my reputation."

"What?"

"One of them called me 'that pervert wizard.'"

"He's just jealous," Rivka retorted with a toss of her brassy hair. "Come on!"

In as much silence as possible, the team rode to the intersection, then left the horses at the corner as prearranged. Experience and training was on their side, keeping their feet as quiet as cats' as they traversed the peaceful neighborhood. Isaac lit up the path with faint traces of magic so that they could avoid stepping on crunchy leaves or tripping on stray rocks.

"Remember," Rivka hissed, "the letter. Above all, we need it for the queen."

"Everyone else alive?" asked one of the men.

"Absolutely. If possible." Rivka fired off those last two words like arrows. "Take up your positions."

"We ready?" Isaac asked once the men stationed at the windows were in place.

"Mm-hmm." She looked around at her men and saw several pairs of wide-awake eyes shining back at her. "Now!"

Rivka slammed her shoulder against the door. Ignoring the bruising as if her arm and side were made of stone, she pushed it aside and charged into the room with her men at her sides. The men in the room, all light-skinned and black-haired Imbrians, sprang to action, but she unsheathed her sword as soon as she had clearance to not hit one of her own.

"Surrender to the queen's forces and we won't hurt you!" she bellowed.

"Shit, it's the Perachis!" shouted a man with a missing tooth.

Over in the corner, a Perachi woman started to cry. She darted toward the back room, but Rivka yelled, "Her too!" and one of her men blocked her. "Get her out of here."

A young, skinny Imbrian drew a dagger and headed straight for Rivka, but she easily threw him off and toward two of her other men. "Isaac, where's the letter?" she called out in their native language.

"Over there!"

The oldest of the Imbrians had wrestled himself free of two Perachi soldiers and was rushing toward the fire. He reached into his coat, but Rivka, abandoning her sword, leapt onto his back with all four limbs and snatched the paper out of his hand.

No sooner had she popped off him and shoved the letter down her pants—for lack of a better idea—than he was on her. His fist tried for her face, but she dodged and grabbed his arm. Pouring all her weight into her upper body, she flung him down and tried to withdraw—now that she had the letter, it was vital that she get it to safety. But from the floor, he grabbed her ankle, and soon, they were in the dust wrestling together.

In between slamming his head into the floor and pulling his hand off her waistband, she looked up to see Isaac grappling with one of the other Imbrians. His left hand was closed in a fist; the fingers of his right, which could not close, were splayed out and shooting off whips of light. Sweat shone from the curves of his exposed skin.

Well, good, Isaac was taking care of himself, so Rivka could fully focus on her own fistfight. And just in time too. Once again she found herself pulling the Imbrian's hand out of her pants, where she'd stashed the letter. He was determined to retrieve it and drove his arm forward even against her grip. She gripped harder.

And harder.

And *bent*.

She knew Isaac would look over when he heard the horrible cracking snap, so in their own language, she shouted, "I'm okay; it's him," as reassurance.

"That's some well-guarded—" she heard him begin, but then all she could focus on was the glint of the huge dagger the man in her grasp suddenly produced. He brandished it with the arm she hadn't broken—*yet*—and was aiming it straight at her face.

The next few moments were a tangle of leather and hair and skin and metal, but then, with a thump of finality, Rivka stood up from the floor. At her feet was the leader of the Imbrians, his broken arm hanging off strangely at his side and his own dagger wedged in his chest.

Isaac and the other Imbrian were still punching each other, so Rivka came up behind her husband's opponent and aimed a flying kick at his back. As he went down, Isaac was able to get a full zap from his finger lasers at the man's face, safely stunning him.

"That was the man who was killing all the lizards," Isaac explained calmly, sweat pouring down his face. He pursed his fingers over his nose and mustache to wipe some of it away.

"He just missed the most important one," Rivka commented as she retrieved her sword and sheathed it.

"But barely!" Isaac smirked. "You have the letter?"

"Where only you can get at it."

Isaac lifted one eyebrow. "Dragon's privilege."

"Where are we? Where's that woman?"

"She's outside in custody."

Rivka nudged the body at her feet with the toe of one boot. "And there's this guy."

"Rui."

"Oh, that name I remember from Ezra's notes."

"And this is André," said Isaac, holding his hand out at the unconscious man in front of him. "He was their messenger."

They looked over to the doorway, where a group of Perachi soldiers were subduing a sweaty, angry Imbrian with a missing tooth. "You got him?" Rivka called out.

"We're fine, Captain." The soldier who'd spoken winced. "Oof! His breath."

"He can sober up in the local jail."

"Aren't we taking them back to the palace?"

"Sure, in the morning." said Rivka. "But let's put 'em in the jail overnight so we all have time to recover from this. And some of us can sleep there too, in case they try anything."

The guards nodded. "Yes, Captain."

Rivka and Isaac quickly examined the remainder of the house and found no more conspirators. "I think we're done here, for now."

"Yes, Captain."

On their way out of the house, Rivka let everybody else go ahead. Finally alone with Isaac in the starlight, she looked up at his smiling face. "*Now* I can look at you."

"Look all you want, Mighty One."

She planted one palm on his chest, feeling warmth and a beloved heartbeat. "You said to get that letter."

"It was the most important part of the mission, and I knew you could."

In the darkness of a now-slumbering Grapefruit Street, she aggressively kissed him. Her intensity inflamed him, and he encircled her with his strong, bare arms. As she held him she reveled in the novel sensation of gripping his naked back while she stood there, fully clothed.

As they walked toward the jail, arm in arm, she asked him, "What about your tail?"

"I imagine I'll have to spend enough time as a lizard to grow it back," said Isaac. "I definitely can't fly without it."

"Sleep on my chest, then."

"My paradise."

"Will you sing to me?"

"Where the Imbrians can hear?"

"Fuck the Imbrians."

"What about the letter?" Isaac asked. "Are we going to read it before we take it back to the queen?"

"I think she should see it with the seal intact." Rivka led him back into the main thoroughfare, and they walked off together in the direction of the jail.

Chapter 22. The Letter from Imbrio

Morning found Queen Shulamit in a sun-dappled corner of her salon, cuddled happily on the sofa against the soft flesh of Aviva's side. Two hired musicians, middle-aged women with kindly faces, serenaded the ladies with flute duets. Naomi was playing on a woven cotton rug on the floor with cloth dolls that looked like different-colored cats, safely cordoned off by a little wooden fence just like the one in the kitchen-house.

Shulamit applauded against her thigh between tunes so she didn't have to drop Aviva's hand even for a moment. "I love what they're playing." She took a drink from a cup of ginger-lemon tea resting on a side table.

"It's like a basket of little cookies," Aviva agreed. "Each one's different, and sweet in its own way, and then—whoo! It's gone in one bite, and on to whatever's next."

Shulamit smiled. "It just fills me with this…" she paused to sigh happily. "…feeling of joy and peace, like maybe everything's going to be all right."

"Maybe it is!" Aviva kissed her on the nose.

"I'm sure Riv and the Guard captured whoever they found last night," said Shulamit. "Soon, we'll be able to question them, and stop the sabotage at the source."

"Dig it right out by the roots."

"And you know, Aviva? This flute music is so hopeful, I can almost believe it's not going to be Carolina. You'll see—Riv will get the men to crack and we'll find out it's her Prince-Consort." Shulamit's eyes flashed and her speech grew rapid with excitement. "I don't know how they handle divorce in Imbrio, but in any case he'll be entirely discredited as royalty, and maybe she can marry João after all, like she always wanted. And *then*, then, Aviva—" She leaned her head dreamily against Aviva's shoulder and blinked up at the ceiling. "—the Imbrian working class will finally be set free and live as Perachi farmers do."

"I like your garden," said Aviva.

"That place badly needs it," groaned Shulamit. "I was terrified when we were there that someone would catch on from somewhere that you're my chef and—"

"I know."

"Also, if Carolina had nothing to do with the bugs, then I can stop feeling guilty about—"

"Shulamit." Aviva took both of the queen's hands in hers and looked into her eyes, her voice quiet but firm. "No matter how many flowers you grew around her portrait, you're not, you're *never* culpable for anything she did. Not then, not now, not ever. Even if it does turn out to be her."

"Everyone keeps saying that," said Shulamit. "Now I just need it to sink in."

She relaxed once again into the caresses of the music until she heard familiar noises in the palace's inner courtyard. "Hey!" she squealed, jumping up. "They're back! Riv's back."

Aviva scooped up the baby as Shulamit quickly dismissed the flute players with a handful of coins. "I've got to get back to my kitchen work anyway," said Aviva, kissing Shulamit on the cheek on her way out. "Good luck!"

"Thanks!" Shulamit scampered into the daylight, holding her cup of tea carefully so she wouldn't spill anything in her agitation.

Rivka stood under the coconut palm, holding a rolled-up paper tube. Her eyes brightened when she saw the queen. "We got 'em."

"All *right*!" Shulamit made a little cheering motion with her free hand, then drank more tea. "Whoo! What's the outcome? We have prisoners?"

"Three men and one woman taken; one man killed," Rivka reported. "All Imbrian except for the woman."

Shulamit nodded. "Good work. Thank you. What's that?"

Rivka looked down at the paper. "I took this from their leader. It came directly from Imbrio. I could be wrong, but you might recognize the seal."

Shulamit took the tube from her and turned it over to see. Blood flooded out of her face and her cheeks felt cold. "Yes," she murmured, clutching her tea more tightly. "Um. You didn't read it?"

Rivka shook her head. "Under the circumstances I thought it would be good if we could say honestly that the Queen of Perach had witnessed the untampered seal."

Shulamit nodded. "Good thinking. Well, let's see what this is about." She handed the letter back to Rivka, who used one of her smaller daggers to slit it open before returning it to the queen.

As Shulamit read the words on the page, her heart sank and collapsed into her stomach. Each sentence made the picture clearer for her; she gritted her teeth and kept scanning. Her sips of tea were automatic more than anything else; they brought little calm except through the mechanicalness of the motion. She felt as if she were tea herself, the bad taste in her soul slowly growing as if the letter were the leaves and she was the water quickly becoming overbrewed.

"So, *nu?*" Rivka asked with wide eyes.

Shulamit passed her the letter without a word, trying to remember how to speak.

Rivka held up her hand. "Could you read it to me? Their alphabet will take me too long to remember."

"I can do that." Shulamit licked her lips. "You want me to translate?"

"Sure."

Shulamit drained the rest of her tea, sat the cup on the ground, and clutched the letter with both hands.

My loyal friends, my Imbrian compatriots,

Thank you for your success in our plan. The market news already speaks of shortages—soon, there will be no more talk in Perach of boycotting Imbrian goods. Our hardworking farmers will be the ones to directly benefit from your efforts, and Imbrio's new burst of prosperity will be shared first and foremost with those whose toil grew our crops and our trees.

I commend you for getting rid of the Perachi spy. I have had to do the same—I have killed rather than let our plans reach the queen's ears. Our most pure and beautiful, noble Queen Carolina! You should drink to her praises when you read this letter. I took her on a tour of Imbrio's most prosperous but unequal farms and I believe our truth has finally grown in her heart. Her reign ushers in a new glorious age for Imbrio, one full of riches to be shared among its own workers and not dependent on foreign products.

Gods bless you, Gods bless her, and Gods bless Imbrio. Imbrio forever.

Your friend,

João Carneiro de Façanha, Visconde

"There's another one of those ram's-head things from his ring at the bottom, under his name," Shulamit added. She gave Rivka back the paper.

"You have to stop him," said Rivka. "She needs to see this."

"I know, but…" Shulamit played with her lip. "Yeah. I—thank you. I'm—I'm glad you were able to get your hands on this. Um. I'll have orders for you later." She turned toward her library.

"Where are you going?"

"I have tax papers I need to look at." Shulamit hurried away.

"What?" But Rivka was talking to the back of her head.

❖ ❖ ❖

Rivka gave Shulamit space, occupying her time by washing her feet in the stream behind the palace, changing her clothes, and splitting a roast chicken with Isaac in the

218

main kitchen. Nourished and cleansed, she sought out her heart-sister with new energy.

She found her at her desk in the library, piles of papers stacked in every direction. "Hey. You look busy." For once, she wished Shulamit could see the smirk she was aiming at her from behind her cloth mask.

Shulamit didn't look up. "I'm trying to figure out the difference between these two proposed trade agreements with the City of Lakes."

"You should take a break. Come on—work out with me." Rivka flexed a muscle.

Shulamit cast her a skeptical stare, her mouth an angry little line.

"We don't have to talk about it," Rivka added.

Shulamit looked back down at her papers. "But what would I wear?"

"*That* is the silliest excuse ever, from the queen with the biggest wardrobe since—"

Shulamit threw her head back and groaned. "Okay."

A few minutes later, Shulamit clad in something sleeveless, roomy, and usually forgotten, the two women entered the barracks practice area. With no guards there, and therefore no men, Shulamit seemed to be relaxing in spite of herself—just as Rivka had planned. Rivka handed her the weights she thought appropriate for Shulamit's lack of habitual practice and showed her what to do with them.

On the tenth rep, Shulamit finally spoke. "We have to save our farmers."

Rivka nodded without breaking the rhythm of her bicep curls.

"But," Shulamit continued, "what would Perach be if protecting her meant selling out the Imbrian working class?"

"She'd be your responsibility."

"Then can it really be my responsibility to doom Imbrio to another generation of inequality and torture? We'd be prospering at her expense, just as they would have done to us. And it would be the poorest who'd suffer, not those who deserve it. If I discredit João..."

Rivka transferred her weight to the other hand. "He's killed one of our citizens, even if he was a *chazzer*, and he's trying to ruin our country. What happens if you do nothing and let him keep running Imbrio behind the scenes?"

"Then we fall into economic ruin," Shulamit muttered, and panted with exertion. "I mean, even if we figure out a way to stop the bugs, he'll try something else. He's dangerous." She put the weight down. "Look, Rivka, I want to save us. I *have* to save us. But it would be buying our happiness at the direct cost of thousands of others."

"What would your father want?" Rivka pushed her guilt away into the curls. It was a low blow, and she knew it. She just hadn't realized it 'til the words were out.

"He wouldn't have trusted me with this," Shulamit replied. "Which doesn't exactly help."

"If it does help, *Isaac* trusts you. And he's the one who's seen you grow up these past five, six years. Sometimes your philosophy differs from your father's, and that's okay."

"He wouldn't have understood. He would have wanted me to put Perach first, without thinking."

"Then don't put it first *without thinking*," said Rivka. "Think, first. That's your favorite hobby, right? Overthinking? After reading and picking out new pink and purple dresses."

Shulamit let out a sad little giggle. "I love you," she mumbled, looking away.

"Let's do a little *spiel*. Pretend you do nothing. Then what? Just, pretend that's your final decision."

Shulamit was still for a moment, her eyes focused on an empty corner of the room at which she was obviously not actually looking. "No. That's unacceptable."

"So you have to find a way to expose him to Carolina," Rivka insisted. "Something that you can live with."

"I just wish he wasn't…" Shulamit looked up at the ceiling and sighed deeply.

"Go back to the reps; it'll help you think."

"Things are so screwed up over there, is the thing," said Shulamit as she obeyed. "Carolina only listens to the highborn, and no highborn Imbrian is sticking up for the workers. João was a fluke, a special case. Without him—"

Rivka looked directly into her eyes and spoke with solemnity. "She would still have you."

Shulamit slowly nodded. "You're right. I'm the only other person who could talk to her. I guess this means I have to go back."

"We will of course go with you."

"My God," Shulamit blurted suddenly. "Naomi caught my cold. She can't go up there this late in the year. The Imbrians have a real winter—"

"She'll be safe here with Aviva and the wet nurses."

Shulamit's face quivered with emotion. "I've never been away from either of them for that long. But you're right. I'm the only one left who can reason with Carolina about the working class. I'm the only other person she'll listen to. I mean, not that she really listened to me before, but maybe now it'll be different since she's seen the farms up close."

"It's not going to be a fun conversation."

"If it works, I can save both our countries at once." Shulamit paused. "If she even listens to me after—after."

Chapter 23. The Pale Queen

Queen faced queen in the chill of the sumptuous Imbrian salon. Shulamit stood, waiting, her gloved fingers fidgeting with the fur edging of her cloak as she watched Carolina read the letter. That lovely, pale face grew even paler, almost green; her dark eyes grew larger and seemed to turn into vast, gleaming stones of polished onyx. Her body was still like a statue, but Shulamit could tell that inside the sculpture of nobility there was a woman crumbling to dust.

Finally she spoke, and Shulamit was so tense that the sound startled her. "He should never have taken this action."

"I'm so sorry, Carolina." Shulamit hoped her tone conveyed the full weight of her sincerity.

"No, *I'm* sorry." Carolina set the letter down and took one of her hands in hers. She stared into Shulamit's eyes as she continued. "Imbrio is Perach's ally. We are Perach's friends. The throne does not condone this."

"Thanks." Shulamit's voice cracked, and she sounded adolescent to her own ears. She drew herself up and tried to feel twenty-five. The Imbrian chill wasn't helping; winter had come in full force, and she felt cold inside her bones. It made her want to run to Isaac and hide in his capes, snuggling like a child. But Isaac wasn't even human right now; for reasons of state he'd entered the room in Rivka's hair.

"He worked this plan as my father lay ill and dying, to build my reign on treachery," Carolina murmured, almost to herself. Then, louder, "What fate for his conspirators?"

"Extradition or trial in Perach," said Shulamit. "There's the matter of that man they murdered."

"You may keep them," said Carolina scornfully. "This is not what I wanted for my reign. This is not what I wanted for my country!"

Shulamit paused, knowing she was about to touch the bruise again. "What will you do?"

"He cannot stay here." Carolina's gaze fell. "His lands will be taken and he will go into exile."

"I'm sorry," Shulamit found herself saying again, immediately feeling stupid.

They were interrupted by clattering from the corner. Shulamit looked over to see the Imbrian princess sitting in the middle of a collapsed tower of blocks. The little girl let out a wail of frustration.

"It will be okay, Sophia," Carolina said in Imbrian. "Now you can build something even prettier."

Shulamit's gaze traveled under fluttering lashes back and forth between mother and daughter, fighting a sinking feeling. "Carolina, this isn't... *very* bad, is it?" *This is none of my business, but I so badly don't want it to be true... I have to know.*

Carolina looked at Shulamit with puzzled eyes, then followed her gaze to Sophia and understood. "No." She shook her head slowly. "No," she repeated, and then, in the tiniest of voices, "not then."

"I understand," said Shulamit, full of meaning. A flash of insight reminded her of how vulnerable she'd been, herself, after the death of her own father. She would have gladly run off with any woman who'd held her hand, even an ax murderer.

"We traveled the countryside together," Carolina reminisced, "and he showed me our farms, up close. Not as I'd seen them as a princess, not in the farmhouses stuffed full of treats and waiting for compliments from the landowners. In the fields themselves. We watched the people working, and he told me their stories. He told me, you know, this one likes poetry, and that one is saving up so that he can pay to heal his ailing son. He made them all real for me."

Shulamit took a deep breath. "He was right about *them*, even if he was wrong about us."

Carolina looked dreamily into space. "I had new visions for my country in his arms. Now I wonder if they were all just fantasies."

"What he showed you was true," Shulamit insisted. "He just took it in a horrible direction. I mean—if he hadn't been in love with you since childhood, think, he might have even started an uprising *against* you. But you two were..." She gestured meaninglessly. "...so he had to twist it around in his head and somehow make it *my* fault. Or my country's, anyway. I know this wasn't about me."

"Uprising..."

"Start loving your people, Carolina. *All* of them. You saw what they're really like. Imbrio really *can* be great."

"Of course I love my people!" Carolina's eyes flashed with expressiveness. "But there are different types of people, yes? It is part of the way the world is put together—some people work this way and some that. Would it not be too much for someone from the other classes to try to do what we do?"

"There's no inherent difference. You remember Aviva?" Heat pounded in Shulamit's face as she grew more impassioned. "She's the love of my life and one of the smartest people I know, and she's from the working class. Not even lower landed gentry like João. Her father's a tailor and her mother was a laundress before her back problems started. Would you have known she was working-class if I didn't tell you?"

Carolina, stunned, shook her head. "She has such poise and confidence!"

"She saved my life when I was younger"—Shulamit looked her deep in the eye—"when all you could do was beat the cook."

The pale queen swallowed uncomfortably. After a time, she said, "He will have the Imbrio he wanted, but he will not be here to see it."

"I guess it's too much to ask that he be extradited with the others?" Shulamit half grinned in a grimace.

"I would prefer to strip him of title and banish him to the north, to Zembluss," Carolina answered. "His crimes were all on our soil—the murder he admits to in this letter, and his plotting. So, technically, legally, he is my responsibility."

Shulamit nodded. "That makes sense."

"Oh, dear Shulamit…" Carolina sighed, and rubbed her temples. "These crowns, these crowns, they are shackles for us. To be a queen is to be surrounded by people always, but so lonely. You will stay my friend, yes? Because who else can understand?"

226

Shulamit nodded, but she didn't feel lonely. She didn't want to say it out loud because it felt like bragging, but to love Aviva was to love her people. It seemed just and right and good and *blessed* that a queen should love a woman so representative of all that she cherished about the country she led—hard work, generosity, and the richness of Perachi agriculture. Aviva fed Shulamit just as the land fed her people.

What she said out loud was "You should come and visit us some time."

"When I am no longer in mourning," said Carolina. She adjusted the crown on her head, replacing it from where she'd disturbed it in her dramatics. "Why do you not wear a crown?"

"It's on my bedside table," said Shulamit. "It's too heavy for me and also too big."

"But surely you can have your own made!" Carolina gestured to Shulamit's earrings and the tiny jewels she wore in her hair. "You are so fond of ornaments and fashion."

Shulamit licked her lips. "In my country, that would mean melting down my father's crown, and I'm... I'm having trouble. It's like it's still *him*, somehow. I know it's silly, but I like having the crown there because it's like he's *in* it, somehow."

"I understand," said Carolina. "Maybe, then, could you have your crown made and then with what's left, his portrait in gold? Because there will be some left over if his crown is bigger and heavier. You could wear a circlet like I do."

Shulamit nodded slowly. "That might actually work! Wow." She was surprised at the direction the conversation had taken, but pleased.

Carolina sighed and gazed out the window at the white sky. "I will take my leave of you for now… it is time for me to do what I must, before I lose courage. If I do it quickly, maybe it will not hurt as much."

"Thank you for not hating me," said Shulamit.

"I promise I will visit when things are better."

"Bring your children too! Isaac will tell them all his adventure stories."

"You are lucky to have him," said Carolina. "He did not come?"

"He's downstairs with the rest of my guards looking after the carriages," said Shulamit.

Isaac was not downstairs looking after anything. Right now, Shulamit could see him perched on the wall behind a candleholder, holding still to blend in with the decoration.

"Be careful of him too, I suppose."

Shulamit nodded. She was used to hearing that, and it was only natural, coming from Carolina after the kind of shock she'd had. But she was pretty sure of her loved ones at this point.

"Good-bye, Caro."

"Good-bye, Shula."

They parted with an awkward hug.

❖ ❖ ❖

Isaac watched his wife and the three other guards who'd followed Shulamit into the palace escort her out again. His presence here was vital; was Carolina telling the truth about her shock? Was this all just an elaborate scheme all along? Or, more likely, was she innocent but weak, and wont to forgive João his sins out of her adulterous love?

When the room had emptied of all visible Perachis, Carolina called over a servant. "Please take the princess to her governess to practice her alphabet. Then have the Visconde summoned."

"Yes, Your Majesty."

The little girl was ushered out, leaving her coliseum of blocks half-built in the corner.

The door closed with a click, and Carolina—or so she thought—was alone.

She seemed in a trance, moving slowly at first. Then Isaac saw her breathing grow heavier and heavier. Finally, in a swift and sudden movement she seized a vase from an end table and hurled it against the wall.

As it crashed and shattered, she convulsed with a single sob.

She was facing away from the door when it opened again. João walked in, alone, and began to approach her. "Caro…"

Carolina spoke without turning around. "Did you think you were king?"

"What?"

She whirled around, clutching the letter firmly, and he tensed. "Was it a lie? Was everything lies?" Crouched against the candleholder on the wall, Isaac shivered as he beheld her transformed face. The statue was gone; in its place was a face of flame, trembling in rage and pain.

"When did I ever lie to you?" João spoke quietly, moving toward Carolina with tenderness. "If I did anything, I only kept from you—"

When he tried to embrace her, she threw off both his arms. "When you held me, did you mean it? Or was I just the throne to you? You have seen the woman inside the queen. I gave you what I had no right to give. Was it love that pulled me to that place, or lies? We were children together, yes. But did that beautiful young man from my girlhood ever return from the war in Zembluss, or did he send back his hardened, deceitful double? Was it *ever* about me, or was I just another part of your plan?"

João looked deeply into her eyes. "I have loved you since we were children and that love has never faltered. I swear it now and I would swear it if I were dying. Those years in Zembluss, the thought of you kept my head on straight when I saw nothing but fire and blood. Even now, in your anger, you are beautiful and noble."

Carolina was still, the storm clouds on her face melting into sadness. The silence in the room was so oppressive Isaac was afraid even a lizard's movement would be heard. Finally, she spoke, looking away. "I wish you had lied."

"Why?"

"I wish you had lied and said you never loved me. Or I wish it was true. Either way. Could you not have been less cruel and said this to me?"

"Why would you want me to say I never loved you when I live for you, my beautiful Caro, queen of everywhere but nowhere so much as my heart?" He reached for her hand, but she withdrew.

"Because you must leave Imbrio." Her voice was quiet but firm. "If you hadn't loved me… if these past weeks had been a lie… it would be easier to banish you. But now your exile is my exile. You cruel, cruel, impossible highwayman."

"Why banish me, my darling?" He was smiling at her. "If you hold that letter, then surely you can see that Imbrio's glory is impeded by Perach's success. The flourishing of our people—"

"You killed for this, and what's worse, you could have started a war," Carolina explained wearily. "Plus, Queen Shulamit is my *friend*. I have so few friends."

"That ineffective little clothes hanger?" said João dismissively. "It's the wizard who runs Perach. What can she—"

Carolina shook her head. "You don't know her as I do. She's smart, and she's devoted to her people. If she trifles with clothing, what is it to you? You have been fooled by her awkward manners and her size. It doesn't take a body like a palace to house a queen. You're just used to mine." She was beginning to speak louder and loftier, and these last words were said bitterly.

"But our farms—"

"Can flourish without sabotaging our competition. Really, João!" Carolina sniffed and shook her head. "You speak of fairness, but why do you not consider the Perachis just as human as our own farmers? They may not be Imbrian, but

231

isn't that the same as those class differences you're so fond of erasing?"

"You don't understand."

"No, I understand too much, and it makes me sad. I understand that I lost my father, and you were there with your guitar, and… and that grief is a dangerous drug."

"You wished for it your whole life just as I did. Do not lie."

"Of *course* I did, but do you think I ever wanted to hurt my father, or my husband?" She looked down at the ground, then looked up again resolutely. "Good-bye, João."

"You can't do this."

"Don't worry, it already hurts." Her voice sounded hollow and dead. She sounded a gong, and Imbrian guards rushed in. "Put the Visconde under arrest and then bring me my legal counsel. I have orders and a proclamation to write."

As they led her lover out of the room, she added to them, "And please have the governess bring my daughter to me."

She remained motionless by the window, watching the bare branches outside pierce the white sky. Isaac would have comforted her, had his presence not been a gigantic faux pas to begin with.

But he needn't have worried. Soon, the door opened and little Princess Sophia appeared. She ran to her mother, who knelt and embraced her. "Mamae, what's wrong? Are you crying?"

"I will be fine," said the queen, "with you here."

Isaac used the opportunity to make a quick exit, not transforming into human flesh again until he was well outside the palace and near the carriage where he was supposed to have been all along.

Shulamit and Rivka turned when they heard his footsteps on the gravel. "What's going on up there?" Shulamit hissed under her breath.

"She's your loyal friend," Isaac verified, "but she has a rough time ahead."

"Poor thing." Shulamit stroked the fur lining of her cloak again. "At least her husband will know how to make her laugh. And she's got her kids."

"Sophia is with her now," said Isaac. They all looked up to the window of Carolina's salon, where mother and daughter were visible at the window.

"Who's that?" Shulamit pointed to a second woman at the window.

"Sophia's governess, I think," Isaac answered. "It looks like they're talking."

"Maybe she did take what I said to heart, and is talking to the working people like they're people."

"I knew you could do it!" Rivka clapped Shulamit on the back soundly. "Time to go home?"

Shulamit nodded vigorously. "I miss my girls! Besides, this place is *too cold*."

Chapter 24. Grandmother Swan

Great, sprawling oaks and silent armies of pines gave way to palms and papaya trees as Shulamit's caravan made its way back toward Perach and sunshine. Fleeing the chill of the Imbrian winter, and of Carolina's broken heart, Shulamit was hungry for Aviva's velvety embrace and the rightness of her presence. As the leaves got larger and greener, and the sun more bold, she perked up and dreamed of her love and their baby daughter.

At last the carriage arrived at Home City. Shulamit would have begged Isaac to fly her straight home, to reach them even just minutes sooner, but he lay asleep in the form of the great yellow-and-cream python. He was coiled up around Rivka, his tail spilling out across the narrow floor area, both of them dozing away their night watch. Shulamit didn't have the heart to awaken him.

They reached the palace in the pink of sunset. Shulamit leapt from her carriage, calling, "We're back!" with her face toward the kitchen-house.

Voices from inside surprised her in their deepness, and she hurried closer. The first person to emerge from the kitchen-house was not Aviva, but a wiry, bearded man with a head of unruly curls. Holding the baby princess close to his chest, he smiled and called out, "Hey, Shulamit!"

"Kaveh!" Shulamit exclaimed in happy surprise. "And Farzin! Oh, yay!"

For the Prince-Consort's stout, amiable-faced partner had appeared behind him. "Wow, that's great timing. We've only been here since this afternoon."

"I'm so glad to see you two!" Shulamit hugged them both, kissing her daughter on the cheek in the process.

Aviva came out last, a wooden spoon in one hand. "My absolute favorite queen ever." Without another word, the two women melted into each other's arms. Shulamit almost couldn't move for a few moments; this was the longest they'd been apart in ages. Couldn't they just stay here like this, bare skin sticking together a little, for another hour?

"You smell like home," Shulamit mumbled. Then her brain clicked. "Wait, if *they're* here…"

She unpeeled from Aviva and tore across the garden to see if wishful thinking was lying to her eyes. But, no, *there she was*, the graceful middle-aged lady with black hair graying in streaks, with her striking, unusual long face and gigantic eyes. She sat under the coconut palm holding Halleli's kitten, and Halleli knelt across from her studiously drawing.

Queen Aafsaneh set the cat down and hobbled to her feet when she saw Shulamit coming. "My dear girl!"

"Oh, don't get up for me! Your foot. I'm so—oh, goodness." Shulamit hugged her tightly.

"This young woman of your employ was drawing me," Aafsaneh explained, gesturing.

"Looks great!"

"I can finish it later." Halleli withdrew modestly with the kitten, bowing slightly to Kaveh and Farzin as they walked over. Aviva followed them, holding Naomi against her hip.

"Thank you so much for coming!" Shulamit couldn't stop smiling; she felt surrounded by so much love.

"Of course I came!" Aafsaneh petted her hair. Shulamit noticed with a squeeze of her heart that Aafsaneh was

235

always careful to pet her hair in the direction of her braids, to not disturb them, because she respected Shulamit's quirks. It meant more than she could articulate.

"But your foot!"

"I'm… it's getting better." Aafsaneh demonstrated her limping walk. "Things happen."

"How did it happen?" asked Shulamit.

"I tripped over a cat if you can believe it. On a marble floor."

Shulamit tried not to giggle. "So, how is Eshvat, anyway?"

Aafsaneh smiled. "No, not her. It was a real cat, not a shifter. But she's doing well. The tavern is busier than ever, actually—she got a lot of publicity when two men fought a duel over her a little while ago."

"A duel?" Shulamit's eyes widened.

"I know, isn't it silly?" Aafsaneh brushed a stray lock of hair behind her ear. "Pointless of them to be so possessive when she doesn't want anything like a regular boyfriend."

"I bet it made her want them both even less."

"Well, yes, at first," said Aafsaneh. "When they first talked about it, with all the shouting and posturing, she rolled her eyes at them and looked the other way. She was pretty annoyed. But then, when the actual fighting started and it was clear it wasn't just all talk, and she realized she was selling twice as many kebabs as usual from the attention, she just laughed at them and figured it was part of life."

"And so what happened afterward?" asked Shulamit. "When she, no doubt, rejected them both."

"Well..." Aafsaneh looked at Kaveh and Farzin, her eyelids delicately downcast but her cheeks merry with a smile.

"That's not exactly what happened," Farzin volunteered.

Shulamit, tired from the past few days' journey, looked back and forth between them in puzzlement. "I don't get it."

"Like Maman said," said Farzin, "Mother Cat made twice as many kebabs as usual." He grinned enthusiastically at his own joke.

Shulamit growled as she comprehended his joke, temporarily stunned. "Wow. Well, okay then. Wow!" She looked at Aviva, who was giggling into the baby's hair. "I don't even want to lie down with one man, let alone two at once! No offense, guys, but *yecch*!"

"You're thinking of it the wrong way," Aviva pointed out gently, "since you don't like men. Imagine two women at once."

Shulamit smirked. "You win! That's something else."

"I know the way your mind works," Aviva replied. "Speaking of which..." She painted her fingertips down Shulamit's arm, continuing in a softer tone. "How's Carolina doing?"

"What? Oh, well. Like you'd expect. But she'll move on— and, she's my friend. She really is my friend." Shulamit leaned in closer so that she could whisper in Aviva's ear. "But don't worry; we don't need a bigger bed."

"Girls?" called Queen Aafsaneh, interrupting their tête-à-tête. "I know I'm needed out in the olive groves, but it's late and getting dark, plus I'm tired from the flight. We can leave in the morning if that's all right."

"That would be *amazing*," said Shulamit.

"In the meantime, does anyone want to play Pirate's Payout?" suggested Farzin.

"We can go in the salon," Aviva suggested.

"I think I'll just watch and nurse," said Shulamit. "I don't have the mind for games right now, but I want to spend time with everyone. I'm sorry we don't visit you more often, Aafsaneh. I wish that we did, but I don't think your husband can stand me."

Aafsaneh cocked her head and smiled sadly. "His loss!"

Shulamit settled comfortably into the sofa in the salon next to Aafsaneh as Aviva, Kaveh, and Farzin set up the board and game pieces on the floor. Within a few moments she had Naomi latched, and overflowed with relief as her breast fed her child again and not a stranger's or bare earth. Good she'd expressed often enough out there in her travels. She'd been so scared of drying up.

"Treasure!" Aviva shouted from the floor. Kaveh stuck his tongue out at her, and she mock kicked his leg.

"Oh, goodness, that's two bad rolls in a row," Aafsaneh exclaimed, looking at her dice with resignation.

"Maman is showing off how virtuous she is by not using magic," Farzin joked.

"I would *never*!" But Aafsaneh was smiling.

"Notice how you don't see Isaac in here playing board games," murmured Kaveh.

Surrounded by so many people she cared about whom she saw much less than she liked, Shulamit felt like there were rooms of her heart thrown open and illuminated by a wondrous glow, rooms that were usually shut up and left to grow dusty. The light filled her near to bursting, and she hugged her nursing infant.

A guard's boots thumped at the doorway. "Majesty?"

"Yes?" Shulamit turned to look his way.

"A message for you—update from the northern farmlands."

"Thank you." Shulamit took the roll of paper and sent him on his way. She opened it, then sighed with dismay.

"What's wrong, dear little one?" Aafsaneh wasn't absorbed enough in the game to miss her distress.

"I feel so out of control. Here." Shulamit gave her the paper to read.

Aafsaneh scanned it with solemn eyes. "So the bugs you mentioned have crossed the burnt farmland."

"They're already eating more of our crops. And now there's nothing between them and the Lovely Valley but more olive groves."

"Come here, sweet thing." Aafsaneh held out her arm, and Shulamit snuggled into her inviting side, craving something motherly. "I've handled worse. I have an idea, and if it works, everything will be fine in the morning."

"You promise?" Shulamit found herself saying in a voice that reminded her of a child's.

"I'm not promising, but I'm hoping. Is that enough?"

Somehow, between her gentle confidence and her maternal warmth, it was.

Chapter 25. Dragon and Dragonfly

Shulamit's dreams were so miserable that night that she was glad when Naomi woke her up to nurse. She clutched her close and felt like crying, the guilt and shame of the nightmare still lingering even though it was obviously untrue.

She looked over at Aviva, and was surprised to see open eyes. "Did I wake you?"

"I don't know," said Aviva, caressing Shulamit's feet with her own. "It's good to have you back. Sometimes we slept in Ima and Aba's room while you were gone."

"I'm so glad to be back with you two that I can't even describe…" Shulamit sighed. "My dream just now—it had something to do with the new infested farm, and how it was somehow all my fault because I'd gone away for so long without my baby, or because of my complicated history with Carolina."

"That just proves that you're the real Shulamit and Imbrio didn't capture you and send us back a golem replacement." Aviva kissed her shoulder lazily. "I'm sorry that you're stressed out, but it's only because your heart's in the right place."

"I just have to trust in Aafsaneh at this point, I guess."

"Let's take it as it comes."

"In my dream," Shulamit added into the silence of the night, "they were eating…"

They had been eating Naomi. She couldn't bring herself to say it out loud.

"Shh… you have to think about other things. Maybe pray a little?" Aviva was petting her hair.

Together, they mumbled their way through the familiar lines, until Shulamit was soothed back to sleep.

❖ ❖ ❖

Another day, another grove, another infestation. Shulamit tried her best to keep her eyes away from the afflicted trees, instead scanning the skies for any sign of the great swan that was one of Aafsaneh's shapeshifting forms. She stood with the farmers, an elderly husband and wife, with Rivka and the other guards they'd brought close beside. Over in front of the farmhouse, the farmhands admired Isaac, who hadn't bothered to become human once depositing his ladies on the lawn. Not while there were compliments to be had.

"Will she be here soon, Majesty?" asked the old woman, wide-eyed with anxiety. It was for good reason. Her trees looked like someone was grinding peppercorns over them, so thick were the bugs in the air.

"Any minute," Shulamit answered. "We just got here first, because dragons fly so much faster."

"Oh, she's not a dragon too? I don't know, I guess I thought they were all like him." She cocked her head at the preening Isaac.

"She does birds," Shulamit murmured distractedly. "Wait! Look!"

Her pointing finger toward the sky heralded the approach of the Swan Lady. She was like a piece of sky come to life, come down to them with blue feathers gleaming in the sun.

Shulamit heard gasps from everyone around her as they marveled at the sight.

Aafsaneh transformed as she landed in one graceful, coordinated motion and walked toward Shulamit, smiling and hands outstretched.

Shulamit took her by the hand and led her over to the landowners. "I present Her Royal Majesty Queen Aafsaneh of the City of Red Clay. She's the Prince-Consort's stepmother," she added, in case they needed reminding how the great lady was connected with Perach.

"Your Majesty," said the old woman breathlessly.

The old man simply kissed her hand and bowed.

"Can you help us?" the old woman asked earnestly.

"I plan on it," said Aafsaneh serenely. She looked over at the insect-laden trees, cocking her head to one side, then the other as she peered around.

With a flap of her arms she suddenly disappeared into the form of a tiny songbird. Swift on the wing, she was in the middle of the olive trees within moments, and was off catching bugs.

A wave of panic rose in Shulamit's gut. "We tried that already. Aafsaneh! Isaac already—"

Then a hand squeezed her shoulder protectively. She looked back at Rivka. "What's she doing?"

"Let maybe the expert work, all right?" Rivka's eyebrows were lifted.

Well, if Rivka had faith, maybe there was faith to be had. After all, what virtue has faith when all is already sure and comfortable?

Maybe birds have better stomachs than lizards for these awful things, she mused.

But then Aafsaneh was walking back toward them in human form, pulling something from her mouth. It was the insect. As everyone stared, she studied it in her hand.

Her face lit up. "Yes, I know these. They're just what I thought. Perfect."

Perfect?

Aafsaneh stood back on the bare ground and held her hands in the air in front of her. With palms outstretched upward, she began to breathe deeply in solemn rhythms.

"What's she doing?" Shulamit asked Isaac.

"You are an impatient little chipmunk," he replied obliquely, and she fluttered her eyelids in bewilderment.

Oh, wait, he has no idea either, and he doesn't want to admit it. Shulamit grinned. *I love my family!*

Something tiny zoomed through the air. It came from the east and headed straight for Aafsaneh. Another just like it followed close behind, then a third from the north.

Soon, dozens were whizzing all about her head. What *were* they?

"What is that?" Shulamit called out.

With a little smile and a nod, Aafsaneh sent one of them over.

Shulamit held out her hand, and on the tip of her middle finger alighted—a dragonfly. Two sets of translucent wings glittered like sunlight on the stream in which it had undoubtedly spawned.

"I don't get it. More bugs?"

"There's our cavalry," gasped Rivka in wonder and appreciation.

All eyes were on Aafsaneh, with now at least a hundred dragonflies crossing the air over her head around and around, over and over. Then, with careful deliberation, she changed the aim of her hands, flipping her palms down and aiming her fingers straight at the olive grove.

The dragonflies followed her command and made straight for the trees. The red-and-blue pestilence was like candy to them, and they devoured the other bugs as if breaking the fast. Shulamit's mouth dropped open and she was unable to move. The whole thing was so beautiful and so perfect that she could almost feel the earth hum.

"This is the best thing ever" was the totally unintelligent thing she said when she managed to find speech. "I am... wow."

"Queen Aafsaneh is a genius!" Rivka bellowed, and the other queen smiled deferentially.

Isaac came up behind them as a human, folding his arms across his chest. "Neat trick! I never would have thought of that."

"Can she get more?" asked the old woman who owned the farm. "There are so many more trees than the ones they've reached."

"Aafsaneh!" called Rivka. "Can you summon any more? This batch is doing great, but they're staying in that one area."

Aafsaneh, her eyes wide in concentration, bit her lip. "I'm trying. Maybe we'll just have to work slowly."

Isaac marched over to her. "Can I help?"

She nodded vigorously. "Oh, definitely! If you give me a boost, I can reach every dragonfly in the kingdom."

"Just stop if you get funny like last time," called Rivka.

Isaac knelt to the ground and pressed his hands to the tops of Aafsaneh's feet. Once again, she turned her palms upward and regulated her breathing.

This time, with his powers magnifying hers, she began to glow slightly, and even rose up off the ground. He maintained contact with the tops of her feet, but she hovered four or five feet in the air. With her face radiant in the morning light, she performed her magic once again.

Soon, the air was thick with the angular swoops of their tiny saviors. Shulamit stayed close to Rivka, out of the way of their flight path, and wished for an idle moment that Halleli were here so that someone could record this beauty forever.

Aafsaneh cast the dragonflies over the olive grove once again, and this time, Shulamit could tell that with so many of them, the red-and-blue insects would be entirely consumed.

The elderly farmers hugged each other, and the husband kissed the wife on the cheek. "We're saved," she whispered back.

PERACH is saved, Shulamit's thoughts echoed.

Now Isaac and Aafsaneh were both in their shifted forms, he a dragon and she a swan, flying over the grove.

How does it look?" Shulamit cried out.

"It's working!" came Aafsaneh's call from the distance.

"We'll see you in a little while—we're taking this show on the road!" Isaac added.

Together, swan and dragon soared into the distance.

"Where are they going?" asked the old woman.

"To the other farms," Shulamit realized with a grin. "This mess is over."

Chapter 26. Time of Rededication

The courtyard of the Frangipani Table was alive with conversation and the noise of happy customers enjoying their food. Halleli stepped out into the perfectly cool, balmy night and approached one of the outdoor tables. "Well?" she asked as she cleared away plates. "Weren't those *the* best sufganiyot?"

"They really were," said the customer through a hearty smile. "You know, I wasn't even going to get any—I was so full from that incredible chicken! But then I saw them over at another table and I just couldn't help myself."

"I'm so glad. Come back again before the holiday's over and you can have some more."

"Oh, definitely! Here's the money for our dinner."

"Thank you! Happy Chanukah!"

"Happy Chanukah, Halleli! Tell Yael I said the same."

"I will." Halleli waved them off into the tall palms, their path illuminated by outdoor torches.

She hustled back inside the kitchen, knowing there were plenty more parties to see to.

"Table 3 outside really loved the sufganiyot," she told Yael as she burst into the kitchen, already looking for the next set of plates to carry out.

"*Everyone* loves my sufganiyot," Yael snapped back with a grin. "You take some home to Hadar, you hear?"

"Wouldn't dream of forgetting!"

"She reminds me of a girl I loved, way back before either of you had a spark of life. Way before I met my husband too." Yael paused to concentrate on her plating. "You're really such a big help around here, Halleli. Anyone else would fuss about missing the big menorah-lighting ceremony with the queen over at the Square. Your counterpart already begged off."

"Well, I'm assuming you'll let me go at least on Shabbat," Halleli pointed out. "She does it all eight nights, right?"

Yael nodded. "But this is your first time, since you just moved here. I'm just saying, I'm grateful you passed that up to make sure all those wallets out there got fed."

Halleli giggled at the brazen mention of money. "You're not as hardened as that. I know better." She was intensely grateful to the older woman for making sure that her transition away from the only life she'd ever known was easier than it could have been. "So, what's it like over there? What am I missing?"

"Sometimes people come up after Her Majesty lights the candles," said Yael, "and share the miracles that have happened to them since last Chanukah."

Halleli sighed poetically. "What a beautiful tradition!"

Yael handed her the next plates to be taken out. "Here are the tabouleh and bourekas for table 2."

"Outside or inside?"

"Outside."

"It's such a beautiful night tonight. Not sticky at all. It's… wonderfully cool and refreshing. I feel like I could dance!"

249

"Dance with Hadar when you get home, child. Lord knows she's got the energy," said Yael. "For now, that food's getting cold."

Halleli whirled off, careful not to spill her fresh plates.

As she served the customers, she daydreamed about what she might say on her night off, if she had the courage to speak in front of that many people. Even in this season of wreckage she was all too aware of the blessings she still had.

Maybe I should just draw my miracles, she mused. *Then I won't have to explain them in front of so many people.*

A busy night meant time ran swiftly, and soon, the restaurant closed for the night. Halleli carried all the outside tables in, one at a time. After they were all back in their usual spots, she scrubbed them down.

"Well, kitchen's clean!" Yael emerged from the kitchen carrying a chanukiah and two candles in one hand. "You'll stay and do this with me? You can do it again with Hadar when you get home."

"Sure!" Halleli answered.

Yael held one candle against a torch on the wall, then used it to light the other. "Bless You, Our God, King and Queen of the World, who kept us alive, sustained us, and enabled us to reach this season."

Halleli murmured along, intrigued by the gendered quirks in Yael's prayer and for some reason shy about reciting the words any louder.

A knock sounded at the door. "We're closed!" Yael and Halleli shouted in unison.

"I know!" called a familiar voice. "I'm not here for food."

"The queen!" Halleli leapt to her feet, blinking rapidly.

Yael opened the door. "Your Majesty! Happy Chanukah."

"Same to you!" Queen Shulamit stepped inside, a vision in lilac silks. On her head was the dainty new circlet she'd taken to wearing; candlelight glinted from its gems. Captain Riv and Isaac hovered behind her as usual. "I've just come from the ceremony in the Square, and since it was on our way, I figured I'd stop by and see if you needed a guard escort home."

Halleli inhaled in wonder. "Well, sure! Wow, thank you, Your Majesty."

"I also had something for Yael. It's symbolic, really, but it does matter." Shulamit reached behind her, and Captain Riv handed her something.

As she handed it to Yael, Halleli saw what looked like a small jug.

Yael uncorked it and sniffed it. "Oil? Olive oil?"

Shulamit nodded solemnly. "Can we sit down and watch the candles together? I'm worn out from the shindig in the Square."

"Absolutely! Right here." Yael pulled a seat out for her right in front of the lit menorah, then sat to one side. Halleli deposited herself quietly and primly in the seat to the queen's other side.

Riv and Isaac remained in the doorway, speaking in low tones with each other in some foreign tongue and ignoring the ladies. Farther outside in the darkness, Halleli sensed the presence of more guards. But after a few moments of meditating on the two lit candles, she noticed them less and less. Only the three women at the table existed, just for a time.

"I brought you that oil, Yael, because you saved the country." Shulamit's voice was solemn but serene.

"Me? What?"

"If you hadn't come to me when you did, we'd never have known to look harder in that murdered man's papers," Shulamit reminded her. "What we found helped us stop the spread in time."

"Did we really catch it in time?" Yael asked. "Oil prices are up, and I've been lighting less torches in my dining room this winter. Everybody is."

"It's hard to have Chanukah without oil," Halleli commented.

"But that's just it," said Shulamit. "We *do* have oil. It's not all gone; yes, there's a shortage, but there was a reserve and the groves will rebuild. Don't forget the whole point of this holiday is that miracles are possible."

"Hadar, this job," Halleli found herself rattling off, to her own surprise. "My kitten Olive, my friends on the palace staff… customers who really like my artwork."

"Sitting down after a long day in this place," Yael commented.

"My loved ones," said Queen Shulamit, joining in. "My daughter. Not being horrible at this job!" She chuckled at herself. "Anyway, it's more than perfect that I spend part of *this* first night of Chanukah in the presence of the two women who saved this country."

Halleli gazed into the candles on the table, watched them flicker and burn. They were tiny, two flutters of white-gold in a dark world, but they existed all the same. She thought of how tomorrow night there would be more lights, and then more and more, until finally a week from now all nine places on the candelabra would have joined in chorus.

Tears formed in her eyes when she imagined all the olive groves that had fallen to the Imbrian plague's devastation doing the same thing, each rebuilding—each *rededicating*—one by one.

Queen Shulamit stood up. "I have to go home and nurse. Halleli?"

"I'm coming!" Impulsively, Halleli hugged Yael good night, and followed the queen into the starlit palms.

END

❖ ❖ ❖

A neverending well of thank-you's for

My spouse, who is the cutest and the smartest. My family, especially my mom, always my first audience and my greatest inspiration.

Kate, "Kate the Great", my Chief Executive Beta. The careful yet loving corrections you gave all four Mangoverse books proves to me that you are going to be the best possible mother to your brand new "new release", already a bestseller in your and his father's hearts.

Cousin Kate, for your calm wisdom, your guidance in writing my trans woman Yael, and for your friendship. And to Cousin Lizzy—"if I'm the bi cousin and *you're* the bi cousin, who's flying the plane???"

Dr. Jennifer Gillett-Kaufman, the expert in insect pests in olive production who spent a morning of her time showing me trees, slides, and even a perfect way to wrap up my story.

Nicole, who asked for a trans woman in the Mangoverse (and Alex, who wanted more with Micah!) Never be afraid to ask your faves for characters like you, folks. They might say no—or they might invent Yael.

Maricruz, the original Sad Princess (now Dr. Princess!), and Brooke, the original Little River of Stars. Both of you are freaking gorgeous and brilliant and I wish you the best. Much appreciation to Brooke, Emilia, and Martina for the Portuguese sensitivity beta.

Eliana and Becca, lesbians who checked over the scenes where Baby Shula acts out Baby Shira's adolescence, as well as the Hadar/Halleli farm chapters. Eliana, your enthusiasm for the Mangoverse has kept me running when I was on empty. Becca, your artwork *is* the Mangoverse, for me and for many others. Speaking of artists, not only Becca but also Caroline, Laya Rose, and Yeaka for their incredible, inspiring art. You've brought Shulamit and her crew to life and in color.

Jane, Kat, and of course, my Number One Fan Ducky for being the Very First Readers. Caitlin for helping with supernebular dragon flight. J.L. Douglas for never shutting up about Farzin, and for friendship and validation, and other writer friends like Kayla Bashe and Claudie Arseneault. My online Waffle community, for helping with details—especially "Other Jane" for perpetual support.

The black cat we loved and lost, and the calico who bit her way into our hearts (....wait.) Incidentally, Tabletop Tova was released and now lives by herself in the woods. Well, except for the cats.

Jaymi, JoSelle, and Yet Another Jane for editing and proofreading, and Joanna and Kristi for hosting my Perachi children during my years at Prizm Books.

And, as ever, Richard Wagner, Anna Netrebko, Hibla Gerzmava, James Morris, Joyce DiDonato, Jonas Kaufman, Boaz Daniel, and the incomparable René Pape for the musical shawl in which I wrap my stories.

Glossary of non-English words in *The Olive Conspiracy*

Some of them seem like English to me, because they were a constant part of my upbringing and remain a constant in my life! But, I realize that many Gentile (non-Jewish) readers would like more information about some of those words, and likewise that not all Jewish readers share my background. It was my hope that I had incorporated them organically, so that they could be understood in context the way one would understand invented words in any other fantasy novel. But why not give people the opportunity to learn more?

The conceit of the Mangoverse is that Perach, the setting, is a Hebrew-speaking haven of tropical agriculture, and that up north, several countries away, there's a country whose primary language is Yiddish. "Perach" itself means "flower" in Hebrew, and is a reference to Perach's being based on South Florida, where I grew up. (Florida also means "flower", in a way.)

What follows is an informal glossary. I don't claim to be an expert in Judaica, but I'd like to offer what I have.

Aba – Dad in Hebrew (Mom is **Ima.**) Imbrio is Lusophone, so there they use **Mamae** and **Papai**. In Farsi, Mom and Dad are **Maman** and **Baba** so that's what Kaveh and Farzin and Aafsaneh would use, but I seem to have copped out with the City of Red Clay folks and not had them actually speaking the rest of Farsi as I did with the Imbrians and Portuguese. I'm sorry!

Malka – Queen (with Malkeleh meaning "little queen", commonly used for a little girl in one's life, even if she's not royalty–the way my dad used to call my little half-sister "Princess." Rivka's use of **Malkeleh** as a pet name for the queen is therefore a pun.)

By the way, the -eleh ending for a name to make a diminutive is a Yiddishism. Shira turns into Shiraleh, for example. And the cat was "**ketzeleh**" to my grandmother.

So "Malka Shulamit bat Noach" is "Queen Shulamit, daughter of Noach", Noach being her deceased father. "**Bat**"—sounds like *bot* as in robot, not the Halloween flying puppy–is the "daughter of" name syllable. For "son of" it's "**ben**."

Ir Ilan means Oak Town in Hebrew.

Yom Kippur is the holiest day of the year, the Day of Atonement. It's right after our new year's and it's where you get to get yourself scrubbed clean, spiritually, and promise to do better. There is fasting involved. There are more holidays right after, that are part of the same season: **Sukkot**, an agricultural holiday commemorating wandering the desert, when we hang out in a cool hut called a **sukkah** (or *sukkas* in Yiddish) like the one in chapter 1, and **Simchat Torah**, rejoicing in the scriptures and absolutely nothing to do with fasting hence Shulamit lying through her teeth to avoid having to discuss her medical problems.

Speaking of Sukkot, the **lulav** and **etrog** are symbolic fruit and vegetables associated with the holiday. I've compared the etrog to a "gigantic dinosaur of a lemon, with a clitoris" (sorry) and the lulav is a bouquet made from branches of palm, myrtle, and willow. Etrogs have the most amazing citrus smell.

257

Shabbat (or **Shabbos**, in Yiddish — Shabbat is Hebrew) is Friday night and Saturday morning. The Jewish Sabbath, involving compulsory rest, special food, candle-lighting, going to **shul** (Yiddish word for temple/synagogue which is the same as the German word for school), and supposedly, marital sex

Kippah (Hebrew)/**yarmulke** (Yiddish) – those teensy hats that Jewish men wear in shul and at holidays and weddings.

Shtik drek = "piece of shit" in Hebrew. "You can't put that in a book!" my grandmother protested. "But she's a *warrior*," I tried to explain…

Which reminds me… "**Oy vey**" = literally, Oh woe, so **Oy vey iz mir** is "oh, woe is me." Sounds overdramatic, right? When you've grown up hearing it in another language it just blends in, though.

Mammeh – Yiddish for "Mom". (Dad is "**Tateh**", and they're both the same words in Polish, which makes sense — Yiddish is in a lot of ways Polish-flavored German written in Hebrew letters.)

Nu – it's Yiddish, and it's kind of like "So?" It's a prompting word. Like if you're waiting for someone to answer you and they're just staring into space.

Schmendrick – another one of those undefinable Yiddish insults

Maror – horseradish. Well, "bitter herbs", anyway.

Kaddish – prayers for the dead. I said them for my dad. (2016 edit: and my grandparents, sigh.)

Mi Shebeirach – prayers for healing

Abscheid und Feuerzauber—German words meaning "farewell and magic fire." This is a reference to Wotan's Farewell and the Magic Fire Music from the end of Richard Wagner's opera *Die Walküre*, where some very sad things are happening that result in Odin (Wotan, in German) having to say goodbye forever to his favorite daughter. Fire surrounds the rock where she lies in an enchanted sleep, hence the image of Isaac's fire protecting Perach in the same way. There are other opera references in this book but not as many as in *Mango* and *Date Palm*.

Sufganiyah—Donuts without holes. Plural is **sufganiyot**

Shivah—Jewish mourning period. You hang around your house with the door unlocked so people can just let themselves in and love on you—bring you food, listen to you talk about the person you lost, etc. You're supposed to wear old or torn clothes that don't matter and cover your mirrors. When this word comes up in *The Olive Conspiracy* Rivka is thinking of the mourning Imbrians in her own terms; they're not Jewish and wouldn't themselves be thinking of what they were doing as sitting shivah. She just has no reason to call it anything else.

Shayne maydeleh—Pretty girl, a Yiddish term of endearment.

Rugelach—Little pastries with filling. I've seen chocolate, raspberry, and more interesting flavors. They're about the size of a business card. Someone should take advantage of that and use them as a business card. Isaac would be a big fan of this idea.

Riachinho Estrela – in a fit of affectionate punning, I named the Imbrian capital after a friend, whose name in English means "little river of stars." It seemed appropriate since her Portuguese heritage is one of the reasons Imbrio

259

is Lusophone. I don't know if her parents had this in mind but in *The Olive Conspiracy*, Princess Carolina tells Princess Shulamit that the "little river of stars" means the Milky Way.

Sherwani—NOT a Hebrew or Yiddish word; this is an Indian men's long dress coat.

Schnorrer—Yiddish for someone begging on the street.

Oud—Middle Eastern/North African lute-like instrument

Obrigada—Thank you in Portuguese

Sim, sua Alteza Real—Yes, your Highness in Portuguese

Minha adorada—My beloved in Portuguese

Boureka—Many cultures have a savory "pastry pocket with stuff in it"; this is ours.

Farshtinkener—Yiddish has so many insults! I think this one means "stinking" but, like, not literally. **Meshuggah/meshugganah** is another one.

Kindeleh—"Child" with the diminutive -eleh added to the end. Yiddish.

Chanukiah—the menorah specifically used *for* Chanukah

Yud י and **Tzadik** צ are the first two letters of Isaac's *actual* name, which is יצחק (Yitzchak, with the ch being the guttural "clearing your throat" noise English doesn't readily access.) There's a whole conversation on why I used Isaac instead of Yitzchak in all five books if that's his real name but at the end of the day: you are valid if you are assimilated; you are valid if you are *not* assimilated, and I love him—and us—either way.

Tales from Perach

by Shira Glassman

*Appreciation to J.L. Douglas, K.D. Lubeck, Ducky Newcamp, Claudie Arseneault, Colette Aburime, Najela Cobb, Desireé Heyliger, and my spouse for beta-reading and Black hair/trans sensitivity reading.
All remaining errors are mine.*

Your Name is Love

Cast: Hadar/Halleli from *The Olive Conspiracy*

For My Nerd; thank you for taking me to see the plants when I was sad

♡ ✡ ♡

"Whoo!" Hadar came smashing across the garden, her face glowing and her sweaty under-tunic sticking to her wiry, muscled frame. She twirled the outer portion of her guard uniform from two fingers. "Free for the rest of the day! Hey, look, it's the prettiest girl in the palace. Guess what? I beat my personal best today."

"That's terrific! I'm so proud of you." Halleli, who had looked up at the first familiar noise, put her sketchpad on the ground beside her and stood up for a kiss.

"You smell like garlic," Hadar blurted out before Halleli could say anything. "Maybe I should snarf you up for dinner."

Halleli giggled as heat flushed her cheeks. "Yael needed extra help in the back today to get ready for a bar mitzvah catering job. Is it really bad? I can—"

"Why would it be bad? Everybody likes garlic! Who doesn't like garlic?"

"I might be able to get some rosewater from the quee—"

"It's fine, I like it." Hadar ran her hands down Halleli's upper arms. "I need to jump in the creek before dinner. You coming?"

"Sure! I already washed up, but I'll hang out." Halleli bent down to retrieve her art supplies and then followed the cutest butch in the world toward the creek behind the palace.

♡ ✡ ♡

Hadar, naked in the water, reached down to scrub dead skin off her foot. "You still working on that drawing with Olive and the flowers?" Olive was their little black kitten, a gift from the queen's bodyguard, who was Hadar's boss.

"It's somewhere," said Halleli, holding her left hand out in front of her and studying it critically. "This one's for the queen."

"More family portraits?"

Halleli shook her head. "You remember I told you that when she was growing up she got into her father's books and found art of women like us, women together in couples?"

"Yeah, but you said it was all shit."

"It was insulting. I saw some of it myself and she was right—it's not us. It's not for us. It has nothing to do with us. It's so obvious the women are being drawn for the audience and aren't paying any attention to each other, and when the pictures got… graphic… that's not how it… you don't…"

"So, lemme guess—she's got you drawing something better."

"Exactly! She wants me to make her a codex—maybe even more, if this one works out. With pictures, that tell a story, and dialogue written in."

"So how's it going?"

Halleli's face twisted. "Eh, I've done so much better. If you want to see what I've got so far —"

Hadar waded to the edge of the water and peered over. "Looks pretty good to me. Who are they supposed to be?"

"I don't know. I just feel like they're—wooden. Flat."

Hadar hopped around, creating complex ripples in the water. "Make something up, then."

"That's the problem," said Halleli. "I haven't made up any new stories in ages."

"Are you sad? Do you need hugs?"

"I always need hugs. But it's not really that, it's…" Halleli paused, her pencil resting against her lip. "I feel like my mind is out of ideas, or out of… out of whatever ideas are made with. Like it's having trouble finding the raw materials."

"Maybe you're working too hard." Hadar patted the water with the flats of her hands in a series of tiny, controlled splats.

"That's part of it," said Halleli. "I love working at the restaurant—Yael's very nice to me, and the customers always gush over their portraits. But there's no *thinking* time. You can't hide inside yourself working in a kitchen. And we don't live on our own anymore. I can go hide in our quarters if I want to think something through, but that's not as inspiring as being out in the open."

"I think I have an idea," said Hadar.

"A story idea for my art for the queen?"

"No, an idea for an adventure," Hadar said. "We'd have to both have the afternoon off at the same time though."

"I'm working all day tomorrow and the next day, but right after that I'm only on until the end of the lunch rush."

"That should work!" said Hadar, stepping out of the water and onto the soft grass of the bank. She began to dry her shimmering, golden-brown skin with a piece of cotton cloth.

"What are we going to go do?" asked Halleli, intrigued.

Hadar pulled a clean tunic over her head and toweled off her hair with a flourish. "It's a surprise!"

♡ ✡ ♡

Three days later, Halleli hurried home from the restaurant full of anticipation. Chopping vegetables, carrying plates, and sketching patrons had left little time in her morning for conjecture. But now in these last few minutes before Hadar appeared, while Halleli tied her hair behind a fresh scarf that didn't smell like kitchen grease, she reveled in the unknown. Was Hadar taking her shopping? Were they going out beyond the city to look for wild flying goats?

264

Maybe they were going to the other side of town, to the river docks, to watch the longshoremen unloading cargo ships.

From her perch at the foot of their bed, Olive the kitten chirped and rolled onto her side. "Aww, who's cute? *Who's cute?*" Halleli was still petting her when Hadar appeared in the doorway. "Hey!"

"You ready?" Hadar grinned. She had already changed into her civilian clothes.

Halleli nodded. "Hurray, I finally get to find out what you've been up to!"

"I hope you like it." Still beaming, Hadar knocked her fists together with nervous energy. "Look under your pillow."

Halleli furrowed her brow, then slid her hand between the pillow and the sheet. She was surprised to find a paper there. That hadn't been there last night, or it would have crinkled. "What's this?"

"I made you a scavenger hunt," said Hadar. "That's the first clue."

Halleli's mouth dropped open and she glowed, impressed. This was not to be *one* adventure, but several! A swirl of glee rose within her. "Thank you!" She unfolded the paper and read from it, in Hadar's writing. "*The queen's sanctuary.* Are we even allowed in there?"

Hadar jumped from foot to foot. "You have to go and see! I'm not helping. I'm just along for the ride."

With a final caress of Olive's fuzzy face, Halleli led Hadar from the room and shut the door. They waved hello to some on-duty guards as they crossed the courtyard to the royal suites, and ducked to the side for a moment to avoid a pair of laundresses scurrying past with armfuls of clean sheets.

Halleli could see the queen in her bedroom through the open doorway when they arrived. Queen Shulamit bustled around gathering and sorting documents, the baby princess strapped to her chest in a golden sling. She lifted a hand in greeting when she saw the other women. "Spending the afternoon off together?"

"Yes, Majesty!" said Halleli, her insides pleasantly warm. "Hadar made me a scavenger hunt, and I think the first clue leads here."

Queen Shulamit's heavy eyebrows jutted forward. "In here?" She looked toward Hadar. "Did one of the maids hide it?"

"No, no—" Hadar drummed her fingers on her other hand. "Sorry, Majesty. Halleli, it's not in here. I should have said something before we bothered you."

"It's no bother! I think this is really sweet, that you made clues for her. I just don't know anything about it."

"I'm sorry," said Halleli, her cheeks hot with embarrassment. "I just thought it had to be here."

Queen Shulamit reached toward her. "Can I see the clue?" When she read it, her face spread into a burst of a smile. "Oh! I see why you came here, but I know what Hadar meant."

Halleli's eyelashes fluttered. "But you have only one bedroom, and the whole palace is your home."

"Think about what the clue would mean," said the queen, "if it were *you* she was talking about. Anyway, good luck and have fun!" She retreated back into the sumptuous little bedroom, leaving Hadar and Halleli outside.

"If it were me…" Halleli licked her lips. "*My* sanctuary. Well, I mean, there's our room, but it still doesn't feel like home yet… home is…" She turned to face Hadar, realization pouring into her. "Home is *you*. Home is you, you're my sanctuary, and Aviva has the second clue!"

Hadar stuck her tongue out at her. "I was talking about the kitchen-house, since she eats in there except Shabbat and holidays, but close enough."

"Oh, that makes sense."

The kitchen-house of the queen's wife did indeed look every bit the hidden royal sanctuary as they approached, with its cream-colored walls peeking out from behind trellises of passion vine and cucumber. Halleli was momentarily distracted by the assortment of herbs growing on both sides of the path to the door—mint, cilantro, lemongrass, and a basil bush so leafy and lush she almost wanted to lie down in it like it was a pillow.

The door burst open and Aviva emerged holding a pair of clippers. "Oh, you're home already!"

Halleli nodded. "Hadar's taking me on an adventure."

"Yes, I know," said Aviva with a twinkle in her eye as she snipped and collected bits of lemongrass and cilantro. "I have the next clue inside waiting for you."

"We're allowed to come in?" Halleli's cheeks flushed and she felt shy.

"You both have to promise that you're not bread," said Aviva with just the *hint* of a smile on her pretty face. "Or chickens."

"Not today, anyway!" said Hadar, and Halleli giggled.

They followed Aviva inside. "Ooh, what are you working on?" Halleli asked when she saw the pile of pecan shells.

"Sweet potato pie," said Aviva, "with a pecan crust."

"So the whole crust is nuts? Neat!" said Hadar.

"That sounds healthier than a regular crust anyway," said Halleli.

"Here, try some!" Aviva held out tiny bites to each of them.

"It's wonderful," Halleli breathed once her mouth wasn't full of sweet, sticky nuts.

"Kinda like baklava," Hadar said through munches.

"Here's your clue, by the way," said Aviva, handing over a folded piece of paper. "Sorry about the, um, that one looks like it's probably goat grease. And… black beans."

"Don't worry about it," said Halleli. Her heart was still fluttering slightly from being in a place *this important*, at least for a few minutes. The queen might be her friend, but she was still very conscious of the difference in their life circumstances.

"That sounds really good though," said Hadar. "Makes me want to lick the clue!"

Halleli smiled nervously at the comment and unfolded the paper. "'You can't buy sunshine, except from her.' Buy sunshine? Oh! I know! The juice stand at the entrance to the marketplace!”

“And it’s orange season, so it really does taste like sunshine,” Aviva affirmed as she scraped nut shells into her compost bin.

♡ ✡ ♡

Of course the young ladies had to buy juice the minute they arrived at the woman’s stall; one couldn’t be surrounded by piles of fresh, glowing oranges like that without being tempted. They hadn’t brought cups with them, so they had to drink them while standing there, but Auntie Juice was used to it and didn’t mind. She stood at her countertop, squeezing more fruit against her special bowl as she watched them with a face full of satisfaction.

“Who was it who first said this is the taste of sunshine?” Halleli asked between sips.

Hadar shrugged. “My sister, but so did your dad, and Eliana, and that traveling salesman peddling blankets.”

“I remember him!” Halleli exclaimed. “He said it was what really made him feel like he’d arrived in Perach.”

“That’s why I have free samples,” said Auntie Juice. “Once they taste it, travelers always want a cup. It’s irresistible!”

“Thank you for the juice,” said Halleli, setting the cup down and folding her hands respectfully. “Do you have the next clue for me?”

“Now where did I…?” Auntie Juice rummaged around in both pockets of her apron, then looked behind a stack of fruit crates. “Oh! Here.”

"Thank you!" Halleli straightened out the paper, which was crumpled and a little juice-speckled. "'It's bad to break things, but it's good to break these. In some cases it's all they're good for.' Um… breaking… promises… dates… no, that's still bad. Breaking dawn? I'd think you wanted me to watch the sun come up with you but it's afternoon."

Hadar watched this musing monologue with merry eyes as she danced around a little in front of the stall.

"Oh!" Halleli exclaimed suddenly. "Eggs! Of course."

Hadar threw up her hands in celebration.

"Are they all going to be food?" Halleli asked.

Hadar grinned sheepishly. "No, I must have been hungry when I started making up clues. But I'm not saying they're *not* food—I don't want to give you too many hints."

"You two are cute," said Auntie Juice.

"Thank you," said Halleli, looking at the ground and slinking backward slightly until her shadow overlapped with Hadar's. But she was smiling.

Several people in the marketplace sold eggs, but Halleli knew Hadar was talking about the stall they usually passed on the way to their favorite tiny public park, which was only big enough to hold one bench and two rosebushes. The egg man was explaining something to a customer when they arrived, and they waited their turn.

"Well, if you *say* so," said the man buying the eggs. He looked confused. "But I'll see what my wife says when I bring them home."

"I *promise* the brown shell doesn't mean the chickens are getting too much sun." The egg man waved in farewell, his face a study in controlled exasperation. Then he turned toward Hadar. "Oh, it's you!"

"Too much sun?" asked Hadar. "That's a new one."

"Hey, there are no silly questions—just silly customers." The egg man retrieved a strangely folded paper from beneath one of his egg baskets. "Hope it's okay that I did that. Have to keep my hands busy and I didn't realize that wasn't one of mine."

"Oh, that's so cute, you made a flower out of it!" gasped Halleli in delight.

"That's great!" said Hadar. "I want to learn to do that. I can't keep still either, and that sounds like a really fun way to handle it." She studied the flower, then presented it to Halleli with a gallant flourish.

"I like this adventure you cooked up," said the egg man. "This is your sister, right?"

Halleli felt fire in her cheeks and she wanted to fade into the trees, but Hadar responded promptly. "No, this is my wife. We're like the queen."

"Oh, right, I didn't know that." The egg man nodded. "You look alike."

"No, we don't," Hadar whispered in Halleli's ear after they'd walked away.

"I'm so glad Queen Shulamit is so open and straightforward about her life and family," Halleli murmured in response. "It makes things so much easier to explain." Their move to the big city had meant

271

introductions happened all the time now, instead of the small farming village where they'd lived together for the past few years where everyone knew they were a couple without having to talk about it. If the queen had not also been drawn to women, Halleli was *sure* things would be more difficult.

"Definitely. Read your clue, love!"

"But I'll have to ruin the flower."

"I'll learn to make my own. Then you won't be able to stop me and our room will be waist-deep in 'em."

Halleli giggled, then read. "'He uses fire, rock, and water to make things.' That sounds… like God. Is the clue at the synagogue?"

Hadar smirked. "I totally wasn't reading that much into it—try less poetic and more literal."

Halleli's eyelashes fluttered, her mind stuck in the mud.

"But," Hadar added as she took her by the hand, no doubt after seeing the frown, "I like the idea, and I bet you'll turn it into something with your art or writing."

"Be careful," said Halleli as grains of pride gathered. "If the queen saw me do something like that she might make me illustrate the whole Tanakh!"

"Starting with the Book of Esther," said Hadar.

"I'm already working on that."

"She's predictable!"

"So, who literally makes things out of fire? The potter needs fire to harden the pots… and earth to make the pots with…"

"I guess my clue was a little too broad."

"It's not the potter?" Halleli asked. "Is it more food?"

Hadar shook her head emphatically.

A cry from the marketplace cut through the chatter. "Toss the horseshoe 'round the pole and win a prize!"

"Oh, it's the *blacksmith*!" Halleli clapped her hands.

"Yay!"

They hurried off toward the forge.

Halleli stopped when she saw a small crowd gathered around a man in sparkly, purple clothing. "Ooh, what's he doing?"

"Looks like magic tricks." Hadar hovered close to her, one hand protectively close to her back.

The man, an athletic fortyish with a braided beard, was holding up a coin to those watching. He showed one side, then the other, before holding out his hand in invitation for audience volunteers. Small children in the front hopped up and down, and he chose one of them. Handing the coin to the youngster with instructions to keep it tightly in one fist, he then proceeded to stand on his head to scattered applause and children's laughter.

He then asked for a second volunteer. This time, he extended his hand to an old woman clutching a basket of vegetables. Before the crowd's eyes, that hand waved in the air and suddenly held a blooming lily. "Ooh!" rose through the audience. The old woman's face crinkled with delight.

"Wait, the flower isn't free!" the magician said dramatically. "You must pay me. Use the coin I gave the little one—it's in your vegetables."

"It is?" she asked in wonder. "Oh, my goodness, it is!" And she handed it over for him to show the crowd.

"Just to make sure it's the same coin, you don't have it anymore, do you?" the magician asked the child.

The little one's fingers uncurled, and sure enough, to the gasps of everyone watching—"It's empty! I just had it!"

"No, she did! And now it's mine again. Thank you, thank you." The magician took a bow, his hands spread wide in each direction, and several people made their way to the front to place coins in a clay pot near his feet.

Halleli and Hadar floated away down the path again before he started another trick. "That was fun," said Halleli.

"Definitely!" said Hadar. "I like getting the chance to see magic like that, instead of Isaac's stuff back at the palace. Something about wizards feels, I don't know, elitist to me. I mean, that purple guy? Anyone could learn those tricks, so it feels different."

"I know what you mean," said Halleli, "but technically, anybody could learn to be a wizard too. Not that I really know anything about it, but both the man back there and Isaac probably got where they are by practicing a lot."

Hadar stuck out her hand and swung her body in a semicircle around the slender trunk of a carpentaria palm as they passed by. "Yeah, but the work's different. I mean, anyone can practice the kind of sleight of hand and tricks we saw back there, but to do what Isaac does you have to concentrate. You know I'm not cut out for that. I couldn't be a wizard, but I bet I could do the coin trick if somebody showed me."

"That's true, but that doesn't mean *everyone* could do the coin trick." Halleli bent down to remove a road rock from her shoe. "There are probably people who'd have an easier time with the thinking type of magic than the coin trick. Like—if they had stiff joints and couldn't move as fast. Or don't like touching strangers."

Hadar chewed her lip thoughtfully. "I didn't think of that!"

"Wizards do act pretty smug sometimes," Halleli acceded. "That's probably a big part of why it feels elitist even if it's not, really." She didn't say anything about it because she didn't really know how, but she felt sort of—*glowy*, and also lucky that she loved someone with whom she could have such interesting conversations.

A second happiness joined the first as Halleli realized that she felt the pricklings of fresh inspiration. The street magician, with his exaggerated movements and flashy clothing, would be awfully fun to draw. Surely she could find a place for him in a visual story for the queen.

Bits of the conversation with Hadar floated into place like puzzle pieces as Halleli imagined a story about two magicians. One would use sleight of hand, like the one they'd just seen, and the other would be a wizard like Isaac. Whose magic would win?

Her eyes widened as she realized the afternoon had just handed her the perfect story idea for her project for the queen. Who needed *male* wizards and magicians when there were witches in the world?

A street performer, using ordinary tricks, and a witch with magic spells. There would be mistrust at first, perhaps conflict, but then—a common purpose—and through it, love?

Common purpose…

Halleli's idea curled up in a ball and went back to sleep. Well, that was normal; she was used to these things coming in unpredictable and uneven waves.

She took Hadar's hand and continued walking to the forge.

The clanking of hammers on anvils greeted their arrival, and for a few moments they stood there in the doorway hand in hand watching the men work. Hadar peered around, then said, "He's the one who has it, but he looks busy." She gestured to a man with his back to them as he worked with his current project.

"Yes, you'll have to… wait a moment," he called back to her without looking. After another minute he turned around, the sun-hot metal shaft of a small blade clasped between his tongs.

Halleli loved watching blacksmiths quench their projects, so she felt a little thrill when she heard the sizzle of its plunge into the water. This was lucky timing.

The smith drew the dagger out of the water and placed it aside. "Now, then!" He wiped his hands on his apron and approached the two ladies holding a folded paper. "You're lucky this didn't fall into the fire. This isn't the right place for games."

"Yes, sir. I'm sorry, sir," said Hadar, slipping noticeably into her Royal Guard posture. "Thank you though. We both appreciate it."

"Nn," the smith grunted in lieu of "you're welcome." "Tell the captain I said hello."

Hadar nodded briskly. "Yes, sir."

Halleli felt like she had a weight on her chest—she never wanted to be a bother to anybody. But just as they were about to turn and leave, the blacksmith seemed to relent slightly and winked at her. She smiled and looked at the floor.

Halleli still waited until they were back outside to do anything about the paper in her hand. "I'm sorry you had to go through all that trouble," she said as she squeezed Hadar's arm affectionately.

"Hey, I know you like to watch the quench."

Halleli unfolded the clue. "'The king who sleeps but never sleeps.' Whoaa... I have no idea, but I really like the way you said that!"

Hadar's arms shot up in exultation as Halleli continued musing.

"King... well, we don't have a king right now because Prince Kaveh's just a Prince-Consort..." Halleli was speaking of Queen Shulamit's political-only husband, who lived with his male companion on a vineyard outside Perach's borders. "We haven't had a king since King Noach died. Oh, this is about King Noach, isn't it? Sleeps, death..."

"I guess it's an obvious one," said Hadar, "but I have no shame."

"Never sleeps." Images flashed into Halleli's mind and she turned to Hadar, wide-eyed. "Are you saying something here is *haunted*? By the dead king's spirit? We—"

Hadar's mouth rose up in a grin. "No, no. Wow, you are, like, seventeen times more creative than I am."

"I should write about dybbuks," Halleli whispered, half to herself.

"He would never be something like that!" Hadar protested. "He was a good king."

"Oh, I know," said Halleli. "But you said *never sleeps*—"

"He's still with us in some ways, right?"

"On the mosaics in the palace, you mean?"

"What else?" Hadar pressed.

"Old coins from before he died?"

"Think bigger. A lot bigger."

Finally, Halleli understood. "*The statue!*" She grabbed Hadar's wrist and took off toward the square.

The monument to the late King Noach ruled over the Plaza of Moses on the far west of town, just before the docks. He faced the river, ostensibly in greeting to those who entered Home City by water. Halleli craned her neck up at him as they approached him from the south, looking up beyond the stone steps and careful plantings to observe his familiar face—bald to the back corner of his head, but then hair to his shoulders, and the bushy eyebrows he'd passed on to his daughter. "Look at the craftsmanship on his tunic," she breathed in admiration. "It looks like real fabric!"

Hadar reached out to touch it, as if to check what she knew to be true against her eyes, as Halleli continued her circle of the statue. Now that she could behold it more fully from the front, she saw that the king was holding a child in one arm, resting on his hip. It was a representation of the young queen, as she'd been at perhaps four or five—that was clear from the braids—but she'd been carved in a different style from the king. The little girl was roughly hewn, all right angles and sharp edges, as if the artist hadn't had time to finish her.

"Because Shulamit's reign had only just begun when this was commissioned," Halleli realized out loud.

"Wow, that is *deep*," said Hadar.

Halleli looked up at the little girl, then at the arm holding her. She was afraid if she told Hadar what she was thinking that she'd hurt her feelings, especially after all this work she'd done to cheer her up.

"Love?" Hadar could always tell though.

"My parents have no statue," said Halleli in the tiniest of voices.

"Oh, *love*." Hadar wrapped her in both arms and scrunched at her with one hand.

"I know this is silly, but..." Halleli breathed in and out slowly, stopping the urge to cry. "They were so good and wonderful in so many ways, but nobody knows about them."

"Then you'll have to change that," said Hadar, continuing to rub her back. "With your pictures and stories."

"They deserve a statue."

"*You're* their statue." Hadar pushed her back slightly so that she could grasp both of Halleli's upper arms and look into her eyes. "You were created to honor them. You're made out of everything good about them, and you're standing here, just like Noach is, to watch the sun over the water."

Halleli smiled through tears. "The idea makes me feel better."

"I'm telling the truth! I'll even find some birds to poop on you if you don't believe me." Hadar patted her lightly with her fingers. "Plop! Plop! You're a statue."

This made Halleli giggle and sniffle. "Sorry."

"It's fine! I miss them too."

Halleli rested her head on Hadar's shoulder. "Where's the clue?"

"Oh! Right. It's under one of the bushes near his feet."

As she rooted around in the dirt, Halleli asked, "What will we do if someone else took it first and threw it away? Since you didn't leave it with anyone this time."

"If we can't find it I'll just tell you the clue myself."

"Oh! Here it is." Halleli shook it out over the soil, then unfolded it carefully to make sure stray bits didn't fall on her simple linen dress. She read out loud as she sat down on the top step of the statue's base: "'You can travel without bags, or horses, or a carriage. You can spend time in the distant snows without a coat; you can ride over the sea without leaving dry land. You can meet Miriam and Queen Esther and the Empress of the Mermaids, without getting out of bed or moving the cat off your lap. And what's better—you, my love, YOU can send people on these journeys. All thanks to this little object.'"

She'd been confused by the beginning, her mind pulled in all sorts of exciting directions by the horses and snowdrifts and sea crests of the clue. But when Halleli reached the end, she was smiling broadly, her eyes smarting with quite a different kind of tears from before. "That was really pretty," she blurted as she looked up at Hadar.

Hadar just did one of her little dances, then reached out and scooped up both Halleli's hands in hers. "It's the truth." She pulled her up and danced her around in a circle.

"The clue's at the bookmaker's, then?"

"Very good! If she hasn't sewn it into a book already."

"I'm sure she's put it somewhere safe," said Halleli.

"Look!" Hadar pointed to the docks. "They're unloading a ship."

"Ooh, let's go see!"

The girls hurried across the square to the street that ran parallel to the river, stopping short to avoid a couple of horses. "We'd better not get any closer; we'll get in their way," said Halleli.

"Can you see anything?"

"Not yet."

"Look!" Hadar pointed. "I think it's carrying textiles. There's Ben the tailor, from the palace. And those two women are also tailors."

"Oh," Halleli breathed in delight as one of the sailors unrolled a bolt of shimmering, red cloth for the Perachi customers. It shone with the richness of wine in the late afternoon sun. "It's so beautiful. I don't think I'd even be able to wear it. I'd just want to look at it."

As Ben and the other tailors negotiated with the sailors, Hadar and Halleli departed, walking along the riverside street. Halleli's eyes were almost entirely on the row of ships and boats, soaking in the inspiration for future projects. Her magician and witch for the queen's romance needed a quest, and quests usually required travel. Maybe a voyage by ship could be involved; then the women would be thrown into close quarters.

They turned left when they got to Flower Street, away from the river and into a ritzier part of town. "Oh, wow, all kinds of fun stuff in here," Hadar pointed out one shop, marked *Curiosities*. In the window they saw a wine goblet clasped in a dragon's paw made of metal, a lamp that looked like a water lily with a vessel inside where you put the oil and wick, and a huge pillow sewn to look like a violin.

"That one's my favorite!" Halleli pointed to a glass-topped table held up by a metal octopus' eight arms and big, bulbous head. "It must cost a fortune."

"You're right, that *is* one of the best," said Hadar. "You should draw it! Then you could take it home without having to pay."

Halleli said nothing as she stared into the shop, memorizing the stormy curves of the beast's great tentacles.

"Thanks for doing all this for me," she finally said as they continued their walk to the bookmaker's. She squeezed Hadar's hand.

"Getting any story ideas?"

"Lots," said Halleli, "I don't think I'm ready to talk about it yet though."

The bookmaker was sewing pages into a binding when the two girls arrived. "Oh, good!" she said emphatically as she stood up. "I was scared I'd have to close up before you got here. But I'm still working on this last set of Haggadahs."

"Can we see?" Hadar asked.

The bookmaker handed them each a finished copy. Halleli opened hers to a random page. *Had He satisfied our needs in the desert for forty years, and not fed us on manna, it would have been enough. Had He fed us on manna, but not given us the Sabbath, it would have been enough.* Dayenu.

Had He given me two loving parents, and not also a loyal wife to cherish, it would have been enough. Had He given me a loyal wife to cherish, and not royal help when the trees failed, it would have been enough. Had He given us royal help when the trees failed, and not delivered us into this beautiful city... Dayenu, thought Halleli. Her daydreams were richly colored and throbbed with energy as if alive, and she overflowed with religious gratitude.

"Ooh, is that Miriam?" Hadar pointed to a picture in hers.

The bookmaker nodded enthusiastically. "My sister draws those, when she has time."

"Halleli draws too!" Hadar announced, which made Halleli's cheeks flush.

"Oh?" said the bookmaker.

"Yes," said Halleli. "Come eat at the Frangipani Table some time, and if you pay extra, Chef Yael lets me sketch your portrait."

"I might just do that! I had no idea," said the bookmaker. "Here's your clue, by the way."

"Thank you," said Halleli, trading the Haggadah for the clue.

"This is the last one," said Hadar once they were outside again.

"That's all right," said Halleli, smiling shyly. "It's already been amazing. 'You couldn't drink this no matter how hard you tried, for five hundred million days. But you can float on it, and drink little things instead.' Float? Are we going back to the river?"

Hadar shook her head. "Too busy. Think more private."

"Quiet Lake?"

Hadar nodded rapidly.

"What kinds of little things?" Halleli asked.

"You'll find out when we get there!"

Hadar took the lead when they arrived at Quiet Lake, approaching the boat rental. Halleli thought she heard a fragment of uncouth humor between the two young men at the counter, but as soon as they saw the two women they stopped talking and played innocent.

Hadar clearly felt like being brazen today. "What did you say about the one about the dancer and the two jugs of rum?"

The man on the left burst into laughter, while the man on the right played the fool. "I don't actually know," he said. "I thought there was a joke like that, but I can't remember it now."

"I can't either, then," said Hadar. "You still have that picnic basket from earlier, or did you eat it for us?"

"We wouldn't do anything like that!" said the man on the right. The man on the left simply produced the picnic basket with a huge smile on his face.

"Thank you! Here's the rest of the money I promised you. Now, where's our boat?" Hadar looked around at the water with her hands on her hips.

"That one there." The man on the left pointed.

"Sure you don't need us to come out there with you?" asked the man on the right. "Not as much fun when it's only girls."

Halleli wanted to disappear inside her hair scarf, but Hadar shot right back with, "Yeah, but we're *women*."

The man on the left chuckled and punched the other man in the side. "Stop being a kidney and go help them, or I'll tell Ima about, you know, the thing, with the girl, and the…"

"Shut *up*," said his brother, and went to go untie the boat.

Wow, thought Halleli. *Hadar could have said 'I'm in the guard!' Or 'Stop that, or I'll tell Captain Riv what you said.' But she just did that all by herself, without using her uniform or scary boss as a shield. She's the best.*

Hadar had the picnic basket, and she handed it over to Halleli once Halleli was seated in the rowboat, so that she could herself sit down. They pushed away from the shore and drifted out into the gentle waters.

"Thank you so much for today," said Halleli. "My soul is fed."

"Now I need to feed your stomach," said Hadar. "Open it, open it!"

Inside the picnic basket were: bourekas, roglit, falafel, chewy dried bananas, and tiny bottles of wine. "It's our whole dinner!" Halleli exclaimed.

Hadar nodded. "I got permission to do it this way. They're not expecting us at the dining hall tonight."

"So we can just relax in our room." Halleli sighed happily. "I think I've figured out my idea for the queen's art story now."

"Tell me!" Hadar bounced slightly, and luckily it was a sturdy boat so nothing bad happened.

"There's a beautiful witch in a shiny red dress, like that fabric we saw at the dock," Halleli began, "but also a woman street performer, who does the sort of magic that isn't really magic. Like the man in purple. They're on a ship together, arguing about whose magic is superior, but

286

then they have to work together to go on a quest for magical treasures across the world."

"Like my clues!" Hadar realized.

"And of course they fall in love."

"Because that's why the queen is paying you," said Hadar.

"Well, because it's what *I* want to write," said Halleli. "Let's face it, if it didn't make *me* happy, do you think it would be any good in the first place?"

"So whose magic is better?" asked Hadar, her mouth full of falafel.

"It doesn't matter," said Halleli, rubbing her foot against Hadar's ankle affectionately. "They're both much stronger when they work together."

No Whining

Cast: Yael from *The Olive Conspiracy* and her husband
Aaron

For the folks at Blue Highway Pizzeria

♡ ✡ ♡

In the 4th year of Queen Shulamit's reign (springtime)

8 Iyar: after sundown

Yael sat at a cleared-off table with that night's box of
coins to her right. She counted them in little piles,
scribbling with an old pencil on a piece of some of the
crumpled paper that had protected the new wineglasses in
their original box. Subtract that morning's egg delivery,
then the cost of the spring onions… Oh, and she mustn't
miss that note about the broken plate. That counted as
debit. Too bad.

"Whew, what a night!" exclaimed Aaron as he emerged
from the kitchen, stretching his great, wiry, muscled arms.
"I hope you're about to show me some glorious numbers
because I feel like a grease stain."

"You do have one—just there." But her tone was more
affectionate than her words, and so was her adoring glance
across his familiar bearded face.

After thirty years, he was used to her feigned coolness, and
squeezed her shoulders from behind. "That, my dear, is a
badge of honor. Three families of six all at the same time?
On top of the usual lot?"

"I know." She pushed aside another stack of coins. "Front
of house was busy too, keeping their wine and water jugs

filled. Speaking of which, someone complained about the wine again."

"The herbalist?"

"No, no," said Yael. "Someone visiting, one of the large parties from out of town. They could tell it had been watered down and accused *me*."

Aaron chuckled. "I bet I know how that went."

"I'm probably going to have a reputation in Ir Ilan by next week," said Yael dryly. "Anyway, I'll speak with Sarah about it at her next sales call."

Aaron's bushy beard moved around his twisting mouth. "I don't know, Yael. I think we should start seriously thinking about switching to Asher."

Yael sighed loudly.

"Look," he started. "If—"

"I mean," Yael interrupted. "Yes. You're right. Jacob and Daniel have been letting us down lately, and something needs to change. But Sarah—"

"Sarah's just the delivery girl. She doesn't make the wine, and she's not responsible for its quality."

"Sarah's more than a delivery girl," said Yael. "How many times—how many times *just this month* has she gone to market for me when we were too busy to spare one of us or send Chana? Plus, that other time when she—"

"Great," said Aaron, "but what about that incident with the bill last week?"

"Well, that was either a mistake or Jacob Straw-Hat showing his ass," said Yael, without taking her eyes off her neat line of figures, "but after I was through with him, I bet he'll be more careful."

"Sarah looked embarrassed."

"Sarah looked a right mess! I fed her after that," said Yael. "I wanted her to know I knew it wasn't her fault."

"She's a grown woman," said Aaron.

"Barely," said Yael.

"She'll understand if you try someone else out for a while," said Aaron. He produced a clean glass and a jug. "Let's give this a try."

Yael looked up and saw an unfamiliar picture of a bee. "What is it?"

"Mead," said Aaron, "made from orange blossom honey. Lovely Valley. It's from Asher."

She gasped with exasperation. "You've been talking to him already?"

"No, a barmaid from the Delight ran over here halfway through dinner looking for lemons," said Aaron. "A rat got into their basket and it had to be thrown away, and they needed them for drinks. All she had to trade for it was a bottle of mead. But *she* got it from Asher."

"I'm not saying I'm comfortable with switching," said Yael, "but I would be *awfully* comfortable with you pouring me a glass of mead." She looked up at her husband with a wily smile. "You aren't having any?"

"If we drink from the same glass there'll be less to wash," he said cheerfully. "And then maybe Chana won't be here 'til dawn." He put the glass down on the table in front of her.

"So considerate."

"Or maybe I just want to follow in the wake of your lips."

"All right, all right, big talker. Are you sure you haven't talked to Asher yet?"

Aaron threw up his free hand. "When have I ever hid anything from you?"

Without looking at him, she marked off another number on her scratch paper. "That time, with the thing."

"Shut up, woman."

They gazed at each other with delighted eyes.

♡ ✡ ♡

Yael listened for the sound of deliveries at the door as she peeled onions on the prep table the next morning. Today was her turn to cook, and she had plans for stuffed squash and lettuce wraps. As her gnarled, golden-brown fingers split each papery husk, she recalled the sweet yet well-balanced taste in the glass she'd shared with her husband last night. After a day on her feet, the mead had been shockingly pleasing, but with a refined palate that gave her visions of the great houses of nobility. She wondered why Jacob and Daniel hadn't been able to get something like that.

Well, maybe they could. She'd talk to Sarah. Maybe that was her at the door.

"Good morning!" the tiny woman with the huge hair called out, waving, as she climbed off her pony and circled around to the cart he pulled.

Yael nodded, leaning against her doorframe. "They got you working hard today?"

"That's every day," said Sarah as she counted bottles and compared them with her scribbled list. "Um."

Yael knew that "um." Yael knew that meant Jacob-or-Daniel had made another mistake in her order. Particles of stress settled on her aging limbs like sawdust, irritating her and clouding her mind. She walked up to the back of the cart.

Sarah looked up to face her. "It's the dry red from Two Trees." She pursed her lips. "I thought it was here, but those bottles must have been part of the Delight order."

Yael rolled her eyes. "They're filling these orders while they're asleep, aren't they?"

"I'm sorry, I really am," said Sarah. "I have to make my deliveries in the order they give me. Also, I have to tell you—we *did* get that new shipment in from Aram and Swan, and I talked about it with Jacob and he agreed we'd save the semisweet red for you like you asked, but this morning Daniel insisted it go to the Silver Goat and the Marquis' manor."

"Shit!" Yael rubbed her forehead. "That's my bestseller."

"I know, and I'll talk to them again." Sarah held out her list. "Want to check what's left?"

Yael forced herself to do this part carefully, because who knew what other mistakes lay in store. Luckily, nothing else had gone wrong. Dry white, sweet white, sparkling pink… "That's not mine." She pointed.

Sarah crossed the other dry white off her list. "That's Jacob's writing. Maybe he wrote that instead of the dry red you wanted."

"All right, child, let me get you your money."

Yael and Sarah carried the bottles of wine inside, and then Yael counted out coins. "You tell that Jacob I'm coming down to see him again if I can get a minute away from the kitchen. I'm always grateful for everything you do around here, but Aaron—he's been sniffing around at Asher's stock, and after enough of this I can see why."

"Yes, Chef," said Sarah, her eyes downcast.

"I hope those bosses of yours appreciate you," said Yael sharply. "Putting up with their mistakes."

Sarah was gone, and her visit had left a big red stamp, the color of the missing semisweet wine, on Yael's mind. How much longer should she have to endure missing orders, wrong orders, and generally being treated like other, wealthier customers mattered more than she and Aaron did? This was becoming ludicrous. Sarah seemed like a tiny wall trying to hold back a flood of incompetence all by herself. She meant well, but she was somewhat powerless.

At least Aaron could be the one to placate the customers looking for Aram and Swan today, while Yael worked her magic in the kitchen away from socializing.

♡ ✡ ♡

The steady hum of lunch conversation surrounded Yael in meaningless waves as she worked in the kitchen, plating stuffed squash for the next table. "Order up! Table one, outside," she called.

Chana appeared in the kitchen and collected the plates in a row on one lanky, practiced arm. "Table four inside wants to ask you questions about the stuffing."

"That's fine. If you can put those lettuce cups on plates, they're ready to go out to two and three inside." Yael smoothed back stray pieces of her tied-back hair, then left her waitress in the kitchen as she crossed forward into the dining area.

"What can I do for you?" Yael approached table four with the air of a queen—protective, confident, and welcoming.

"Oh, yes, thank you, Chef," said an unfamiliar woman with lighter skin than the locals. "Could you please tell me what's in the stuffing for the stuffed squash?"

"Rice, sultanas, nuts," Yael ticked off ingredients by tapping one finger with the fingers of her other hand. "Preserved lemon, carrots, onion, celery, garlic. You're not asking me for my secret herbs and spices, are you?"

"Oh no! You see, I'm from the City of Red Clay, and this is our Month of the Sun," explained the customer. "We don't eat *any* meat during this time. The rice wasn't cooked in meat broth, was it?"

Yael shook her head. "The stuffing is entirely pareve, neutral."

"I'm sorry, what?"

The woman's dining companion, who looked native Perachi, put his hand on her forearm. "Remember, I told you? Neither meat or dairy."

"Oh, I see," said the woman vaguely. "But not even cooked in broth? I wanted to make sure."

"I can assure you there's only plants in—"

A throaty scream followed by the sound of broken dishes stabbed the conversation in half. "Oh shit," Yael muttered under her breath. Aaron was at one of the outdoor tables pouring wine—she was closer. "I'm so sorry, ma'am," she called over her shoulder as she rushed back to the kitchen.

The first thing Yael saw when she burst through the swinging kitchen doors was the huge, ugly dog whose wolflike bulk took up most of the moving-around room between her countertops. "What in the name of Joseph's coat—"

Chana crouched in the corner, shaking like a leaf with her eyes closed, plastered to the walls as if she were paint. Meanwhile, the stray dog gobbled up the remainder of the lettuce wraps with eager wuffling noises, his tail slashing from side to side. Behind all that, the open back door at least partially explained what had happened.

"*SHOO!*" Yael shouted, her arms in the air. "Git!"

With great effort she finally succeeded in expelling the strange animal from her work area. Then she approached Chana gingerly. "It's gone. You all right?"

Chana almost couldn't speak at first, but then she finally nodded jerkily and opened her eyes. "I'm so sorry. So sorry. Scratching noises at the door—thought it was the children again, so I opened it and it just—barged—I'm sorry about the food. I don't handle dogs well."

"I know. Shhh." Yael rubbed her back with motherly tenderness. "It's all right. It's all right." She didn't know

295

the story about Chana and dogs, but she did know there was a story—unlike her own lizard phobia, which was just a simple disgust reflex. "You feel well enough to go chop me some more filling after we clean up?"

Chana squared her shoulders. "Yes, Chef."

"I need five more orders."

"What about the lettuce? We need more from the market."

"I'll handle that," said Yael. She peered into the kitchen. Aaron was racing around filling water and wineglasses, but even had he been a young man still, handling front of house by himself would have been a tall order.

She stuck her head out the back door and called to one of the tiny children, always idle in the afternoon after their schooling hours because they were too small to work. "You! Come here. Take this coin and fetch me Sarah the wine seller."

♡ ✡ ♡

Shabbat fell on the following evening, so the wine wagon didn't stop by because the restaurant was only open for lunch. They could use what they'd gotten the day before. In Sarah's absence, Yael chewed on her decision, dissatisfaction and loyalty each rising to the top of her mind in turn.

She hadn't had time to go to the wine cellar and have it out with Jacob or Daniel, but it didn't seem like that great of a loss since usually her visits just resulted in a lot of empty promises and air. The question hung over the approach of evening like a bad smell, and she hoped Shabbat would provide a welcome sanctuary from her dithering.

Aaron rested on the sofa while Yael changed into nicer clothes that never saw the grease of a kitchen. He looked awfully comfortable when she emerged, with his eyes closed. "You're working too hard," she pointed out.

"Just tired. Long week." He opened his eyes. "Is that the new dress? It suits you!"

Yael nodded, holding out her arms to show off the burgundy fabric. "We don't have to go though," she added, looking over his posture. "If you're tired."

"No, no, I need to," he said, pulling himself upright and then standing up.

"We can light candles at home." She tried not to show her worry in her face too much, but he was wearing out more easily than usual lately. These things were normal—but this didn't *seem* normal.

Ah, well, maybe she was just in denial that they were *both* growing old! As one did. Hopefully.

"It's less distracting with everyone else there. They keep my mind on the prayers." He retrieved his kippah from a side table and headed toward the door.

Aaron had a kitchen shift today, even if it was only the lunch service. "If the restaurant is wearing you out maybe I should spend more time in the kitchen," Yael suggested. "I don't mind."

"It's nothing! Let's just take it easy, like we're supposed to." He turned around to smile at her as she followed him out the door.

At the synagogue, they said hello to the dressmaker, who admired her handiwork and looked suitably proud when

297

Aaron showered her with compliments, and to Nava, who was the other woman there who was like Yael. There would have been three of them if Chana was there, but she claimed she preferred to go to the more traditional services at the synagogue near Quiet Lake—and then often skipped anyway. Poor Chana. Yael hoped she was back to normal after the incident with the stray dog.

  Yael and Aaron sat down in their usual spot all the way over on the left near the potted lime trees, and soon the rabbi started everyone off with song. How sweet, as the song said, to worship together with your community. Yael let the repetition roll around in her mind, blocking her workday cares. What a lovely thing Shabbat was, that someone should come and gently take your rolling pin from your hands, your chef's knife, set them down carefully and lead you to the soul's nourishment.

  Shabbat wasn't impenetrable though. Aaron stood slowly and with great effort whenever the congregation was called to rise, and Yael tried her best not to react to his quiet but alarming huffing and puffing.

  "Blessed is our God who separates day from evening," Aaron's deep voice bellowed beside her, as if nothing was wrong. And maybe nothing was, but still, when they reached the *Mishebeirach*, the healing prayer, it was Aaron's name Yael infused into it—even if she did so without announcing it, to save his ego.

♡ ✡ ♡

  The restaurant wasn't open the following evening since Shabbat had only just ended at sundown, but Yael and Aaron came in anyway to get things ready for the next morning. Yael was taking inventory of the dry goods when

Aaron poked his head into the kitchen, a rag in his hand from cleaning tables. "Sarah's here."

"Oh." They'd had *such* a wonderful peaceful Shabbat, and Yael wasn't really ready to go back to the conundrum.

"We're really going to keep putting up with them?" He meant Jacob and Daniel.

Yael paused. "I don't know. I really do need a few more days to think about this."

Aaron shrugged, his hands out to both sides. "We need that semisweet Aram and Swan."

"I know." She wiped her hands on a clean cloth and went to go meet Sarah.

The wine seller waited patiently in the torchlights of the street just outside the restaurant. "Good evening, Yael!"

"Peace, Sarah," said Yael. "I'm not sure that I need anything for tomorrow, unless you can promise me my semisweet red."

The flickering torchlight revealed a smile trying desperately to cover a frustrated emptiness on Sarah's face. "I don't think there's any there." She licked her lips. "I'm sorry."

"Look, I feel bad for you," said Yael, "and you're a big help when we're in the weeds. I'd hate to lose that. But the biggest thing I need from a wine seller is wine, and…"

"I understand, and I'm sorry," said Sarah. "I'll talk to them."

"I wish you *were* them," said Yael. "You're the only one around there who actually gives a shit." An impulsive thought landed on her tongue. "Aaron works too hard. What if I offered you a job here? Would you come and work at the Frangipani Table?"

"Oh, Yael!" Sarah laughed sadly. "That's so sweet of you. I… I don't really want to work in a restaurant. But if I ever get stuck, I may take you up on that. I know you'd be a fair boss."

"Thank you." Yael looked down at the tiny woman and saw her past selves, from last week and the week before and so many other weeks, rushing back to them in the afternoon with armfuls of lettuce, of live chickens, of a stack of pita bread half as big as her own height. "Look, I'll give you an order, but I'm not lying when I say I know where Asher lives."

"I understand."

"What happened?" asked Aaron when Yael was back inside with the door closed.

"I think I'm giving them one last chance."

"You're getting soft in your old age," he remarked.

"Not really," Yael countered. "This way, when they screw up it'll be easier for me to make my decisions. Oh, and by the way? *Don't* call me old, old man." She aimed a heavy-lidded smolder in his direction, then picked up one of his untouched cleaning rags. She draped it around his neck and used it to draw him closer, with mock sensuality.

Maybe Shabbat could last just a few moments longer.

♡ ✡ ♡

"Good morning, Yael!" It was Jacob Straw-Hat himself, standing in front of his wine wagon.

"You're late," said Yael, crossing to the back of the wagon where the wine was. "And where's Sarah?" It was far too close to her lunch opening for her to feel safe standing out here messing around with vendors. If she thought of the okra and walnuts she still had yet to chop she felt so agitated she almost couldn't breathe.

"Oh, I had to send her to Ir Ilan with a delivery," said Jacob breezily, lining up bottles on the back of the wagon.

"What?" Yael crossed her arms and peered over his shoulder at the line of jugs. "I thought she was local distribution."

"We had an issue we needed to resolve and she's off taking care of it." He counted silently with one pointed finger. "Three jugs of Two Trees dry red, right?"

"Yes, that's right," said Yael, "but what about the Aram and Swan?"

"Right here." He tapped a jug.

"That's dry."

"Yes, but dry is actually *better*—"

"Jacob." Yael glared directly into his eyes, taking advantage of her height for once. "I don't really care what *you* think is better, or what Daniel thinks, or what wine snobs think is better, or what Aram thinks—"

"Aram's dead, his son runs the—"

"That is so far away from the point it had to hire a messenger boy just to find out what the point *looked like*." Yael knew her rising voice was attracting the attention of people on the street and she didn't care. "What matters to me is, my customers *like* the red semisweet, it's my top seller, and for some reason they seem to think it goes best with my food. I lose money every day I don't have it to offer them. I work too hard to lose money. *Do. You. Understand. That?*"

"Absolutely, Yael. We all do, and I'm sorry." Jacob held out both his hands, smiling shallowly like the impervious wall he was.

"Does Asher have it?"

"What?"

"Does Asher have the wine I want?"

"How should I know what Asher has?"

"Never mind. Where's the rest of my order?" Yael perused the row. "Is that white sparkling? I stock pink sparkling."

"It says pink sparkling on the invoice," said Jacob. "Daniel must have—"

"Do *either* of you two know how to take responsibility for anything?"

When Yael went back inside, Aaron greeted her with a smirk. "I could hear you in here."

"Oh." Yael stuck out her tongue at him. "Oops. That man, though. He could stub his toe and blame the queen."

"Why was he here?"

"He sent Sarah on some errand and now he's making her deliveries for her."

"In the wrong order, sounds like," said Aaron. "It's nearly lunchtime!"

♡ ✡ ♡

That night, Yael and Aaron sat on their bedroom's balcony, watching the stars come out while she rubbed his aching feet. This wasn't unusual but her silence must have been, because Aaron asked, "What are you thinking about?"

"Mead."

"Oh." He chuckled, pointing to the west with one finger of a hand wrapped around a cookie. "Well, Asher's is that way."

"Mead," Yael continued, "and Sarah."

"I thought you said if they messed up one more time, never mind Sarah."

"I know," said Yael, digging her thumbs into tough, tired skin. "But today had nothing to do with her. I didn't expect that."

"All today shows is that you can't count on them to let the one thing keeping your loyalty even be there for you." He finished the cookie.

"Every time I make up my mind to do it one way or another, I start feeling even more strongly in the other direction."

"I can see that."

303

"How are you feeling?"

"Better, now you're doing that."

She smiled up at him. "It's like I said. You're on your feet too much. Wish Sarah'd taken that job I offered her."

"She might still, if she didn't like being sent all the way up to Ir Ilan."

Yael sighed. "I hate having this hanging over my head. Who invented wine, anyway?"

"Most people find it relaxing."

"Smartass."

"C'mere." Aaron patted one of his massive thighs. "I just want to hold you and stop thinking about the restaurant."

♡ ✡ ♡

The next day, Yael still hadn't made up her mind. For two days she told Chana to tell Sarah she didn't need anything, barricading herself behind a pile of kitchen busywork. On the first day she made excuses for herself in her mind, that she was too busy right now, but on the second day she knew she was deliberately avoiding Sarah. After all, how could she cut her off after so much eager and helpful service above and beyond her actual job?

But she knew she had to do it. Aaron was getting older—she was, too, she couldn't deny it—and it wasted so much of their precious time to deal with incompetence and inconvenience.

Sarah didn't stop by on the third day, but they were slow. On the fourth day, business picked up, which was great, except now they were starting to use up the stores of wine held in reserve. Yael knew the restaurant would soon run out and this time it would be entirely her own fault.

Well, never let anyone say Chef Yael backed down from difficult things.

Aaron sat at one of the front tables counting the money from lunch, and he looked up when she kissed him on the forehead on her way out the door. "Where are you going?"

"Asher."

She heard his satisfied grunt as she left.

Thoughts swarmed around her like gnats as she walked through the sunny city. What would she do if she got stuck for product in the middle of the day, now, without Sarah? It really was time to hire a second person to help Chana. Aaron should be resting more, should be greeting customers and pouring wine, and leave all the rushing around to the young ones.

"Peace, Yael!" called a man who was standing at the juice booth waiting for his drink.

He was a regular customer, and she waved back at him. She felt vaguely guilty, almost like she didn't want him to know where she was going. Well, that was silly! Her customers would stop eating at Frangipani Table if their quality declined, so they would have no reason to expect any differently of her and Aaron's purchasing decisions.

Besides, there would be benefits to this, beyond just Asher's purported reliability. There would be mead. She longed to share another bottle of it with Aaron, this time on the bedroom balcony.

Asher's business office was in the front of his home, a small but immaculately white building with the same red curved tile roof as most of the rest of Home City. Yael admired the bottle palms flanking the doorway, and she wondered idly if they were intended as a pun.

Probably, because his door knocker was shaped like a bunch of grapes. She smirked as she rapped it.

Fumbling noises on the other side heralded someone's approach, and then the great door swung open. "Oh!"

Yael's mouth dropped open in surprise, for standing on the other side, her great big hair bound up under a deep pink scarf, was Sarah!

"Who's that, Sarah?" A pleasant tenor voice came from behind her, and in a few moments Asher himself appeared. He was a sprightly, handsome man in his midforties but with the air of eternal youth, curly, dark hair, and a romantic dusting of scruff.

"I—" Yael took a moment to gather herself. "Are you here now?"

Sarah issued an embarrassed smile, and Asher laughed warmly. "She's here."

"Things were bad over there," Sarah said finally. "I mean, you knew. You could see. And then they sent me upstate, which was—they didn't even give me money for lunch. If they'd only given me money for lunch I would have felt appreciated but—never mind, I'm being unladylike. I'm sorry. And then, I knew I was losing *your* business, and that hurt the worst of all, and I just—" She looked up at Asher, who was behind her. "He's so *organized*!" This last exhalation was spoken in breathless joy.

306

"Well, ain't that just the thing." Yael grinned, splashing around in her own relief like a kid in the lake and not really knowing what else to say.

"Would you like to come in and see what we have?" Asher held his hand out toward his office. "I know you like Aram and Swan's semisweet red, and I put some aside for you as soon as I hired Sarah."

Yael followed his hand without a word.

"I was going to come see you, but I'm still moving my things," Sarah explained meekly.

"Now, then," said Asher once the door was closed. "What would you like to taste?"

Yael smiled firmly. "Let's share a bottle of mead."

Every Us

Cast: Kaveh/Farzin

whose love story is told in Climbing the Date Palm

For J.L. Douglas

♡ ✡ ♡

Farzin found himself awake.

After a moment of disorientation, he realized that he had stirred not, as usual, from the gray light of dawn and the recitations of various songbirds in the vineyard, but from the irregular thrashing of the perfect specimen of masculinity beside him in the bed.

"Hey." Farzin shook him gently. "Perfect specimen of masculinity."

"Huh? Huh?" Kaveh woke gasping like a man saved from drowning. "Fa-Farzin? Oh thank goodness." He rolled over and enveloped Farzin as if he were auditioning for world's tightest blanket.

Farzin grinned from ear to ear, selfishly happy to be seized with such ardor even though he could tell something was wrong. "You okay, Prince Charming?"

"No more extra-peppery chicken right before bed," Kaveh groaned.

Farzin rubbed his back gently. "You tell that cook he's not allowed to hurt my companion anymore." As usual, Kaveh was the dubious culinary artist in question.

"I'll get right on that," Kaveh mumbled. "I am… I am just so glad to see you. The real you."

Farzin's brow wrinkled. "I didn't know I'd made any clockwork duplicates."

Kaveh chuckled. *Good, I made him laugh* was Farzin's gut reflex, as it had been since he was a boy and Kaveh was his sad-eyed classmate.

"I bet you could," Kaveh replied. "Just like that little dragon you made last week. But that's not what I mean. I had this dream... it was so real."

"It was obviously so not," said Farzin comfortingly. "What happened?"

Kaveh shook his head. "Everything was—well, first of all, you and I were just friends, like before... but I still loved you, like I do now. I was so sad that we weren't together. I was devastated. It was like... hunger, and emptiness, and, I don't know, missing a hand..."

Farzin kept holding his prince and methodically massaged his back. He was used to these periodic bouts of negative energy, and he always tried to transform himself into three hundred pounds of comfort and love. "That sounds distinctly unpleasant," he said lightly. "I don't recommend it." The goal was to get Kaveh laughing.

"That's not all," Kaveh added. "It was like none of it had ever happened, and I was married to Azar."

Farzin drew in his breath sharply. Now he understood Kaveh's panic, and he tried not to think of the way Azar had forbidden the two of them from meeting their baby nephew on account of some insulting notion of love for men being contagious. That was enough to wipe the smile off even his face, and he needed to be strong for Kaveh right now.

"She's still pretty," Farzin commented. "Unless you've stopped being attracted to women and just like men now."

"No, that's not it at all. I'm still the way I always was," said Kaveh. "I just—she'd put me in a box and never let me out. She thinks my love for you is some kind of sickness in real life—imagine how much worse that was in the dream world where she was supposed to be my ultimate companion."

That did sound absolutely terrifying, Farzin had to admit, so he pulled out all the stops and went full-on clown. "Oh, but you were right the first time!" he said in a haughty tone with uncharacteristic feminine inflection. "I am Azar, your proud princess."

Kaveh chuckled. "Oh boy. Wow, you have that down!"

"Of course I know how to talk to you," Farzin continued, energized by that sacred sound. "We are man and wife, just as it should be in my incredibly tiny mind."

"It's more of a tiny heart," Kaveh countered. "She's smart enough."

Not smart enough to marry you, Farzin didn't say out loud. "I am very smart because I cut wonderful people out of my life because I don't understand them."

"How do I get Farzin back?"

Farzin pulled the blankets up over his head and shifted around. "He's hiding. You'll have to find him!"

Kaveh sniff-laughed and put his hand down on some random part of the great lump into which Farzin had transformed himself.

"Congratulations, you have won the left buttock of a Farzin." With each of Kaveh's chuckles, Farzin felt like he was shooting a perfect score at some field sport.

"How do I get a matched set?"

"There are no matched sets. We have only left buttocks in stock today. Right buttocks tomorrow. Will you take two lefts?"

"How can you tell they're both left?"

"I don't know," said Farzin. "I've never seen my own behind."

"You are a thoroughly ridiculous and adorable man."

"Some say."

"You're right, that was a stupid dream."

"You ever wake up and find us in that situation, you come find me and say something about it, okay?" said Farzin, restoring himself and his blanket to normal sleeping posture. "Because I guarantee that I'll still love you with everything that I am, and we can run off together anyway."

Kaveh was silent for a moment. "Promise?"

"There's no world that exists where I don't love you as much as I do right now," Farzin reassured him.

Take Time to Stop and Eat the Roses

Cast: Micah/Ronit (Esther's little sister)

We first met Micah and Esther in *A Harvest of Ripe Figs*

For Alex

♡ ✿ ♡

Micah lay flat on the sofa, his arms and legs starfished out against the plush fabric. "If I eat one more festival I'm going to diiie."

"Then stop eating," Ronit and Miriam chorused together, which happened often enough in their sisterly hijinks that they'd long ceased laughing about it.

The three Perachi teenagers reposed in a quiet salon, away from the noise and clamor of the party in the next room. That was where the food was, along with several of their future-brother-in-law's aunties. In true "older female relative" tradition, they were more than ready to insist that Micah, or any of the rest of them, eat even *more* festivals or ackee or fried breadfruit.

Part of the reason all three of them had overeaten was the novelty of Sugar Coast food.

"But if I don't eat any more festivals, I'm going to diiie." Micah's face contorted in mock pain. "They're so good."

"It's literally just fried meal," said Miriam. "How are you so skinny?" She and her older sister were comfortably round, and their eldest, Esther—the one who was getting married tomorrow on the beach—was possessed of a graceful and imperial fatness.

"Oh, don't be a goof," said Ronit. "You know that has nothing to do with it and never has. God makes some

312

bodies gain weight when they eat, and some don't. Esther eats the least of all of us, and she's always been the biggest."

"She's going to make such a beautiful bride!" Miriam's face lit up, and she stared dreamily into the corner.

♡ ✡ ♡

"Hey, Micah!"

He lifted his head from the pillow—he'd been staring out the window instead of sleeping anyway, mesmerized by the undulations of the waves in the moonlight. "Can't sleep?"

"Haven't tried!" The candle Ronit held lit a face ripe with devilish glee. "Are you too tired to go on an adventure?"

"I'm not sleepy yet." Micah sat up and ran his hand through his hair in case it was messy from tossing and turning. "What are we doing?"

"I thought it would be a really beautiful surprise for Esther if she woke up and found flowers all over her room."

"Sounds like fun! Where are we going to get the flowers? Tzuriel's aunties will be mad if we touch anything for tomorrow."

"Other people's gardens!" said Ronit. When Micah opened his mouth to protest, she added quickly, "We can leave coins in return. Tzuriel's ima gave me a bunch of change when we got here, little stuff that she didn't need."

"That sounds fair," said Micah. Stealing food when he was a street kid wasn't the same as a girl from a prosperous farming family stealing flowers, and he was relieved that he didn't have to bring that up.

313

"I was thinking we could tie them by their stems to a big ribbon and then wind it up all around the room."

"Let's try it!" Micah scribbled a note that said *back soon* and left it on his bed, just in case anyone got scared he'd turned street again, and hopped after her. "What about Miri?"

"She threw a pillow at me when I tried getting her out of bed," Ronit whispered as they crept through the dark hallway, "but I'll try again." She slid open the door to the room where she and Miriam had been given bedrolls. "Hey! Miriam! We're going on a flower hunt to surprise Esther."

"Fuck *off*," Miriam whimpered. "My insides are exploding and I just want to sleep."

"From the food?" asked Micah.

"No, I'm bleeding," said Miriam.

"I'm sorry." Ronit knelt next to her and massaged her shoulders. "Do you want us to get you anything before we go?"

"Chocolate?"

"There's some in a dish on the table where we were hanging out earlier," said Micah. "I'll go get it." He knew, first-hand, how awful she must feel.

"Thanks," said Ronit when he returned, and she fed the uneven nibs to Miriam before kissing her on the forehead. "Hope that helps. Sorry about the bad timing."

"Could be worse." Miriam smiled up at her weakly. "Could be Esther."

"*Worst* timing," agreed Micah.

Ronit stood up. "Come on! Let's go cause trouble."

The air outside Tzuriel's parents' house was vibrant and alive with the night breeze coming off the sea. Micah, who was used to the much stiller, muggy nighttime air in Perach, breathed deeply and relished the feeling. "This was a good idea," he commented. "I'm glad we're out here."

Ronit dug her hand into her purse and retrieved a handful of coins. "Here's your lot. Leave one every time you take a flower."

Micah squinted at the coin in the full moon's broad light as they trudged along the sandy path. "That's the queen of Sugar Coast?"

"Yes," said Ronit. "You can tell it's only the one-piece coin because the twists in her hair are coiled into a knot. On the ten piece her hair's a big, soft cloud around her head, and on the crown coin her twists are down around her shoulders."

"Good thing we don't have to see all that in the dark." Micah kept watching for good flowers in the yards of all the sleeping houses, but his eyes often flickered to the bits of ocean he could see between house and shrub. Maybe tomorrow night he and Ronit could walk on the beach, once all the fuss was over.

"Ooh, there's some hibiscus!"

"Good catch!"

The blooms were large and showy. It was hard to tell in just moonlight, but Micah figured they were some variation on peach. He picked a few, and so did Ronit. "Here, I'll put them in my purse." She took them from him, carefully cradling them in her fingers.

 As Micah left coins on the fence, he noticed that there was a mezuzah on it—on the *fence*, not the door, as in Perach. Curious, he peered at the door to the stranger's house. Another mezuzah sat in its usual place in the doorframe. "Did you see? The house has an extra mezuzah."

 "Oh, that's to protect the garden from fairies," Ronit said casually. "Tzuriel's family has one too, to keep them out of the cacao trees."

 "*Fairies?*" Micah raised his eyebrows.

 "Yes," said Ronit. "Sometimes they leave out bits of leftovers for them, so they won't cause mischief, but the mezuzot keep them out of the walled areas where people live."

 "Who told you all this?"

 "One of the aunties," said Ronit, "and Tzuriel's aba."

 "Well, I guess it can't keep *us* out," said Micah.

 "Right, but we're paying. They don't."

 "That garden was just hibiscus," Micah realized after they'd walked away. "What would a fairy want with flowers?"

 "Oh, they eat them," said Ronit placidly.

 "Oh, look at that!" Micah pointed, grinning with glee. "Ylang-ylang!"

 "Nice," said Ronit. "This is working out great! These are even bigger than the hibiscus." Together they picked out three of the prettiest flowers, inhaling the dazzlingly sensual scent as if there was a way to get the smell to stay in their noses forever if they breathed deeply enough.

Micah left three coins on the fence, eyeing it to see if— yes, there it was, the extra mezuzah.

"What about those?" Ronit pointed to a tree in the garden of the next house. Its flowers looked either red or orange— it was hard to tell—and they ran thickly through its broad, squat branches. "I can't reach."

"I've got to teach you how to stand on my shoulders one of these days if you insist on being so short," Micah teased.

"Save it for *our* wedding night," Ronit shot back as Micah climbed, catlike, onto the stone garden fence with one leap.

Micah retrieved a handful of poinciana flowers, then steadied himself and jumped back down to the sandy path. "This enough?"

Ronit nodded. "Perfect landing! Now do it while playing fiddle."

"Only if you stand in the street and milk the crowd."

Ronit waved her hands theatrically as they passed more houses, sleeping under seagrape trees and coconut palms. "Lad*ies* and gentlemen—"

"—and everyone else," Micah interrupted.

"Them too," Ronit agreed. "Step right up and see the death-defying leaps he takes while playing violin! Will he miss a note? Will he break his neck? Only your coins know the answer." She shook her empty hand at the air as if asking for the price of admission.

"I'd have to practice with a junk violin first, obviously."

"Or just a piece of wood, at first. Wait." Ronit looked around her. "Did you hear something?"

"You chattering," Micah shot back.

"Shut up. I heard a flittery noise."

"Moths?"

"It sounded bigger than that. Maybe a dragonfly?" Ronit kept looking around, her little bow mouth pursed up suspiciously.

"Or the wind in the leaves," said Micah. "Or—wait! Do they have bats around here?"

"Yes, they do! I'd love to see a bat." Ronit's eyes flashed. "If I could do magic like that wizard who helped you have the right body, I'd want to do bat magic."

"Like... turning into a bat?"

"Maybe." Ronit was silent for a moment as she thought about it. "Or have bat friends. They're so cute."

"Hey, look, more hibiscus." Micah pointed to a bush studded with pink blossoms. "Those look like nice healthy ones."

"This is so much fun!" Ronit exclaimed.

They continued much along these lines for the next little while, collecting passion flowers—"Careful with all those delicate parts!"—and plumeria—"Watch out for the sap."—as well as more and more hibiscus. Micah's pockets grew lighter and lighter of coins, and he imagined the flowers lounging in delicate disarray within Ronit's purse.

They'd look amazing strung up all around Esther's room when she woke up in the morning!

"Micah!" Ronit suddenly whispered in a loud hiss. "My purse—it *moved*. I think something's in there."

His time on the street spoke for him. "Is it a rat?"

"Eek!" That was the wrong thing to say, because now Ronit was afraid of her purse. "Get away from me!"

"Maybe it's only a bat," Micah quickly interjected.

She held her purse at the end of a trembling arm, squinting at it through narrowed eyes. "I don't want to hurt it, whatever it is."

The bag moved again, and both of them yelped.

"Right," said Ronit.

"Right."

Slowly, they drew together and Ronit opened the purse.

Sitting on top of what was left of the flowers was a tiny, wide-eyed person with skin that looked like dolphin's flesh—slick, gray-blue, and shimmering in the moonlight. As it moved, cringing from them in fear, Micah realized that some of what he'd thought was flowers—there were so few of them left!—was the creature's wings, camouflaged to look like peach and pink hibiscus flowers.

"Micah," Ronit breathed, unable to move. "It's a fairy."

"And it ate our flowers."

The fairy burped.

"Ylang-ylang," Ronit commented sadly.

"So much for all those garden mezuzot!" said Micah. "Once we took the flowers out there was nothing else keeping it away."

"Now, look here!" Ronit addressed the fairy sternly. "We *paid* for those flowers, so they're ours now. What you did was stealing, and it's wrong."

"So?" The fairy looked up at them with big, round eyes with vertical slits like a cat's. It spoke in a mosquito's whine of a voice, and it had no nose. Micah was fascinated. "I don't care. It was delicious."

"Well, I *do*," Ronit insisted. She suddenly grabbed the bag away from Micah and closed it as hard as she could.

"Wait!" shouted the fairy from inside the purse. "You can't do that! I have to be back in the sea by the time the sun comes up or I'll dry out."

"Not my problem," said Ronit airily. Micah cast her a questioning eye, but she winked at him and smirked. She was bluffing.

"But I'll become driftwood," the fairy wailed.

"What can you do for us to make up for the flowers?" Ronit demanded.

"I can give you back your coins," said the fairy. "I can summon them since I was there when you left them."

"I don't want the coins back, I want decorations for my big sister's bridal chamber!"

"Something that'll really make her smile when she wakes up," Micah added.

"Then, it will be as you wish," said the fairy. "Take me to the room, and then cast me back into the sea."

"Also, can you take away my little sister's cramps?"

The fairy sighed. "You humans."

"You could always just eat wild flowers and not deal with us," Ronit pointed out.

The fairy did as they wanted, and when they returned to the house, the two of them snuck carefully into Esther's guest room as quietly as they could. Ronit moved the bag—still clenched shut in her fist—around the ceiling and four walls until sparkling ribbons of magic seafoam and tiny strands of shells entwined the room. Starfish and corals completed the effect. It was too dark to smile at each other and even whispering might wake the sleeping bride, so Micah just squeezed Ronit's hand in wonder.

They held the bag over Miriam too, before leaving again to take the fairy back to the sea. She relaxed in her sleep, and Micah's heart felt warm.

"I guess I got my walk on the beach with you earlier than I expected," Micah commented as he took Ronit's hand, after dumping the fairy out onto the tide at a safe distance from the human houses.

Once they returned and crawled back into bed in their respective rooms, Micah slept deeply from his exertions and dreamed about rescuing bats from fairies. When high-pitched voices roused his ears the next morning, he opened his eyes to a broad stream of sunlight and went to find Ronit.

She was in Esther's room, where today's bride was awake and beaming at the sea magic surrounding her. "It's so beautiful!" Esther said, over and over. "Oh, I'm so happy. Today is already a dream come true."

The Generous Princess

Cast: the Royal Family of Perach

For Tof and Nikki, and our sweet godchildren

♡ ✡ ♡

"Come on, sweetheart, either eat those last few bites or say you're done with lunch," said Queen Shulamit to the eldest of her children. "There's no more time to play with your food; I want you to go through your room with Safta and find some things we can take down to the orphanage later."

"I'm not playing!" said Princess Naomi, placing another cube of papaya on top of the already-precarious tower on her plate. "I'm *building*."

"You can build later, with your blocks, after we get home," said Shulamit, moving one-year-old Princess Ilana to her other breast.

"I want to build a house with fruit," Naomi insisted. "Lots of fruit make great blocks. Melon and papaya, and…" She thought for a moment. "Cheese…"

"I bet she got this idea from her baba," said Isaac, who was holding the youngest, three-month-old Prince Aram, whom Aviva had carried. Aram's biological father was Farzin, the innovative engineer who spent his life at the side of Shulamit's in-name-only husband, and together they were fathers to all three children. Aram was originally intended to be born alongside Ilana, but the oil, as Aviva had put it, had taken a while to heat up in the pan.

Naomi nodded enthusiastically. "Mm-hmm! The last time he was here he built me a wagon out of apples and it *actually rolled*."

323

"But now it's time for *you* to 'actually roll,'" said Shulamit. She waved a hand at her elder daughter as if the motion would waft her out of her chair.

"Why do I have to give things away?" Naomi asked.

"We're a very lucky country," said Shulamit, "but sometimes people still go without. You know I do my best to make sure nobody in Home City goes hungry, but I bet there are children who haven't had a new toy in years, or clothing they got third-hand that doesn't fit. It's Purim, and we're all going to have a party and be happy, but we're supposed to make sure other people have a chance to be happy too."

Naomi stuck out her lip, considering her mother's words. "I have lots of toys."

Shulamit nodded. "You bet. In fact, since you're the Crown Princess, I bet you have more toys than anyone else in Home City."

Naomi's eyes widened. "Really?"

"When I was your age," called Aviva from the kitchen counter where she was cleaning up, "I had only two toys, and one of them was really an old spoon with a mitpachat on it to make it look like a woman!"

"Because you were poor," said Naomi bluntly. "And then you grew up and married a princess and got to live in a palace!" she added, flinging up her hands and sending the top half of the papaya tower flying across the room.

Isaac lifted his hand and made a great show of stopping them midair. With a smirk he slid them across the air to Rivka, where he let them hover in front of her mouth.

"What?" she twinkled back. They had a silent conversation with their eyes before she opened her mouth and chomped down the fruit.

"You two are *so weird*," said Naomi.

"You understand, now, right, sweetheart?" asked Shulamit, rocking Ilana gently. "We're sharing because some people don't have what we have. We work really hard for our people, but it wouldn't be fair if we had lots of things and they didn't have anything, right? Especially if there's enough to go around?"

"Yes, Ima," said Naomi.

"Bring your plate to the counter, please."

Naomi hopped off her seat and did as she was told.

"You're training a good queen," Isaac told Shulamit in his native language, which the children didn't understand, not wanting Naomi to start imagining she was already perfect.

"I try." Shulamit smile-grimaced, happy that her near-father recognized her efforts but sad that her real one would never know his grandchildren.

♡ ✡ ♡

Later, in Shulamit's salon—

"But," Farzin said with breakneck excitement, "when they actually *built* the fence, they realized they'd forgotten to take into account how much water they'd need to keep the mud pliable while they were working, so it actually—"

"I thought you said there was a pump!" Shulamit exclaimed.

"The pump—"

"Wait, wait." Shulamit held up one hand, the one that wasn't holding a copy of the script. "We'll never learn our lines if we keep getting distracted like this."

"Sorry!" Farzin grinned sheepishly and peered at his script. "Um… something about…"

"Just take it from the beginning again."

"All right, all right." Farzin stuck his tongue out at her. "Wait, the *beginning*, beginning? Or after—"

"No, after Vashti leaves. The beginning of our scene."

"Vashti's one of *our* names," Farzin mused. "If any of this really happened, it was probably over near our city."

"Yeah, that's what the scholars think," said Shulamit animatedly. "And Esther's one of your names too, technically. She's really Hadassah."

"How old are all of these stories?"

"Oh, shoot," said Shulamit. "Hundreds… thousands… of years."

"Every once in a while when we're tilling a new field on the vineyard, we turn up some bits of broken jars from something that was there back in the day."

"That's so exciting!" Shulamit's eyes sparkled with interest. "Any idea how old it is?"

"Going by legend and records, probably between eight hundred to a thousand years."

"Wow," she breathed. "So was there another farm there or was it something else?"

"Well, back then, there was actually a whole village, but at some point, there was a plague, and then everyone who survived just sort of drained into the City of Red Clay," Farzin explained. "It went back to nature for a while, but the soil's too fertile not to attract attention. So, eventually, here we are."

"You're making me want to hire some sort of state expedition to find the real Esther." Shulamit's mind was only half in her salon now; images of organized rows of workers examining the dirt on the empty lands between Perach and the City of Clay flashed through her mind. She imagined one of them standing up, holding a crown in a trembling hand, brushing the dirt off with the other— *Majesty! Look what we've found!* "I wonder if King Jahandar would let me look at the state records or if he thinks I'll contaminate them with my deviance." Her face was a sarcastic knot.

"I bet he has nightmares about little Shulamit sneaking into his bedroom window at night and infecting him with love and acceptance," Farzin teased. "But, hey, what about my mother?"

"That's *perfect*," said Shulamit. She clapped her hands in excitement, hopping a little. "I'll study our records and then tell her what I'm looking for."

"Hey, aren't we supposed to be practicing lines?"

"Arrgh! Now you've got *me* doing it!" Shulamit's hands worked aimlessly at the fringed edges of her decorative scarf. "Look, let's just skip to the exciting part. Maybe that'll keep our minds on the play so we can work backward to the rest of it."

"Where should I start?"

"From the part about 'I will give you anything you want.'"

Farzin puffed out his chest and spoke in his idea of the booming voice of a king. "I will give you anything you want, my Queen Esther. Because you have a sexy husband," he added in his normal voice.

Shulamit burst into giggles. "Oh my *God*."

"You already changed the Vashti part, right?" said Farzin. "You could change this too."

"I changed the Vashti part because he—*you*—wanted her to dance naked in front of random men and that's why she got kicked out. I don't like that part."

"I am *so* all right with girls not wanting to dance naked for me. Look how all right I am." Farzin held out an arm to either side.

"You look devastated," said Shulamit dryly.

"In fact, think of the scandal if the kingdom knew the queen was alone in her salon with her husband's lover!" Farzin was already laughing at his own joke by the time he finished his sentence.

"Think of the scandal if the queen's heart-brother forgot *all of his lines in the Purim play in front of everyone*," Shulamit teased.

"My Queen Esther!" Farzin had resumed his pompous tone. "You may have whatever you want, except of course pita, and chicken, and that cardboard stuff from the other holiday, and—"

"*Stooop*," she said through more giggles.

"You may have whatever you want, *even including* your hairstyle remaining as smooth as you want it for an entire day!" He emphasized these words with a pointing finger.

"You know what, I like your version. We should do this in front of everyone."

"Oh boy," said Farzin, taken aback. "I don't know if I could do it on command!"

"My King," said Shulamit, her skin growing a little hot at the idea that she was pretending to be that beautiful and brave queen who'd been her childhood crush, "it has been commanded that my people are to die, and I beg you to have compassion and save us."

There was a pause. "Wait, what's next?"

"You ask me who said."

"Oh, yeah," said Farzin. "Who is behind these orders?"

"Our enemy is Haman, who stands there!" Shulamit pointed dramatically.

"That lime tree?" Farzin was over to the big clay pot in three bounds. "Say the word, and I'll knock it over!" He swung a fist "at" the tree, wide enough to miss. "I shoulda known. Look how *sour* he looks."

"I'm going to cry myself to sleep over how nobody will ever see this version. It's comedy gold."

"I shall ban all lime trees," Farzin continued, "and—hey!"

"Why are we banning lime trees?" Kaveh stood in the doorway cradling a squirmy, mewling Princess Ilana.

"They're not as sweet as you," Farzin quipped.

Kaveh beamed, and handed the baby over to Shulamit. "Sorry to interrupt, but she's hungry and Aviva's already nursing Aram."

"No, it's fine!" Shulamit scooped her baby into her arms. "I guess we'll have to finish this sitting down."

"It's really only the lines we have to practice, anyway, not the moving-around bits," said Farzin.

"Kaveh, can you hang around and keep us on task?" Now on the sofa, Shulamit maneuvered Ilana around her chest so that she could latch.

"Yeah, we keep getting off topic talking about inventions and discoveries," Farzin explained.

"For you two, science is the real holiday," Kaveh observed.

"Ooh, that's a great idea!" Shulamit exclaimed. "I should look into creating a holiday to celebrate science." Kaveh smiled at her, and she realized she was still finding new tangents. "I can't help it, Kaveh, I'm just so happy to see you guys."

"We love you too." Kaveh grinned.

"We'll both try harder to stay on task," Shulamit resolved, concentrating on the soothing vibes coming from her nursing infant. "So, at the beginning of my part, when Mordecai brings me in…"

♡ ✡ ♡

Torches lit up the palace courtyard so that everyone in the audience could see Farzin's face clearly against the night air as he delivered his lines. "Since Vashti and I could not get along, I will seek a *new* wife."

"Shulamit changed it," Aviva whispered to Kaveh. They sat in the front row, each with a baby on their lap. Ilana was a banana and Aram a pod of garden peas, each in a costume made by Aviva's father the tailor.

"I know," said Kaveh. "She told me. The original version is weird."

"Well, it's weird, but it's ours," said Aviva. "But growing with the times is also ours." She adjusted Aram against her ample chest.

"Your Majesty," said Rivka, who was supposed to be Mordecai, "may I suggest my cousin?"

"Wait 'til you see this dress she asked from my father for Queen Esther," Aviva murmured. "She's a *pineapple*."

Kaveh looked like he didn't know what to make of that, so they continued watching the play. He would see soon enough!

The crowd gasped into oohs and ahhs as Queen Shulamit took the stage in her exotic costume. It was a gown of gold with brown accents, made in the fashion of the court of Imbrio with their enormous skirts. She walked slowly, and since the dress was so long they couldn't see her legs, she seemed to glide by magic. "Whoa," said Kaveh.

"I know!" Aviva grinned happily. "I'm glad she finally came up with an excuse to get one of those northern-style dresses."

Isaac stalked around the stage in a big black pirate hat as the evil Haman, and every time the actors said his name, the crowd shook their noisemakers—*groggers*, in Rivka's language—to block out the word. Aviva pressed her noisemaker into Ilana's hand and showed her how to shake it, but this proved to be a shortsighted idea because she didn't know when to stop. "I guess she's too young for that!" the amused mother said as she took back the noisemaker.

"You have to do it only when they say his name," Naomi explained to her little sister. Ilana looked up at her with big brown eyes as if she understood, but then reached for Naomi's noisemaker and tried to shake it while Shulamit was saying one of her lines. "No, not now!"

"Shh," said Aviva.

"Our enemy is Haman, who stands there!" Shulamit flung her pointing finger in Isaac's direction, and he looked at Shulamit and Farzin in mock fear.

"But, Your Majesty—" he began.

"Quiet, you!" Rivka, as Mordecai, burst on to the stage with her sword out.

"Oh, is *that* how it is, eh?" Isaac drew his own sword with his left hand.

"This is just our version, right?" said Kaveh under his breath.

Aviva nodded. "She's playing to our strengths."

The crowd went wild as Rivka and Isaac's blades clanged together back and forth across the stage, with Shulamit and Farzin clinging together in a show of mutual terror and solace in each other. Isaac had dropped the pretense of being an evil mass murderer and grinned like he'd already won, his face glowing.

Naomi's clear voice rose over the cheers. "If there was a real person like that I'd be so scared of him and I'd fight him and put him in jail, but that's just Zayde in a hat, so it's fun to watch him do things."

"Yes," Aviva agreed. "Bad people can be a little bit fun when they're only make-believe."

"How come when Riv and Zayde play-fight it's like when you and Ima kiss and cuddle?"

Aviva met Kaveh's eyes, and he chuckled. "That's how God made them," she told Naomi, "just like you're made to like cheese and Aba likes lamb. People like different things, and their minds work in different ways. We match, and *they* match." She nodded to the couple on the stage.

"Like when Baba makes a joke and Aba gets all smiley?"

Kaveh reacted to this by "getting all smiley" and ruffling her hair. "Smart kid."

"I don't always get Baba's jokes."

"Then you can look forward to something to grow into," said Aviva.

♡ ✡ ♡

The Purimspiel was over and the palace's inner courtyard rested quietly under the full moon's benevolent glow. Even

333

the third-shifters who busily cleaned up all the fuss and confetti from the crowd were long done. Rivka stood at her post, on guard duty tonight in front of the sleeping queen's door. She'd be here for another few hours, but that was okay—the little Crown Princess had a room to herself now, just next door, and Isaac was there standing guard.

Moonlight glinted off the gray winding through his thick hair and turned the whiter strands silver. He answered her gaze with a heavy-lidded smile. "Here we are, like something out of one of those legends," he commented. "A dragon, guarding a princess."

"You're cute, for a cliché." Rivka waggled her eyebrows at him.

"I have an important job!" Isaac retorted. "I'm on guard against danger. You never know when a brave, muscular warrior might appear and… attack my pants."

"Oh, so you've added foretelling the future to your magical talents, wizard?" Rivka shot back, her body tingling pleasantly.

"Maybe it was foolish to spar in public." Knowing exactly what he was doing, he parted his lips slightly and lifted one eyebrow. It was all very subtle and small, and yet Rivka felt starved for him.

"When we get off duty—"

"Tell me, Mighty One."

Rivka took a deep breath but in that silence she heard whimpering. "Wait."

Isaac heard it too. He leaned his head to Princess Naomi's door. "*Kindeleh*? Are you all right?"

There was a thump and running footsteps, and then the door flung open. Naomi, in her nightgown and her dark hair a thoroughly messy cloud of curls, rushed out and clung to Isaac's leg. "I don't want to give anybody away," she bawled, and buried her crying face in his clothes.

Rivka leaned against the wall in front of the queen's room and watched as Isaac bent down to wipe first one of her tiny eyelids, then the other, clean of tears. "What's wrong, Princess? That's quite the crying fit."

"Ina wanna wahhhhhh." She hiccuped and put her arms around his neck as he lifted her into his arms. They stood like that for a moment as she exhausted her crying. When she was calm enough to speak, she asked, "Can you be a dragon?"

Isaac transformed and curled up like a cat, still cradling the little girl. "Tell me what's bothering you and I'll see if I can fix it."

"I don't want to give them away," said Naomi.

"Give who away?"

The new tears resting in her eyes reflected moonlight. "I'm the princess and I have more of everything than the other kids. I have more mothers and more fathers too. And some of the kids we visited have no mothers or fathers at all. I'm supposed to give them mine. But I don't want to say good-bye!" She burrowed into his scales and shivered, even though it wasn't cold.

Rivka couldn't help smiling, even as she felt sorry for her.

"*Shayna maydeleh*," said Isaac, holding both the princess' tiny hands in one of his heavy paws, "one of the most valuable lessons a future queen can learn is that *people*

335

aren't things." Naomi listened intently. "It's good to give some of your *things* away when you have more *things* than everyone else, and that includes food, clothing, and toys. But people aren't things. You don't have to give anyone away."

"You promise?"

"With all my heart," said Isaac. "Aba and Baba will be your fathers forever, and your mothers will always be your mothers. That doesn't mean they'll be *around* forever, but they'll always be yours, and nobody can take that away."

"And you and Riv too?"

"We'll be here too."

"What about those kids? There were so many of them and they had no mothers or fathers, just two old ladies and a young one, and one of the old ladies looked mean."

"Maybe you and your mothers can help people without children or who want more children offer to be their parents," Isaac suggested.

"That sounds like helping." Naomi considered the idea. "I like helping."

"Good," said Isaac. "That's a big part of what being queen is about. At least, for your Ima."

"I wish Aba and Baba were here more often," said Naomi. "They're really fun."

"They wish they could see you more too," said Isaac. "They have to take care of the vineyard though."

"I know," said Naomi. "Baba said if he didn't go to work every day, the vines wouldn't know they were supposed to grow grapes and would start growing watermelons instead!"

"Your Baba is a joke factory."

"I know, I got that one." Naomi grinned.

"Glad to see that smile."

That made Naomi smile even wider.

"You ready to go back to sleep, *kindeleh?*"

"Can you sing to me first?"

Through the clear, dark courtyard, Rivka listened to her husband sing to Naomi the song he'd first serenaded her with over ten years ago, on the night they'd first spoken openly of their love. It was also the song that Shulamit's father sung her as a lullaby when she herself was a child, and now it was Isaac's song for his beloved little princess.

Jeweled stars, pearl stars
Silver coins in olive jars
Glittering deep within the dark
See them flicker, see them spark
Press the olives, pool the oil
Golden sunlight, golden royal
Press so olive oil will run
Press the night, collect the sun...

Shira Glassman is a bisexual Jewish violinist living in North Florida with a labor activist and a badly behaved cat. Her books, inspired by her heritage, upbringing, present life, and favorite operas, have made the finals of both the Bi Book Awards and the Golden Crown Literary Society awards in more than one year. Shira misses her grandparents.

Shira Glassman online:

Blog: http://shiraglassman.wordpress.com
Facebook: http://www.facebook.com/ShiraGlassman
Goodreads:
https://www.goodreads.com/author/show/7234426.Shira_Glassman
Twitter: http://www.twitter.com/shiraglassman

If you liked *Tales from Perach*, leaving a review is probably a mitzvah.

Check out the rest of the Mangoverse!

The Second Mango
Climbing the Date Palm
A Harvest of Ripe Figs
The Olive Conspiracy
Tales from Perach/Tales from Outer Lands

Want more f/f fantasy?
Check out:
Daughter of Mystery and its sequels, by Heather Rose Jones
Fairest by K.S. Trenten
Prayer of the Handmaiden by Merry Shannon
Promises, Promises by L-J Baker
and for queer found-family in space:
The Long Way to a Small Angry Planet by Becky Chambers
Fierce Family anthology